OVER TIME
A MM, STUDENT/PROFESSOR ROMANCE

ELLA KADE

OVER TIME by Ella Kade

Copyright © 2022 by Ella Kade. All rights reserved.

ISBN-13: 978-1-950044-31-3 (Ebook Edition)

ISBN-13: 978-1-950044-60-3 (Paperback Edition)

Edited by: The Polished Author

Proofreading by: The Polished Author, Amira El Alam

Photographer: Xram Ragde

Cover Model: Biago Castelo

No part of this book may be reproduced in any form or by any electronic or mechanical means, including information storage and retrieval systems, without written permission from the author, except for the use of brief quotations in a book review.

Manufactured in the United States of America.

This is a work of fiction. Names, characters, places, and incidents either are the products of the author's imagination or are use fictitiously. Any resemblance to actual persons, living or dead, businesses, companies, events, or locales is entirely coincidental.

OVER TIME

Join Ella's mailing list to be the first to know of new releases, free books, sales, and other giveaways!

https://harlowlayne.com/newsletter/

I've been keeping secrets from my roommates, but my one-night stand just outed me. Now they know I am bi and that I just hooked up with one of the professors at our school.

They wanted to know why I wasn't the happy-go-lucky guy I was before going home for the summer, but I'm not ready for them to learn why.
    Everything changed for the worst this summer.

It was a secret that kept me up at night. A secret that devastated me to the point I wasn't sure if I'd ever be the same again.

How could I concentrate on school when my whole world was upside down? I had more important things to worry about—namely, my one-night, very drunken stand who kept showing up in my life.

ONE
FORD

I DIDN'T BOTHER to roll over or say goodbye as I heard him sneak out of my bedroom. I was too busy cursing my hangover and my life to care about the person in my bed who probably regretted our hookup. Once I gave the rando from last night enough time to leave, I crawled out of bed, thankful for my blackout curtains. I had no idea what time it was, nor did I care. The only thing I knew was that I had to get up and cook breakfast for everyone since cooking breakfast and dinner for my roommates was how I paid the rent. Since I had no money, we came to an agreement I was to cook for the house. It was far more beneficial for me than Fin or the others, but I took it, nonetheless. As much as I hated it, I needed every ounce of help I could get. Now more than ever.

Stumbling out of the bathroom as the bright light assaulted my brain, I ran smack into West, who was looking back and forth between the front door and me.

"What?" I snapped, not wanting to deal with anyone's bullshit first thing. "I'm headed to make your damn breakfast right now."

His light green eyes narrowed as he took me in. "I don't give a shit about breakfast. Did I just see Mr. Lawrence do the walk of shame from your room?"

Pushing by West, I headed to the kitchen, where it seemed everyone else in the house was congregating. They were all looking at me with the same shocked expressions on their faces as West. Pulling out the stuff to make a frittata, I started cracking eggs as I listened to them whisper behind my back.

Let them whisper. I didn't care. I didn't care about anything except making it through the day, and the next time I could drink myself into oblivion so that I could forget about the last two weeks. Even better if I could erase the entire summer altogether.

Fin leaned against the counter as I chopped an onion. I could feel his black eyes trained on me. If I didn't know him as well as I did, I would have been scared—or perhaps I should say the me from my freshman and sophomore years would have been.

Now I was irrevocably changed, and there was no going back. Nothing could scare me.

Crossing his arms over his chest, Fin cocked his head. "Are you gay?"

I didn't bother to look at him as I answered. "Not that it's any of your business, but I'm bi. Does that bother you?"

I could feel his stare as I whisked the eggs. I wasn't sure what I was going to do if they decided they didn't need me anymore and kicked me out on my ass. I had nowhere else to go. Literally.

"I don't give a shit if you're gay, bi, straight, or asexual. You never gave any indication you like guys, so it was a shock to see one of Willow Bay U's teachers leave our house early this morning, and an even bigger shock that the teacher leaving was a guy."

Wait a minute. The guy, whose name I couldn't remember, likely because my head hurt too much, was a teacher at our school?

"Ah, I see it's finally sinking in," Fin chuckled darkly. "Did you fuck Mr. Lawrence last night?"

"If that's his name," I shrugged. "I don't remember much about last night. I went to some bar in Loganville and got shit-faced. I remember a hot guy, but I don't remember his name or him saying he was a teacher," I muttered, trying to think back.

I tipped back my beer and finished it off before signaling to the bartender for another. I was already three in and had taken just as many shots of tequila.

I wasn't sure if I made the right decision on coming back to Willow Bay, but I didn't have anywhere else to go, so what was I to do? The house I grew up in was sold, and my brother and sister were hours away from me, ignoring my every attempt to speak to them.

"Do you mind if I sit here?" *A tall, dark, and very handsome guy asked as he pulled out the stool beside me. He smiled brightly and flashed his white teeth, giving me a strange sense of ease. All the thoughts clouding my brain cleared away as he sat down and his leg pressed into the side of mine. Instead of moving my leg away, I pressed it harder into his.*

"It's a free country. Sit wherever you like." *I picked up the shot of tequila and threw it back.*

"True, but I wasn't sure if you were here with… someone or not." *His voice was smooth and alluring, making me take him in a second time.*

Dressed in a pair of dark jeans and a white t-shirt that set off his dark skin, I watched the muscles in his forearm ripple as he motioned for the bartender. After what happened with my mom, I never thought I'd find anything interesting again, and in walked Mr. Perfect. I wouldn't mind taking my frustrations out on him and using him to forget for a little while.

His chocolate eyes turned half-mast as he took me in as well. "If you keep looking at me like that, I might have to take you out to the back alley."

I licked my suddenly dry lips, my dick hardening as he watched my tongue move over my flesh. "I can't say I would be opposed, except I have more than a blowjob I want to do to you, and I'd hate for us to get interrupted when we're just starting to have fun."

Mr. Perfect let out a rumbling laugh, showing me those pearly whites of his again. "I like the way you think." He leaned forward until there were only a couple of inches between us. To the point where I thought he was going to lean in and kiss me, but instead, he only sat there and stared at me. Our gazes remained locked until the bartender sat down a bottle of beer for him. Holding up his beer, he clinked it with mine. "To uninterrupted fun."

"I'll cheer to that."

"I don't think we ever exchanged names," I muttered to myself.

Oz clapped me on the shoulder as he passed by me to the fridge, where he got out the orange juice. "It probably won't be a big deal since it sounds like a one and done."

I glanced around the room to find Lo staring at me while biting on her lower lip and her brows scrunched together. She'd been doing so much better the last time I saw her compared to when she first arrived here around this time last year. She looked tanned and had put on some weight that was desperately needed. I didn't like I'd put the worried look on her face.

"Do you think he knew who you were and took advantage?"

Fuck me. I couldn't let Lo think like that.

"There's nothing to take advantage of unless he's going to turn me in to the Dean, which will, in turn, get him in trouble. Football practice hasn't started, so I can't get in trouble with Coach for drinking. Don't worry about me. If anyone was taken advantage of last night, it was him." I smirked, thinking about pounding him from behind and letting out all of my frustrations.

Lo didn't look convinced, and when Oz saw it, he moved toward her, whispering in her ear.

What I remember of our time once we got back here was damn good. It had my dick hardening at the thought.

Turning back to my task at hand, so no one saw I was getting a semi over this Mr. Lawrence, I poured everything into the pan and put it in the oven. "Breakfast will be ready in twenty," I announced. "I'm going to go take a quick shower before it's done."

And jack myself off to the memories of last night.

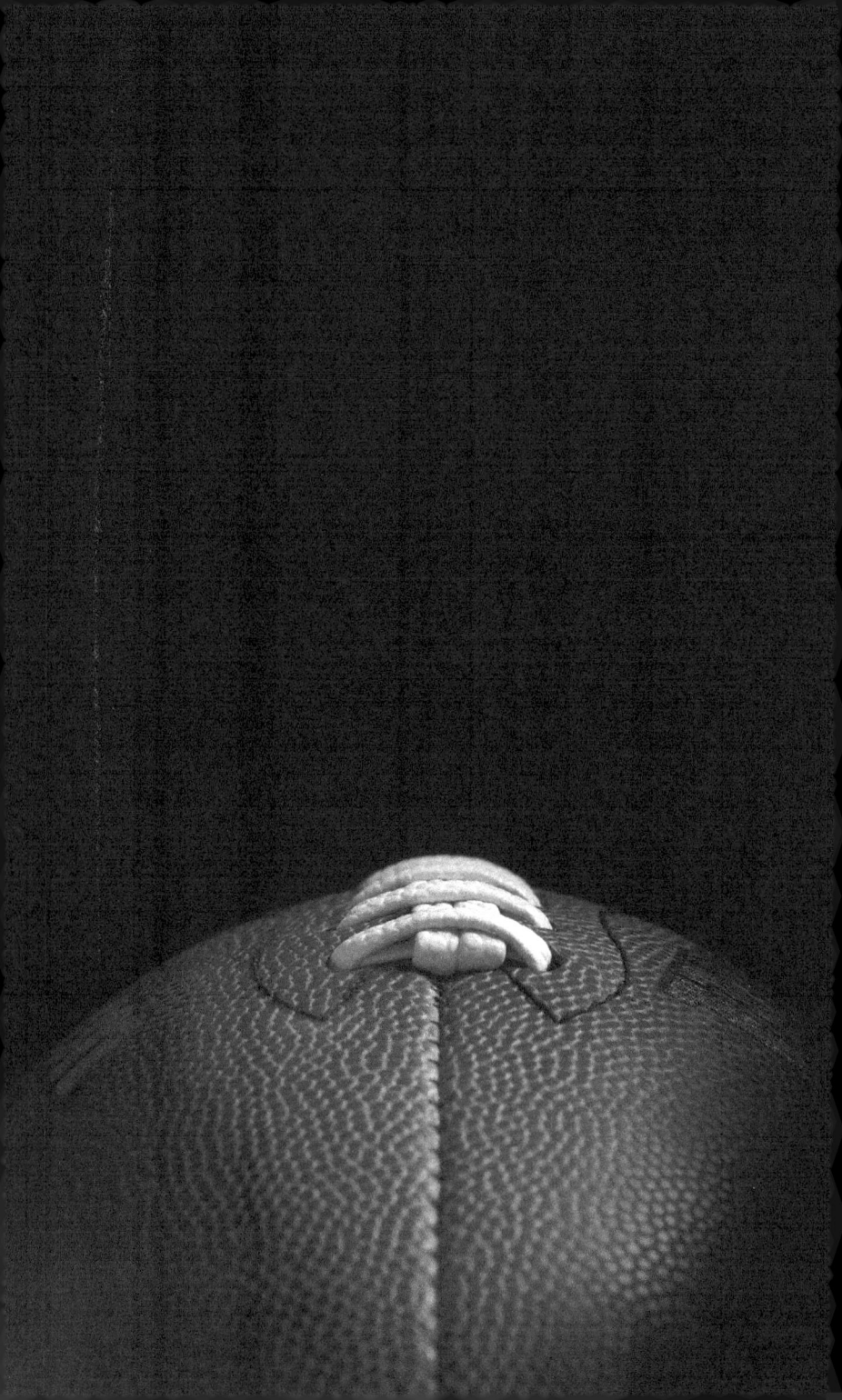

TWO
XANDER

WAS I the stupidest motherfucker on the planet or what? What were the odds I'd find someone at a bar, go home with him, and then realize I was in a house full of students from my school? I slept with a student at my school. If anyone found out, I'd be fired and ostracized.

I wanted to kick my own ass for my bad decision.

I should have known Ford was too good to be true. Finding guys who checked off all my boxes in Willow Bay was next to impossible. Dark hair, check. Dark eyes, check. Tall, check. Bad boy vibe, check. Muscles that bulged in all the right places, check. The only thing that shouted in big, bold, red capital letters was STUDENT. That was a big hell no, and yet I couldn't stop thinking about Ford and the way he manhandled my body like I wasn't six foot two and two hundred pounds of muscle. The rough scrape of his stubble on the insides of my thighs, neck, and face. Hours later and I could still feel every touch. Maybe that's why I was back at the bar where we met last night on the off-chance Ford might show up.

Taking a swallow of my beer, I scanned the room, looking for him. I shouldn't have come back, but I couldn't help myself. I just wanted one more look. One more touch. One more night.

What had gotten into me? This wasn't me. I was cool, calm, and collected at all times. I didn't recognize the fool I was being.

"Are you here for me?" A deep voice asked from the other side of where I was looking.

Turning on my stool, I tried to hide the smile that was trying to take over my face and give me away. "I don't know what you're talking about. I'm here all the time." Lie.

He cocked one dark brow. "Is that so?"

"Yeah, the bartender knows my usual." Lie.

Ford looked at the beer in my hand. "I don't remember a lot from last night, but I do remember that's not the beer you were drinking."

"That's because my usual is whatever's the drink

special of the night." Another lie. "What are you doing here?" It was time I started to ask questions.

"Imagine my shock when I rolled out of bed this morning to find out from my roommates that the man who snuck out of the house this morning is a teacher at Willow Bay."

Fuck, I thought at least one of them looked familiar.

I hated what I was about to ask, but I had to. "They're not going to say anything, are they?"

"They won't say shit."

Good to know.

He motioned for the bartender, and when Ford only ordered water, I was shocked.

"Not drinking tonight?" Shit, was he even old enough to drink?

"Not until football season's over. Otherwise, Coach will have my ass." Great, he was a football player. That explained the attitude.

"I didn't know you're a student." I tried to explain.

"And I didn't know you're a teacher. Not that it matters, I still would have done you."

"Thanks?" I chuckled. I wasn't sure how to take what he said. I wouldn't have gone home with him if

I'd known. Now, I wasn't so sure. There was something about him that drew me to him.

"What?" He shrugged. "You're hot, and there's nothing wrong with a little fun."

Except when it's a condition of your job.

"No, you're young, attractive, and an athlete. You should have as much fun as you can while you're still in school." The words tasted bitter on my tongue. The thought of Ford with other people didn't sit right. None of this did.

"So, you're telling me it all goes downhill after college?" There was a bitter edge to his words I didn't understand.

"No, but life isn't as carefree. Enjoy your youth while you can."

"You sure are cynical for your age." He cocked his head. "How old are you anyway?"

"How old do you think I am?"

He turned and sipped on his water, muttering. "You sure play games like you're in college."

"Did you mistake me for a college student?" I laughed because I didn't look twenty or close to it.

Ford tipped his head my way and rolled his eyes. "I'm not stupid. I know you're not."

"Then why ask?"

"I don't know." He looked down at his water and

sighed. I wasn't sure what it was, but there was great sadness in Ford. "This is pointless. I should go."

The second he stood, my hand shot out on reflex grabbing his wrist. "Wait."

He looked down at me with a storm brewing in his dark eyes. "Why should I?"

My mouth spoke without me thinking. If I had been, I wouldn't have said the next words that came out of my mouth. "I can make you feel better."

"Is that so? Are you not worried about your job? I swore I saw you over here biting your nails before I came over." He laughed, but there was no humor in it—only darkness.

"We've already done the deed, so what's one more night? It's not like this will still be going on once school starts in three weeks." Why did it hurt to know I had less than three weeks with him? Or possibly just tonight?

"I don't know. You already seem addicted to my dick," he smirked, pulling his wrist from my hold. "You're practically begging me to stick my big, fat cock in your ass again."

There was no way I was going to tell him last night was the best sex I'd ever had. How was that possible with a total stranger?

"Tell me... what's your name?"

Fuck me. He really didn't know my name? Maybe it was the alcohol, and after one more night with Ford, I'd realize he sucked in bed and was an asshole, and I'd never want anything else to do with him.

"You really don't know my name?" He shook his head, his brows raised expectantly. "Xander. My name is Xander."

He trailed his finger down the length of my jean-clad thigh. "Can I call you X?"

"Not if you want me to answer," I shot back.

"We'll see about that. I have a feeling once my cock is inside of you, you'll let me call you anything I want." When I didn't answer him, a low rumble escaped him. "Do you want to come back to my place again?"

"*If* we're going to do this, it can't be at your place." I couldn't face his roommates again.

Taking a step back, he grinned wickedly at me. "I'll follow you then."

Pulling out my phone, I woke up my screen. "Give me a minute. I took an Uber in case I drank too much."

"Oh, for fuck's sake. You can ride with me. I drove since I knew I wouldn't be drinking." He walked away, knowing I'd follow him. How had I got myself entangled in this man so quickly?

Ford drove without saying a word, and, oddly enough, it turned me on. I spoke every once in a while to give him directions back to my place, but other than that, I sat back and took in every nuance of his face. His long, dark lashes that fanned out on his cheekbones when he blinked, or his full lips that were set in a thin line, or the way the long black strands of hair fell over his forehead.

Pulling into my driveway, Ford put his car into park. He sat scanning what little you could see of my house in the dark. Without taking his eyes off where I rested my head at night, he asked. "Is this your house?"

"It is. I wouldn't bring you back to someone else's place." Not with what I hoped he had planned for me.

"Willow Bay U must pay nice," he stated with a tick in his jaw.

"Not nearly," I chuckled, grabbing the door handle to get out. "I could never afford this on my salary as a teacher. My parents died a few years ago in a horrible accident. I got a big payout, and with it, I bought this house."

I swore he muttered something that sounded like 'must be nice,' but he was getting out of the car and headed to the front door before I could ask. He waited as I unlocked the door with an intense energy that pulsed off him. It was dark and pissed. If I'd crossed paths with him in an alley or anywhere remotely dark, I would have steered far away from him, unlike now, where I welcomed him into my house and my body.

He stood just inside the door while I kicked my shoes off. "It's a nice place you got here. I can't imagine what you thought of my place this morning."

I stepped back and took in his stiff posture. The man I met last night wasn't the one before me now. This one was pissed and on the defensive. "I didn't think anything of it. I'm not judging you, Ford. I remember what it's like being in college. It's lots of ramen and pizza. A rite of passage, if you will."

"Not for me and my guys. We have to eat healthy. They used to get their meals delivered to them, but now I cook for them. They eat like kings. Healthy kings, but kings nonetheless." I wasn't sure why he was telling me this, but I hung on every word as if I might never hear him speak again.

"That's... good for them." I hated small talk, especially when I wanted to strip him down and get to know every inch of his incredible body.

"Yeah," he stepped around me and started to

head up the stairs. "Why don't we get down to why we came here?"

How could he make me feel so cheap with only a few words? Even with making me second guess what we were doing, I followed him up the stairs and then passed him on the way to my bedroom.

Ford stepped into my bedroom and immediately started to remove his clothes. It wasn't sexy. No, it was robotic and stiff. Let me clarify, Ford was sexy no matter what. It was the knowledge that he wasn't here with me that I didn't like. He could have been with anyone at that moment. He was down to fuck and nothing else.

I accepted my role in this sick game, so what did that make me?

"Take off your clothes," he demanded, stalking forward.

My hands went to my belt on his command without thinking. I tilted my head to the side, taking in his bobbing cock as he moved closer. "Aren't you going to undress me?"

He stopped in front of me with his hands at his sides. All of his beautiful, toned body was on display for me to look at and drool over. "That's not how this goes. If you want something more, I suggest you go back to the bar and find someone else to fuck you."

"I'm not usually a bottom." I let my jeans and underwear drop to my feet.

"Then that's even more of a reason for you to find someone else because there's no way I'm letting you fuck me with anything other than your mouth."

Were all college students this bold and knew what they wanted?

"I assume you have lube," he muttered as he walked over to my bed and started rummaging through my drawers.

"Other side," I directed him. I watched as the globes of his ass flexed with each of his steps around to the other side of my bed.

Pulling it out, he threw the bottle to me. "Lube up your fingers and fuck yourself with them. Get yourself ready to take me in your tight hole," he gritted out.

I did as instructed, climbing onto the bed, pouring lube on two fingers, and pushing one past the tight ring of muscle.

This wasn't me. I wasn't one to take orders but gave them, and I definitely didn't get turned on by someone treating me like shit, but there was something about Ford. The darkness that was inside of him was fresh and raw that made me do exactly as he wanted.

Maybe it was the teacher in me that thought I could help, and right now, letting him take out his anger on me through sex was the best way. Or so I told myself.

The way his eyes darkened and the way he bit down on his full bottom lip as I pumped my finger in and out had me slipping a second finger inside.

"Get up on your knees and face the headboard."

I moved slowly, keeping my eyes on his, which seemed to piss him off, going by the tick in his jaw. I kept looking over my shoulder as I watched him kneel on the bed and move toward me. His dark eyes were cold and burning with lust at the same time. Caging me in from behind, Ford pushed my face until it was flush with the wall and held it there. His other hand gripped my hip with a biting touch that sent a strange mix of arousal and fear through me.

Running his nose up the side of my neck, he growled. "Don't look at me."

This was nothing like the night before, and I wondered what had changed during the day to make me the bad guy. Gone was the playful guy who couldn't wait to rip my clothes off. Behind me was a man who didn't care who he was with, and I was willing to let him use me.

"Ford," I started but was quickly shut down by his hand snaking around and covering my mouth.

"Don't. This isn't going to be nice. We're not going to play like our lives are perfect." I heard the rip of a condom one moment, and the next, he was pushing through my entrance. My body protested. Unable to relax as he rammed all nine inches into me in one move. He didn't give me time to adjust before he pulled back and slammed inside of me. With each punishing thrust, I felt a small amount of his anger waning. But it wasn't enough to prevent him from pounding into me from behind.

It wasn't that I didn't like it. Scarily, I did. I was normally the dominant one in a relationship, but there was something about Ford that had me relinquishing control of that part of myself.

With every stroke, he hit my prostate, bringing me closer and closer to the edge until I needed to stroke myself.

"Don't you touch yourself," he gritted out. "Your pleasure belongs only to me."

His hand ran brutally down my ribs and around my hip. When his fingers wrapped around my straining cock, I let out a low moan. With rough movements, his hand squeezed my tip with every upstroke. My body started to violently shake as pleasure washed over me. I bucked under his harsh hold and reared back, wanting more—needing more—of his expert cock.

"That's right. Choke my dick with that ass of yours." One hand came down, and pain reverberated through my body, sending me over the edge. Ford grunted behind me, moving faster until he impaled me one last time.

His forehead rested on my shoulder for two harsh breaths before he jerked up. "Fucking hell," Ford murmured as he pulled out, my entire being feeling the loss of him inside of me.

I turned to watch as he pulled the condom off and threw it in the trash by my bedside. Ford moved stiffly and robotically, shutting down even more right before my very eyes.

"Ford…" I wasn't sure what to say. We didn't know each other, so why did I expect him to open up to me.

Sliding his jeans up his firm thighs, Ford didn't even bother to look at me as he spoke. "I'll see you soon."

THREE
FORD

"WHAT'S YOUR NUMBER, FORD?" Lo asked the second I stepped foot in the living room.

"I don't keep track," I answered as I walked through and into the kitchen. Pulling out the pitcher of green juice I made this morning, I started to pour it into a glass for me when Lo's blonde head peeked into the kitchen.

There was a deep ridge between her brows as she looked at me. "What do you mean you don't keep track?"

"I don't know how many people I've slept with, and I don't care." Internally, I rolled my eyes. She was asking for trouble. "Please don't tell me you're trying to get your boyfriend's number out of him."

"Seriously, do you all have one-track minds? I'm

not asking how many people you've had sex with." Lo shuddered as she looked at me. "I'm asking what your football number is. I realized yesterday when you all went off to football practice that I didn't go to any of your games last year. I didn't even know Oz's number. Any of yours."

"Are you going to wear my jersey number instead of your boyfriend's?" The thought had a smirk forming on my face. It would eat Oz up if Lo wore anyone's number but his.

With hands on her hips, Lo narrowed her eyes at me. "First of all, he's not my boyfriend. We got engaged, remember?"

Yes, I remembered. I just didn't care. Who got engaged in college? They'd be lucky if they were still together by the time we graduated. "And what's the second thing?"

"Nothing." She stomped her foot like a child, making me want to laugh. "Why are you being so difficult?"

Because life was difficult. I didn't say that, though. Lo knew better than anyone how shitty life could be. This time last year, she was raped at her old school before she came here to live with us. As much as I hated life, Lo didn't deserve my shit.

"I'm number eighty-two."

Her eyes lit up. "That's a high number."

That caused my lips to tip up. "It is. I'm a wide receiver."

"You guys are going to have to teach me all about football. I don't know anything. What's a wide receiver?"

Oz wrapped an arm around her waist. "Come on, let me tell you what all a running back does."

Before they could disappear, I stopped them. "You'll have to come to one of our games and cheer me on."

"Get your own cheering squad," Oz grumbled, pulling Lo to his side.

"Cheer us all on," I amended.

"Oh, I will. I'll be at every home game," she said enthusiastically.

Not a single one of us ever thought about Lo going to one of our games last year. She wasn't in the right state of mind. She couldn't even leave the house without Oz by her side to walk Charlie. "I look forward to seeing you in the stands."

It sounded nice to have someone in the stands cheering me on. I'd never had anyone at a game for me. My mom was always too busy working, and my brother and sister never cared.

Nope. Shutting down that train of thought. I couldn't think about them; otherwise, I'd go mad.

Fin walked by and hit his shoulder with mine. "Why do you look like you want to kill someone?"

I didn't want to kill anyone. I wanted to turn back time and erase the end of summer.

"Does it matter? You walk around looking like you want to murder everyone on a daily basis," I snapped.

Fin shrugged. "I don't like many people."

"Who says I do?"

"I've lived with you for two years, been on the football team with you as well. You've always gotten along with everyone and are in a good mood." He looked me over, his eyes fixed on my crossed arms. "But something happened."

Yeah, something happened.

"And you don't want to talk about it. I get that. In case you're worried, we don't care about seeing Mr. Lawrence walk out of here. We don't care if you're bi either. It's your prerogative." He turned to look over his shoulder and back at me. This time, his voice was quiet. "I know I'm not easy to open up to, but you can always talk to everyone else in the house."

I couldn't talk to them. If I did, they'd all look at

me with pity in their eyes, and I wouldn't be able to handle it.

Fin held his hands up. "Alright, I was just offering. You do you, man. Are you making those shakes for us before we head to practice?"

"If that's what you want." That was easy, and I wouldn't have to think. I'd go on autopilot and then be out the door. Practice, cooking, and fucking Xander, where I exerted every ounce of energy, were the only times I didn't remember how my life had turned to shit.

"Alright, we're leaving in twenty." Fin walked away like he hadn't been nice to me a few seconds ago.

Days like today, I wished I wasn't their slave. I was sure if I said I needed a day off, they'd give it to me, but I'd already had the entire summer off and felt guilty. I kept my stuff here, making it impossible for them to rent my room out for the summer. Not that they would. There was no way Fin was inviting anyone else into his inner circle.

I gathered all the ingredients for a banana walnut shake. It was perfect to have before practice. I made them once before practice, and the guys said they never felt better afterward. Now, they wanted them almost daily before we hit the field.

West clamped a hand on my shoulder as he walked by and started to fill up everyone's water bottles. "You doing alright?"

Turning off the blender, I narrowed my eyes at him. "Did your boyfriend tell you to talk to me?"

West stopped filling up the water bottles and turned to me. "I don't know what you're talking about. Did Fin talk to you?"

"Don't act like you don't know. He came out here acting like he cares about my fucked-up life and then sent you in here."

West's nostrils flared, but that was the only outward sign to show he was pissed off at me. "Even though Fin doesn't show it, yes, he *does* care about you; otherwise, you wouldn't be living in this house. We all care."

"I don't need it. I don't need anything but for everyone to leave me the hell alone. Why are you all so pushy? No one pushed Lo to talk about what happened to her, so why me?"

West's green eyes widened. "Were you violated?"

I almost wished I had been. It might be easier than what I was going through.

"Nothing like that," I brushed him off.

"How could you utter those words?" West bit out. "What happened to Lo is one of the worst things imaginable to happen to anyone. Whatever your little problem is, it's nothing compared to what she went through."

He had no idea, and there was no way in hell I was going to tell him or anyone else. I couldn't. If I did, I'd be more broken than I already was.

Grabbing three of the water bottles, West shoulder-checked me as he moved past. "You know what? I think you should drive yourself to practice."

Practice wasn't the distraction it usually was, and now that I was sitting in my car wondering if when I got home, I'd be told I needed to find a new place to live. I shouldn't have said anything to West. If I didn't explain, they'd think I was an asshole, and I didn't want to tell anyone what happened right before I came back to Willow Bay.

The drive home was short, even though I took my time. We lived close to school and the field. That was why we all drove together on most days. I didn't want to drive around avoiding going home, but when I pulled into the driveway to find Lo sitting out on the front porch with Charlie running around our front yard, I almost put my car in reverse and left.

I wasn't a runner, despite the fact that I was running away from every other problem I had in my life. The second I stepped out of my car, Lo's head came up, and her eyes locked on mine. She gave me a timid smile as I walked up the driveway. I thought about ignoring her, but instead, I sat down beside her on the top step and looked out at our yard and down the street.

I stared straight ahead, unwilling to see the questions I knew were written on her face. The silence was deafening, even though I wasn't willing to break it.

Lo was the first to speak. Her voice was so soft it was as if it came in on the wind. "I know you might not want to talk about whatever's eating at you, but I can promise you that it will make you feel better."

I watched Charlie hop around the yard, chasing an insect or something. "I don't think there's anything that will make me feel better. Speaking those words will only make it more real."

"You can't live your entire life in denial, Ford." Lo placed her hand on my shoulder. I could feel her eyes on me, but I didn't budge. "I don't know what's going on with you, but while it may get harder for a while, it will get better in time."

"You don't know that," I mumbled. How could my life get easier? It had steadily gotten worse for years now and then BAM. My world was swept out from underneath me. I guess life couldn't get much worse.

"Do you remember when I thought I'd never leave the house? When I woke up every night from nightmares?"

"Of course, I remember. I'm not diminishing what happened to you, but this isn't like that."

I caught the tilt of her head out of the corner of my eye. "If you want, I can give you the number to my therapist, or she can give you the name of someone better fit."

"I don't think I can talk to a therapist." I didn't think I could talk to anyone about it—not even my own siblings.

"You know I want to be a therapist, and while I know I have zero qualifications, I'll do everything in my power to help you."

Now I did look at her. Her blue eyes were soft, and there was an understanding there that told me she meant what she said, even though she didn't know what she was getting herself into. "I appreciate that. I don't know if I can talk about it. Every time I think about it, my insides twist, and my heart feels like it's going to stop." I was only alive by sheer anger.

Scooting closer, Lo pressed her leg to mine. "You

don't have to tell me everything. Maybe we can start with something small."

"There's nothing small. It's all horrible, just varying in degrees," I confessed as vaguely as possible, going back to watch Charlie.

"You know," Lo paused with an uptick of her lips. "Charlie is good for the soul. Maybe you should get out and play with him or let him snuggle with you for a while. He's always made me feel better."

Standing, I started moving backward down the stairs. I couldn't open up, nor could I be here. "I'm a waste of your time. Go inside and enjoy your boyfriend."

"He's not—"

"I know, but it feels weird to say fiancé." I shrugged off her anger.

She watched me take a few more steps closer to my car. "Where are you going?"

"I don't know. Someplace to forget." I turned on my heel and got in my car.

"Ford," she called out to me, but I continued until I turned on my car and blasted the AC.

Lo stood and started to follow me out to my car. "Are you going to see your teacher?"

Putting my car into reverse, I denied any association. It wouldn't be good for any of us if they knew of a second night with Mr. Lawrence. "I don't know what you're talking about."

"Sure, you don't," she beamed at me.

I might not have known what I was going to do to forget about my life, but with the mention of Xander, I knew exactly what I needed. I was going to fuck him until I forgot all of my problems.

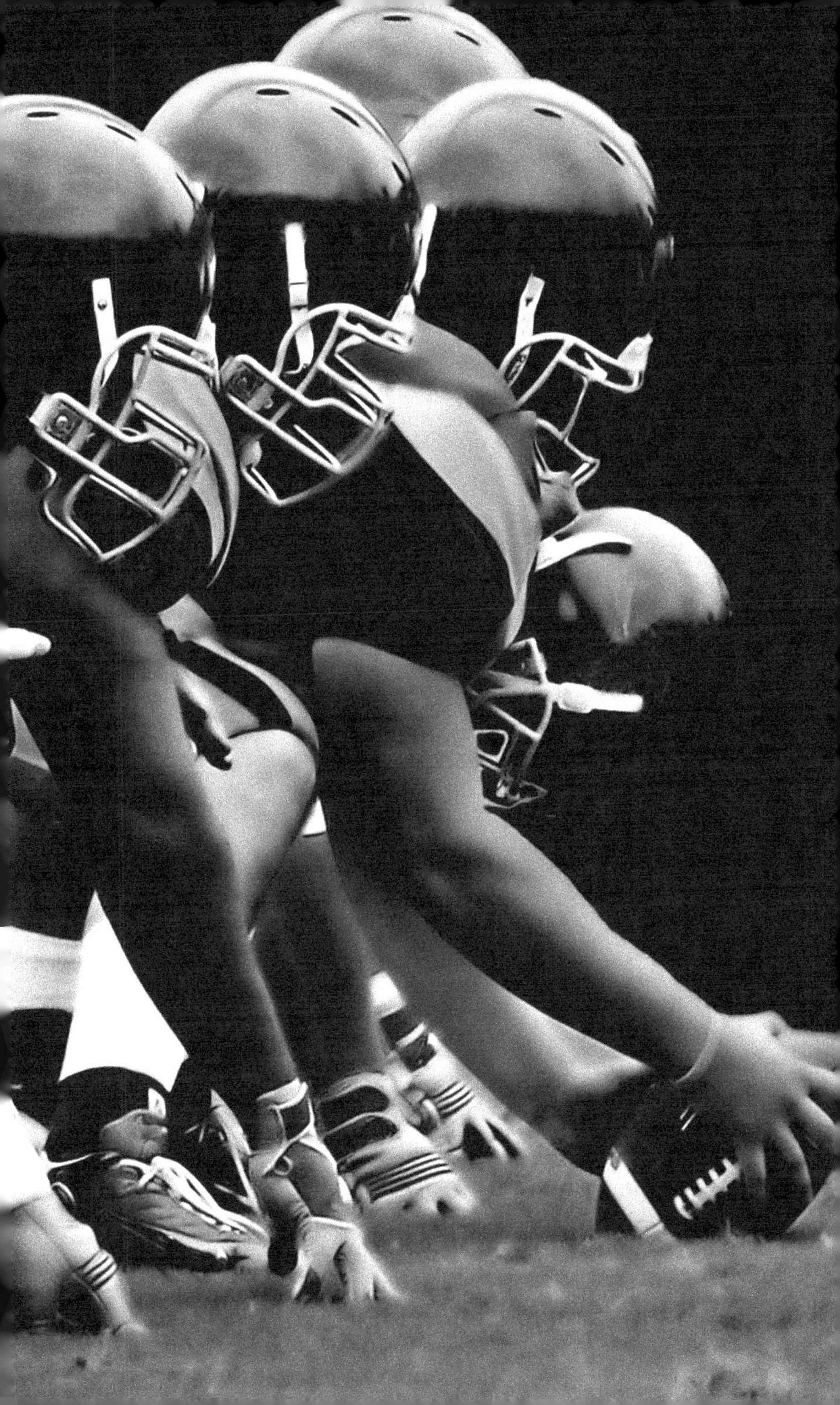

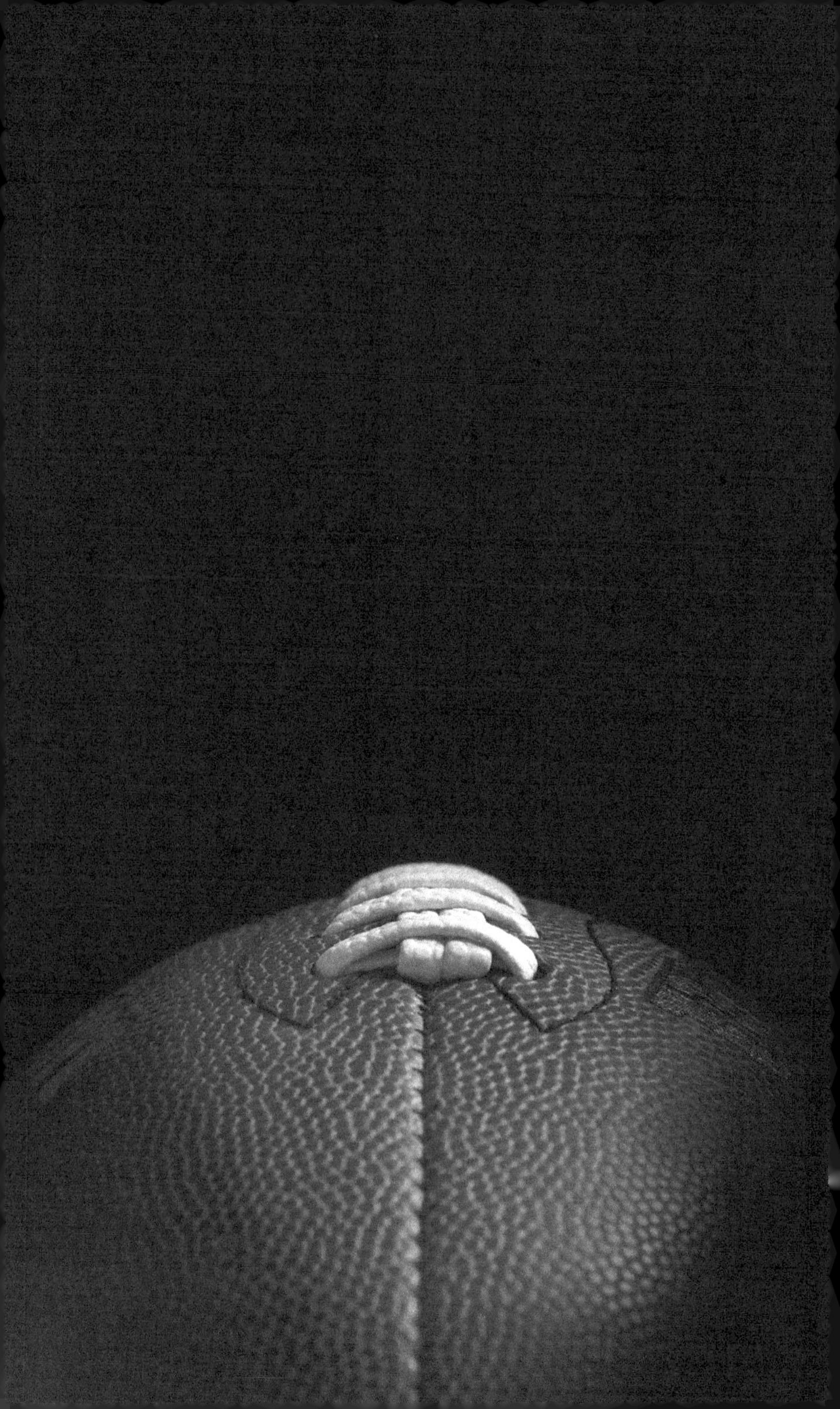

FOUR
XANDER

A DARK FIGURE stepped from the shadow as I made my way up to my drive from my walk. My steps faltered until I recognized Ford's dark hair hanging over his forehead.

I started walking again and passed him. Since Ford's departure last night, I'd thought about the way he treated me. I couldn't set a precedent for letting him think that it was okay to use me and my body. "What are you doing here?"

"I couldn't be at my house, and the first place I thought to come to was here." His honesty softened me, which was dangerous after promising myself I wouldn't give in to him any longer.

I unlocked my door. "Did you get into a fight with your roommates?"

As if sensing my earlier resolution, Ford stood at my front door. The haunted look in his eyes had my defenses falling a little more. I was in so much trouble when it came to Ford by letting him into my life and risking my lively hood for a few minutes of exquisite pleasure. "You can come in."

Ford hung back by the door, looking around my place like it was the first time he'd been here. Before, we were both too filled with want to even have a conversation when he was here. "If you're busy, I can leave."

"I'm not going to let you manhandle me and treat me like shit. But if you want someone to talk to, I'm here."

His shoulders slumped as he moved into the living room and sat down on my couch. With his elbows resting on his knees, Ford held his head in his hands. "I'm not sure I can even get the words out."

I wasn't sure if being near me would help him talk or hinder him, but I took the chance and sat down beside him, giving him a few inches of breathing room.

"Okay, let's start small. Why can't you be at home?"

His body sagged even further. "I said something I shouldn't have."

Was I going to have to drag every little thing out of him?

"You can tell me anything, and I won't judge you."

His head popped up, and his dark gaze landed on me. "You're already judging me."

"Not on this. I can put away our previous interactions," I vowed.

"Is this the teacher in you?" Those dark eyes of his seared me down to my soul.

"No, this is the human in me seeing someone I believe is good going through something bad. What that is, I don't know, but I can tell it's something…" It was horrible, but I didn't want to say it out loud. "What did you say to your roommates?" I tried again.

"It was just to one, but I'm sure they all know what I said. In fact, I know because Lo was waiting for me on the front porch when I got home from practice."

The reminder that he was a student at the school where I taught was harsh. I shouldn't have let him into my house or back into my life once I learned who he was.

I nodded for him to continue, but he kept silent. "What did you say to your one roommate?"

"That what I went through this summer was worse than what happened to Lo last year, and if I could pick between the two, I would've chosen her nightmare instead of mine."

I scooted a bit closer until our knees touched. "What happened to Lo?"

Ford was already shaking his head before I finished speaking. "That's not for me to say. That's her story, not mine."

"Okay. That's honorable, and I can accept that." I could tell Ford's roommates meant a lot to him, even without him saying so.

There was a long pause before he spoke again. "She wanted to talk when I got home, but I couldn't speak the words. Not to her or anyone. I'll be lucky if they don't kick me out if I don't explain, but I can't." He sounded so defeated in that moment. How could they not see the pain he was in? Surely, they'd understand. "I can barely think about it without feeling like I'm dying. Once I say those words..." he shook his head and squeezed his eyes closed.

"It makes whatever situation you're in real." I finished for him. It made sense.

His eyes popped open. "That's exactly it."

I didn't want to push, but I nor anyone else

couldn't help Ford if he didn't open up. "I can promise you if you tell me what nightmare you went through this summer, you won't die. It may cause you more pain in the beginning, but—"

Ford jumped up and shouted. "The pain is never going to end. What would you do if your mother lied to you for over a year? A year," he screamed, turning in a circle on my living room floor. His fingers gripped the strands of his black hair and pulled. I was surprised a chunk wasn't missing when his arms fell to his sides. Eyes the color of night turned to look at me. They were glassy, and in that moment, I could feel his pain as my own. "She lied to me. Over and over again, and two weeks before I was set to come back for my junior year of college, she killed herself."

Whatever I thought Ford was going to say wasn't that. I thought maybe he'd say his mom couldn't afford to pay for his college. There was nothing I could say that would make him feel better.

"Exactly," he grunted. "It's out there, and I don't feel any better. In fact, it's just how I imagined it would be if I spoke those words. My insides are shriveling up and dying."

My body was up and moving before I realized what I was doing. Pulling Ford up from resting against the wall, I helped him back over to the couch. I wanted to pull him in my arms, but I had a feeling Ford wouldn't be responsive to some TLC from the guy he's banged a few times.

I had no idea what to say as I sat there and watched as with each moment that passed, pain wracked his body. My stomach growled, making me jump up from the couch. "Why don't I make us some dinner? Have you eaten?"

Ford's head whipped up, eyes wide. "What time is it?"

I pulled out my phone and checked the time. "It's almost six-thirty."

"I have to go and make dinner." Ford stood and started for the door.

"Are you sure?" I stepped toward him. "You were only just saying that you thought they might kick you out."

"And if I don't make them their dinner, I will most definitely get thrown out on my ass." He started to walk away and then turned back to look at me. "Thanks for letting me in. You didn't have to."

I wanted to say I'd go with him, but I couldn't. There was no way I could hang out with a bunch of students from my school, no matter how much I wanted to help him.

"I'm here if you ever need someone to talk to," I called out to Ford's retreating form.

"But not if I want to fuck you?" He questioned over his shoulder.

I didn't answer him. I didn't know if I would say yes or no if he showed up again on my doorstep.

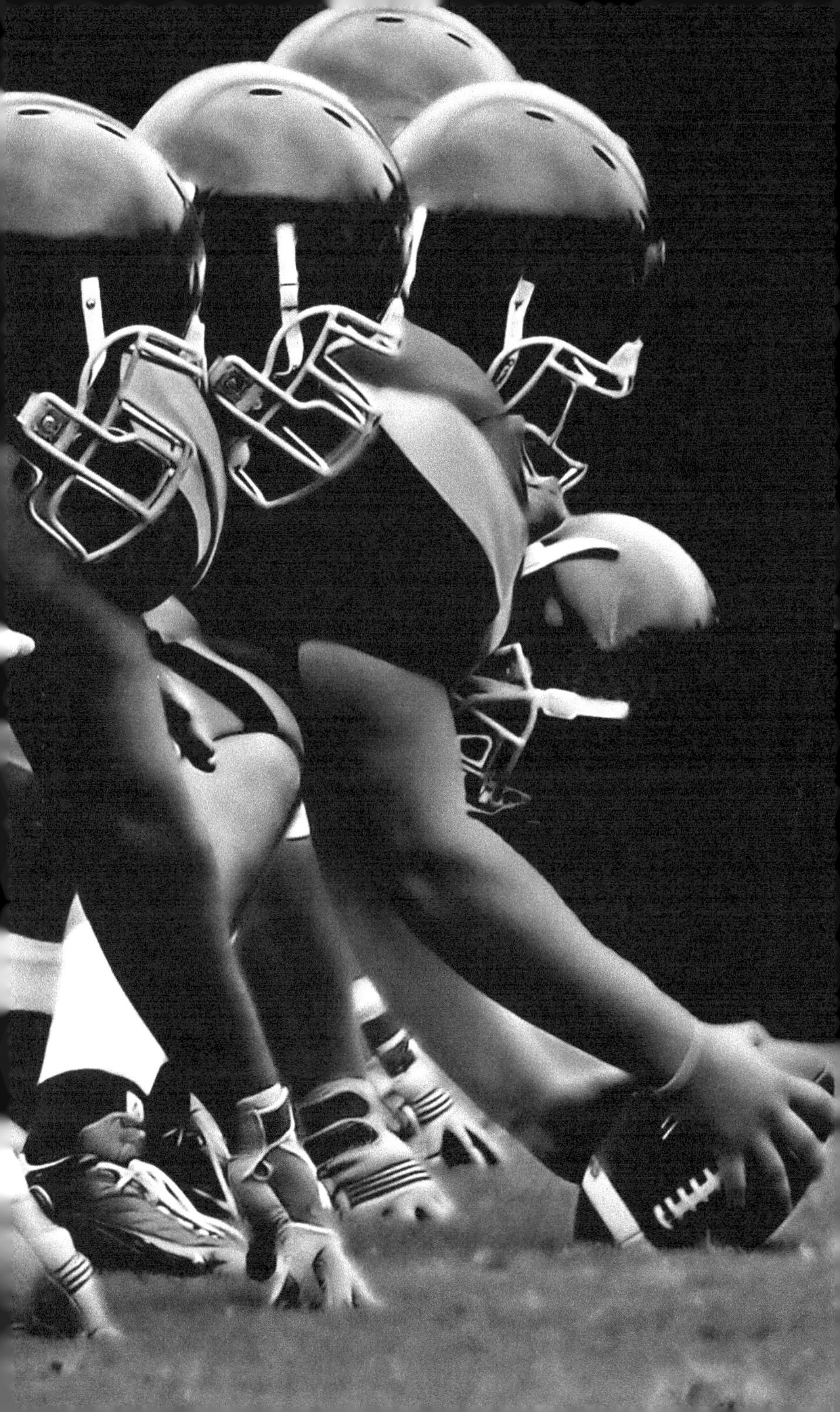

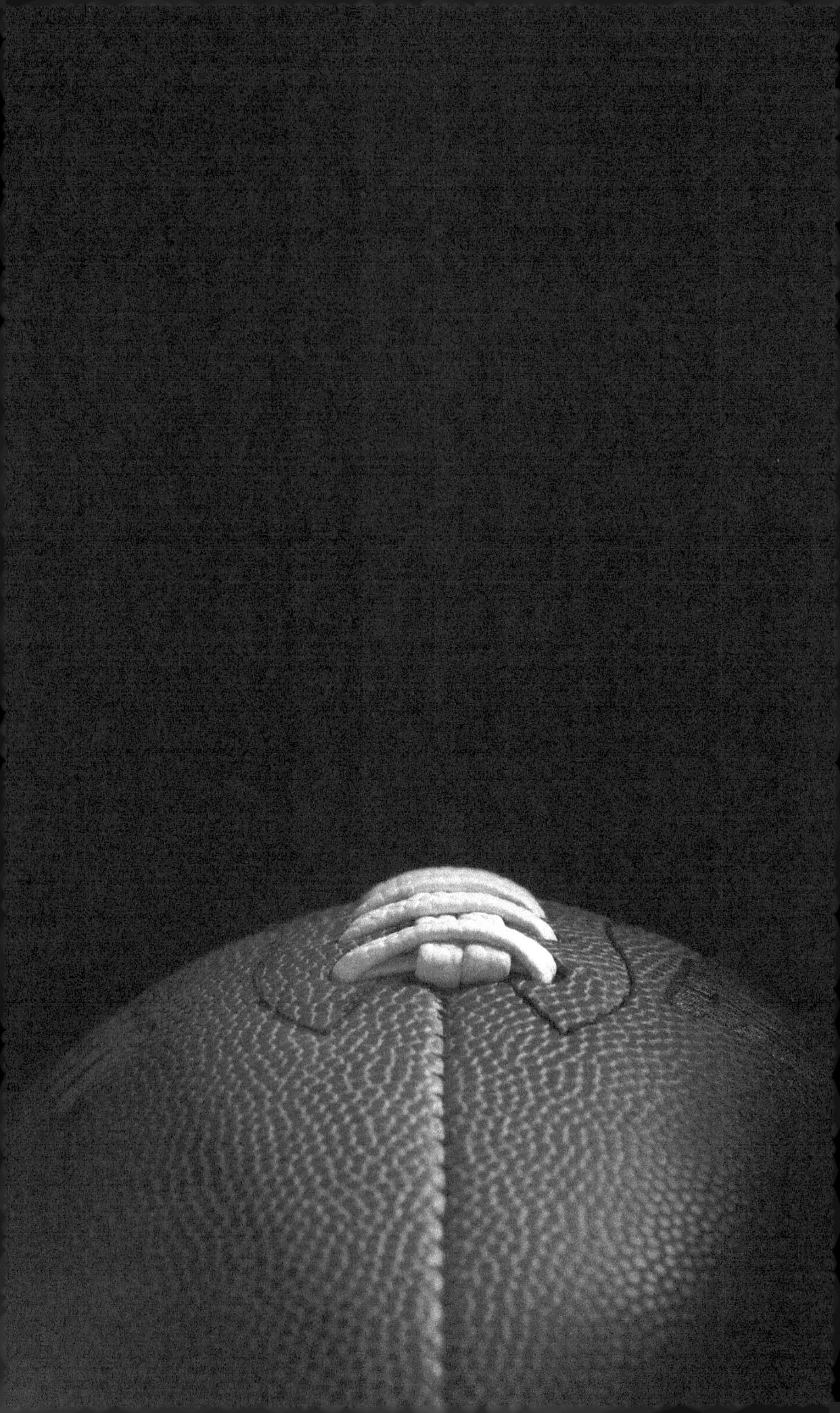

FIVE
FORD

I'D BARELY PUT my car in park before Oz bounded out of the house toward me. His blond hair was disheveled as if he'd been running his fingers through his hair the entire time I'd been gone. His usual happy face was red as he stormed in my direction.

"What the fuck did you say to her?" He barked out. Oz's chest bumped me into the door of my car. I stumbled back, shocked at the show of hostility.

"I didn't say anything to her. That's the problem." I pushed back.

His brow furrowed. "What the fuck is that supposed to mean?"

"She wanted me to talk, and I didn't want to." I shrugged. "West probably told you all that I said I'd rather have what happened to her last year than what I'm going through right now."

"Are you fucking kidding me right now?" Oz slammed his hands on my chest, and I pushed back. Harder. "How could you say that? Lo went through hell."

"And you think I'm not going through hell?" I shouted back. I could feel my face getting hot as my blood started to boil.

"How the fuck would I know? You were MIA for the entire summer, not answering anyone's calls or texts. Then you come back acting like a total asshole."

Death would do that to a person.

"Maybe I've always been an asshole, and I was just good at hiding it?" I sneered.

He shook his head, eyes softening. "Not even for a little bit. An asshole wouldn't have tried making all of Lo's favorite foods in an effort to bring her back."

"Maybe I was doing it to get her to fall for me instead of you." I wasn't sure why I'd said that except to piss off an Oz who was cooling down. I couldn't help myself.

"If I even thought that for a second, I would have killed you," he growled out.

"Ah, there you are. You had everyone snowed as the good guy, but really Oz, you're just like the rest of us assholes. I knew you couldn't be best friends with Fin and be that nice. It was all just an act."

"Enough," Fin boomed from the front porch. He stalked down the sidewalk and pushed us apart. Eyes as dark as mine but now held less malice than when I'd met him my freshman year met mine. "If you've got somewhere to go, I suggest you head there now."

"And if I don't, what happens then? Are you going to kick me out?" Deep down, I wanted him to force me away. For my life here in Willow Bay to be over, just like it was in Las Cruces. I wasn't sure where I'd go if I couldn't live here. There was no way I could afford any of the student housing on campus.

Fin stepped back, crossing his arms over his chest. He took in my wide stance, and fists clenched at my side. "I'm never going to kick you out of here. While I don't know what's going on with you, I do know you're going through something."

"I'm not talking about it."

"And I'm not asking you to. All I'm saying is we're not the bad guys. We're your friends. If you don't want us to know right now, that's fine. Just don't take it out on Lo. She doesn't deserve it."

I hadn't done anything to Lo except not spill my guts to her. I still couldn't believe I'd told Xander.

One thing I did learn was I'd been right. I felt no better. In fact, I only felt worse. If I didn't abhor suicide, I'd kill myself to ease the gut-wrenching sadness and anger that coursed through me from the time I woke up in the morning to the time I laid my head down and tried to sleep. Sleep was an illusion. Every time I closed my eyes, I saw my mother's lifeless body on her bed. Pill bottles scattered around her—all empty. Then the look of my twin brother and sister's faces when I had to break the news to them.

I couldn't wrap my head around why my mother lied to me—to us—for months on end. She said she was fine and healthy when, in fact, cancer had slowly started to eat away at her from almost the moment I stepped foot on the Willow Bay campus.

I wasn't sure I'd ever be able to forgive her for leaving us the way she did. She could have fought, and she didn't even try. Not for me. Not for Christian. And not for Lucy.

Now we were all orphans. At least in my eyes. My dad had moved on. Started a new family and didn't care about his old one. He didn't even offer to let Christian and Lucy live with him when I called him to inform him our mom was now dead. That I had to sell the house to pay off her medical debt, and I didn't have a place for my brother and sister to live.

He only listened to what I had to say, sighed, and then hung up the phone.

If I had the money, I would have sued him or hired a hitman to take him out. Either would have suited me just fine. I could have let the state contact my dad and force him into taking in his children, but Christian and Lucy both hated him as much as I did. They threatened to never talk to me if I made them go live with our dad.

Luckily for them, our aunt Celicia took them in. She'd never been able to have children of her own, and I knew they'd have the best life possible with her. She already had rooms set up for them and was taking them shopping for new clothes for school. Still, I knew it wouldn't be easy to start your junior year of high school somewhere new. At least Luce and Christian had each other. They'd always been thick as thieves, leaving me as an outsider to their group. It's true what they say about twins. They have a special bond no one could break. They didn't need me. Not when they had each other.

My spine straightened until I was at my full height. I looked back and forth between Fin and Oz. They couldn't have been more different, and yet they were somehow best friends. "I didn't do anything to Lo except refuse to talk to her about what I'm dealing with. You should both be able to understand that. You've both had secrets you didn't want to tell."

They couldn't deny I was telling the truth. Oz's secret nearly resulted in him not getting the girl he'd pined after for years on end. Fin's secret kept him miserable for years as well. If I wanted to admit it myself, which I didn't, I could have learned from their mistakes. It was better to have your secret out in the open so it didn't hurt the ones you cared about. Only the thing was, my secret only hurt me. It would destroy me if they knew and acted differently around me, or if I saw pity in their eyes each time they looked at me. They'd probably tell me I no longer needed to cook for them. But no, I wasn't a charity case. And I wanted to cook for them. For me. It was one of the few things that distracted me from my shittastic life.

"I know Lo only deserves the best, and I didn't mean to hurt her feelings. It wasn't my intention, but she and the rest of you need to understand this isn't something I can talk about right now. It's not that I'm trying to hide it from you, but it's too raw." I looked back and forth between them as they stared at me. Fin looked down at me with a furrowed brow. His mouth set in a thin line. While Oz only had concern in his eyes. It was better than pity, but I still didn't like it.

Fin's features hardened before they relaxed. "Like I said. Maybe tonight, you regroup and come back tomorrow with a fresh start." He took a step back and then stopped. "I'm not kicking you out, just trying to let the tension settle."

While I appreciated that, he was taking away one of the few things that let me forget my life for a short time. Maybe I could pick up someone, slip my dick inside a hole, and forget for a little while. But the thought of picking up some random person caused me to only think of Xander. Would he let me back inside if I showed up again?

I guess I would have to take my chances.

"Thanks for not pushing. I think I'm going to try to find someplace else to stay tonight." If all else failed, I could sleep out in my car in the driveway once everyone went to sleep for the night.

"Tomorrow is a new day," Fin said before turning away and going back inside.

"I… I'm sorry. You know how protective I am of Lo, and when I saw her come inside upset, I got pissed. She wouldn't tell me anything, and I assumed you'd done something to hurt her."

"I would never intentionally hurt her or anyone

else in the house. You love her fiercely, and she needs that. I don't fault you for doing what feels right."

Oz clapped me on the shoulder. "Whatever you're going through, I'm sorry. You don't deserve it."

I tried to give him a smile, but I knew I had failed.

He removed his hand and slowly started to walk away. "I'll see you tomorrow at practice."

Fuck, I had forgotten about practice. At least I still had my gear in the backseat of my car.

I watched Oz walk away as I tried to decide if I was going to hit up Xander again or wait it out until everyone was asleep to sleep in the driveway.

Getting in my car, I let my fate make my choice for me.

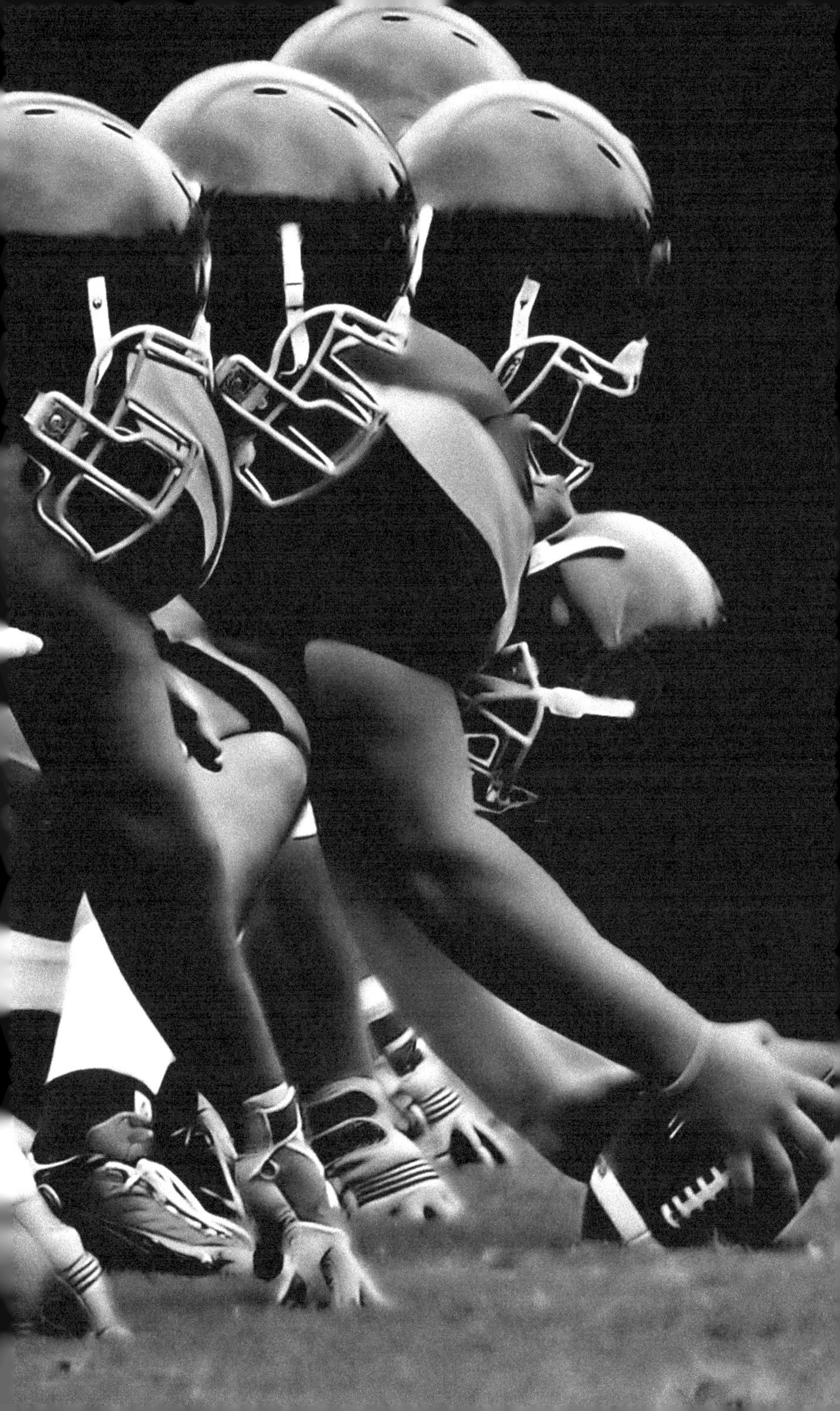

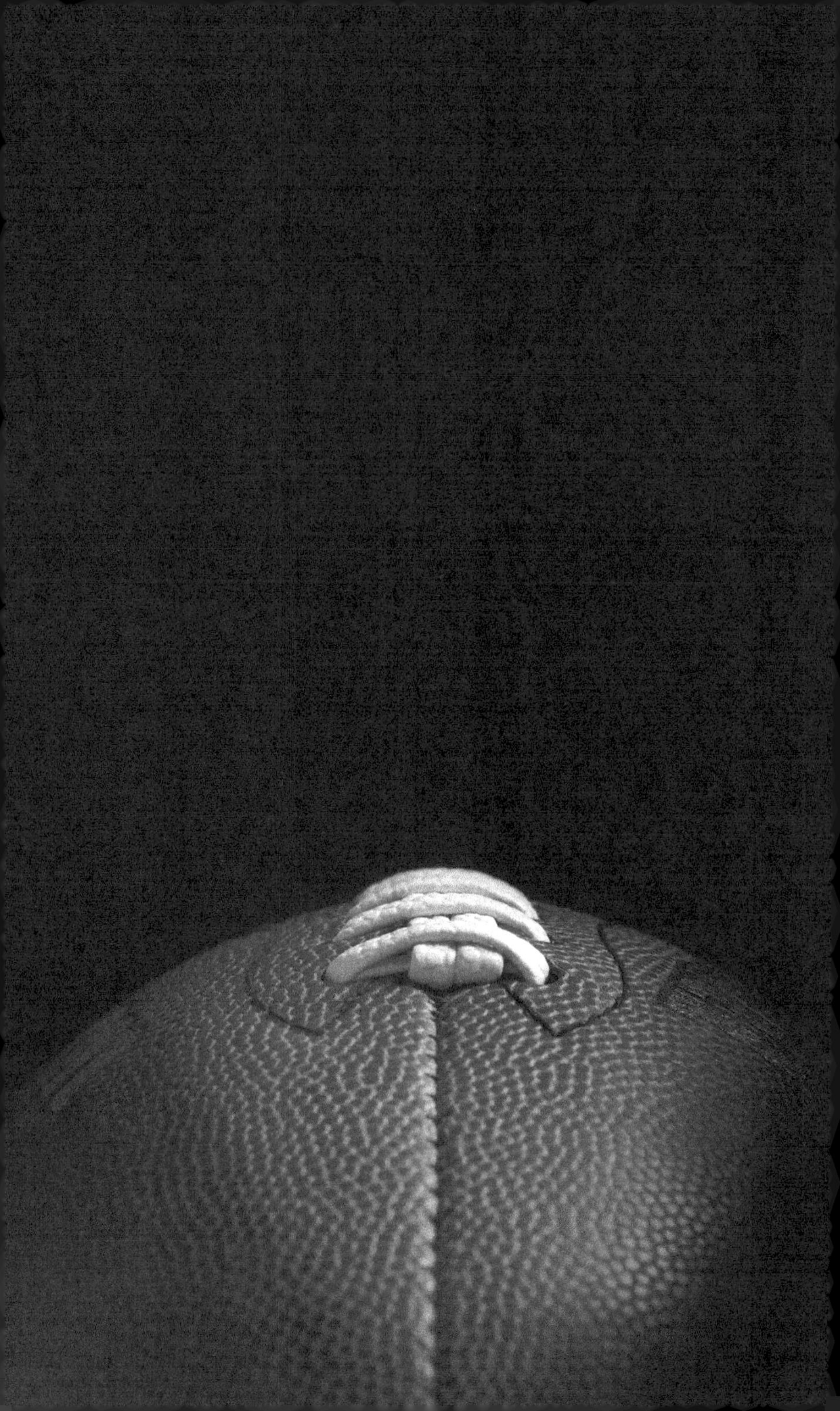

SIX
XANDER

A LOUD NOISE outside had me pausing my movie and going to the front door. I lived in a quiet neighborhood where the only noise came from me. When I pulled the blinds down, I was shocked to find Ford leaning against the column at the end of my front porch.

He hadn't been gone long. Maybe a couple of hours. And what did it say about me that I had thought about him the entire time he'd been gone. I couldn't forget the words he'd spoken about his mom. No wonder he was a mess. Ford was too young to have a parent die. The guilt dripped off him when he spoke about his brother and sister.

I'm not sure how long I stood there watching him looking up at the dark sky. I could feel the anger and sadness from where I watched. Still, I couldn't take my eyes off him. No matter how many times I told myself it was wrong, I couldn't shake how much I wanted Ford or the way I liked how he handled my body.

Had he come back to fuck me, or had he come to unload more of his story?

The second I unlocked my front door, his head swung my way. His dark, troubled eyes met mine before he pushed off and walked toward me.

I met him halfway and stopped short when I saw two brown paper bags sitting on the ground where he'd been standing. "I wasn't sure if you were ever going to knock."

"Me either," was his simple reply.

Lifting my chin, I nodded. "What's in the bags?"

"I thought I could make us some dinner, but if you've already eaten." He stopped and looked toward the house, and for a moment, he looked nervous. Then he was back to his broody self again.

There was no way I was going to tell him only ten minutes ago I'd eaten a bag of popcorn as my dinner. I finally got him out of my head, and now he was back to take over. Trying to play it cool, I crossed my arms over my chest and looked at the bags again. "Depends on what you were planning to make."

Ford's eyes narrowed even as the corner of his lips tipped up. "Cilantro-Lime Chicken with an avocado salsa and quinoa." He lifted a brow. "Is that up to your standards?"

Up to my standards? If Ford made what he'd just said, it would be the best meal I'd had all year. Maybe even in the last five years. Cooking for one wasn't fun, so I usually stuck to pretty basic meals.

"I guess beggars can't be choosers," I said, moving to pick up the bags from where they lay on the ground. "Do you need a sous chef?"

A dark cloud passed over his face as his features tensed. "I prefer to cook alone."

"Perfect because I suck at cooking. I can barely make the necessities."

Normally this would be where someone would say they'd teach you even if they had no intentions of teaching you, but Ford only stared at me, his eyes dead of all emotion. I wasn't sure what happened in the short period of time he'd been gone, but it couldn't have been good. He urgently left, claiming the need to cook his roommates' dinner, and yet here he was.

Ford followed behind me to the kitchen and watched as I carefully laid out all the groceries he'd brought over. Then it was my turn to stand back and watch. He moved like he'd been cooking in my kitchen every day of his life instead of it being the first time.

His knife skills were impeccable. Ford was as close to a certified chef as I'd seen. "Where'd you learn to cook?"

Ford's eyes flicked up to meet mine for only a second before he went back to work on the chicken.

"My mom was busy working to support me and my brother and sister. Someone needed to cook our meals, so I taught myself." He said it in the most monotone voice I'd ever heard from him.

It must have been a touchy subject, and yet I pushed. "Still, most don't learn to cook anything near what you're making tonight. They make ramen, mac and cheese, or chicken nuggets. What you're making could be served in a restaurant."

He shrugged one shoulder as he cut up the avocado. "We got tired of having the same meals all the time, so I looked up recipes on my phone and watched YouTube videos. And then, when I started to play football, I needed to eat healthy, but I didn't want to eat the same meals day in and day out. I've upped my game a lot since being here. The guys like my food and not eating plain chicken with some sort of vegetable every night. I get to explore a little more with whatever I make for Lo."

I cocked my head to the side, unsure if what I heard was right. "Are you saying you make two dinners every night?"

He stiffened, setting down his knife. I wasn't sure what I'd said to cause that kind of reaction out of him, so I kept silent, waiting to see if he'd fill the silence.

"Do you have a grill?" He asked without looking at me.

I did, but I'd only used it once, and I wasn't even sure if it still worked.

"Out back, but I can't promise it works." I guided him out to my backyard, where Ford stood, and took in the softly lit yard and the little oasis in the corner. There was a small koi pond with a fountain and flowers on one side of it. On the other was a covered seating area. It was one of the main reasons I bought the house. It was the perfect place to relax after a long day. It's where I should have gone after Ford left earlier, but I was too rattled by his revelation to even think straight.

"Maybe we could eat out here. It's a nice enough night." Although, I wasn't sure if it was smart to have him in my sanctuary. I didn't want to see Ford everywhere I went in my house.

Ford didn't answer me, though. I wasn't sure if it was because it would seem more like a date or couples thing to do or what. Instead, he inspected the grill, and before I knew it, he had our chicken filling my backyard with its delicious aroma.

I stood off to the side, watching like some creeper as Ford grilled our dinner and placed it on a plate, and then went back inside with the food. I wasn't sure if he had heard me when I made a comment about eating outside until he filled his plate with food and headed out back without a word.

Ford didn't seem like the talkative type of guy, but damn, it was weird for him to be in my space and act as if I wasn't here. Maybe tonight he needed silence, and if that were the case, I'd give it to him. I knew tomorrow he'd be gone, and I'd likely be pining after him while he thought nothing of me.

I took one bite of the chicken and moaned, my mouth salivating for more. "This is damn good." I cut another piece with my knife and fork and was shoving it into my mouth before he could speak.

"It's simple. You could make it anytime you'd like," he muttered before eating a bite of his own.

"You don't give yourself enough credit. This is

damn good. You could be a chef in any of the best restaurants in the state. Hell, the world."

Ford set his fork down. His mouth was turned down as he took me in. "I don't need you blowing smoke up my ass just because I can make a decent meal."

I gritted my teeth, hating he didn't believe me. "While I'm a teacher and it's my job to be supportive, I would never tell anyone something I didn't believe. You're talented. You made this with a handful of ingredients. If I were at a restaurant, I'd pay twenty-five to thirty bucks for this meal." Hell, probably more, but I wasn't sure he'd appreciate me saying so.

His dark, turbulent eyes met mine, and he stared at me for a long moment before he looked down and started to cut another piece of chicken to eat. "Promise you won't laugh at me."

"I guarantee you that whatever you tell me, I won't laugh at you." This was a promise I knew I could easily make.

He gave me a slight nod as he chewed his piece of chicken. "I was thinking about changing my major to culinary arts. I heard they have a good program here."

"Why would I laugh at that? This is something

you're good at and passionate about. I think you should go for it."

"I have to be approved first."

"I don't know why they wouldn't accept you." I searched his face, looking for any kind of clue as to why he'd think he wouldn't be accepted. "Do you have to write an essay or something?"

His black eyes flashed with fire. "Just cook them a three-course meal and present it to them. My food will be my application." He said the words as if what we were eating was garbage and not one of the best meals I'd had in I didn't know how long.

"So, what the problem?" I didn't understand why he doubted himself. He cooked for his roommates and siblings. Surely, they told him how good his food was.

"The closest thing I've ever made was Thanksgiving dinner. They want to be wowed, not bored by mediocrity." His tone was clipped as his jaw ticked with each word he spoke.

"I know you don't have much time until school starts, but you can practice before you present. When's the deadline?"

"It was the day after I moved here."

Now I understood why he hadn't proceeded. "Do you want me to make any inquiries? See if they'll make an exception? I'm sure if you tell them why you didn't submit earlier, they'll let you apply."

"I'm not a charity case," he gritted out.

"And I never said you were. Did those words come out of my mouth? No, they did not. I merely suggested you explain why you were not in the right headspace. They may not have any spots left open, and you won't be able to get in until next year. You'll never know if you don't try." I paused, reaching forward and gripping his hand with mine. "But I can tell by this one meal that they'd be stupid if they didn't let you into their program."

One moment Ford was across the table from me, and the next, he had me splayed on the ground beside the table. He used his body to hold me to the ground as he pressed his mouth to mine. Ford didn't wait for me to open up for him. He shoved his tongue into my mouth like he'd shoved himself into my life and took over. His full lips moved against mine in the most delicious and torturous ways.

I clawed at his shirt, pulling it up and snaking my hand up the back to feel his muscles shift and bulge as he ground himself against me.

Pulling back, he panted. His hot breath fanned across my face. "Fuck, I need to be inside of you. I've never been so desperate as I am with you. What have you done to me?"

I wanted to ask him the same question. Ford had ahold of me in a way that I knew was bad news. This couldn't go anywhere. If anyone found out I was fucking a student, I would be fired faster than I could blink.

Leaning back on his heels, Ford quickly divested me of the sweatpants I'd put on earlier. Never had I been so happy to go commando in my life.

"Fuck, you're ready for me. Pre-cum leaking and everything. Don't ever wear underwear again," he demanded. "I like behind able to rip your pants down and know I can shove inside of you at any moment."

I liked that more than I should.

Rough hands yanked me to my front and then up onto my hands and knees. One hand ran over the globes of my ass as I heard a package rip. Looking over my shoulder, I found Ford coating his fingers with lube. His eyes met mine as he prodded two inside me and started to pump. I continued to watch him as he fucked me with his fingers, all the while keeping his eyes locked on mine.

"I need to be in that tight hole of yours," he gritted out. I could see his erection tenting the fabric of his athletic shorts. I knew I'd feel so damn full with his big cock stuffed inside of me. I moaned at the thought.

Pulling his fingers out, Ford pushed his shorts down enough for his cock to spring out and slap against his stomach. Using the rest of the lube, he coated the condom that covered his dick until it was nice and shiny. He closed his eyes for a moment as he stroked himself languidly.

Shifting, he nestled in, positioning himself directly behind me. His mushroom tip breached the tight ring of muscle. This time he didn't slam inside in one go. He inched in and out until he was fully sheathed. It was like his dick was made for me. With each stroke, he hit my prostate. I didn't even think it was a conscious effort, but damn did I appreciate how he swiveled his hips each time he started to pull out.

This only lasted a moment before Ford started to quicken his pace. His hips slapped against my ass as his fingers dug into my skin.

Wrapping my hand around my shaft, I matched his rhythm, ready to explode. With a couple more strokes, hot cum shot out all over my hand and onto the ground as Ford moved faster.

"You feel so damn good. I love the way you

squeeze my cock," he moaned, stilling deep inside of me. I could feel it as he pulsed and came inside the condom.

Resting his forehead on my shoulder, Ford panted against my back until both of our heartbeats slowed.

"I'm not done with you," Ford grunted as he stood. He reached a hand out to me. Without thinking, I let him help me off the ground then guide me through my own house and up the stairs, where he promptly pushed me down on my bed and climbed on top of me.

He filled my body with his fingers and cock until I was a puddle of bones on my bed, and I fell asleep with him at my side. Sated and content.

When I woke up the next morning, Ford's side of the bed was cold. It was almost as if the entire night had been a dream, but the cycle repeated again and again for the next two weeks until school started.

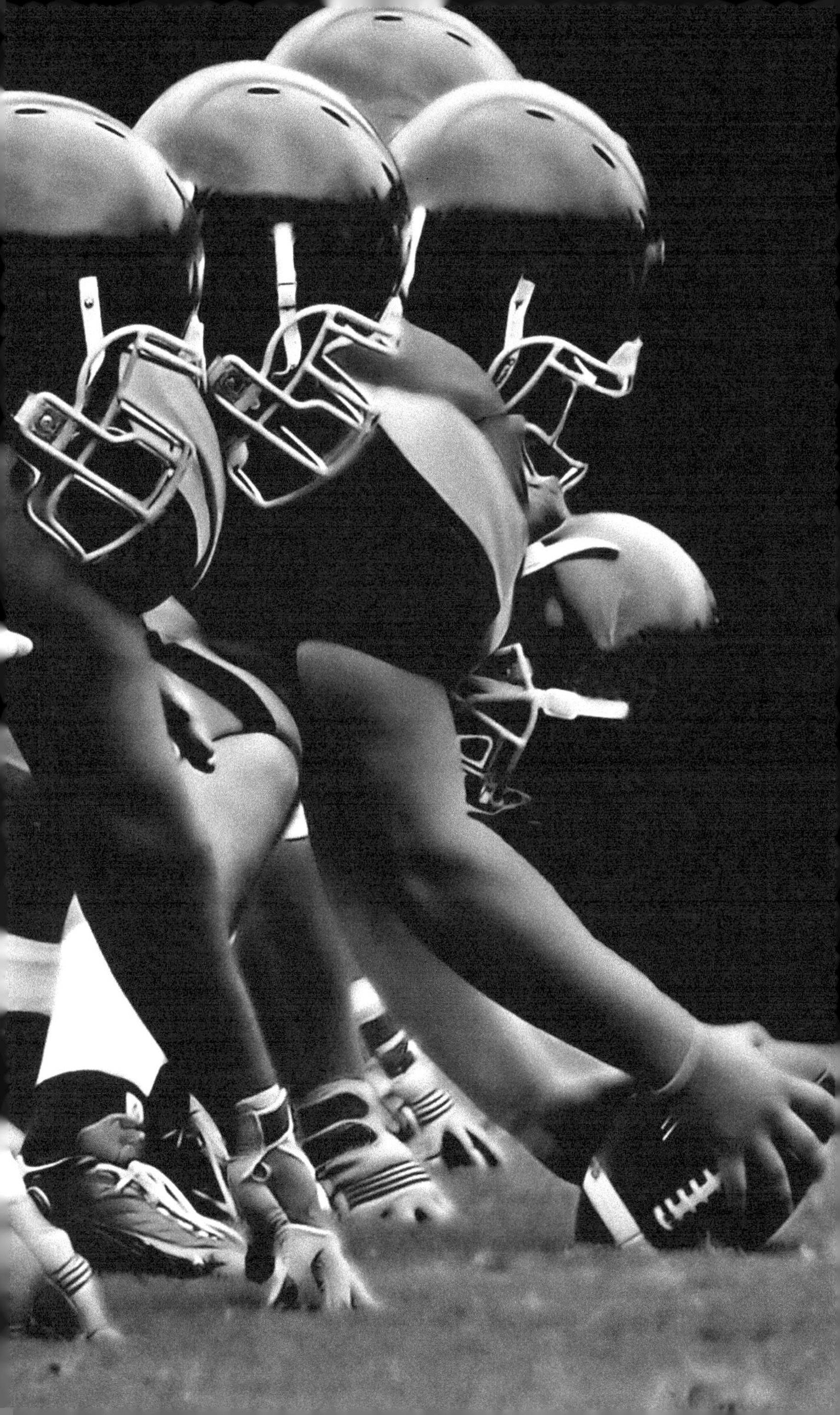

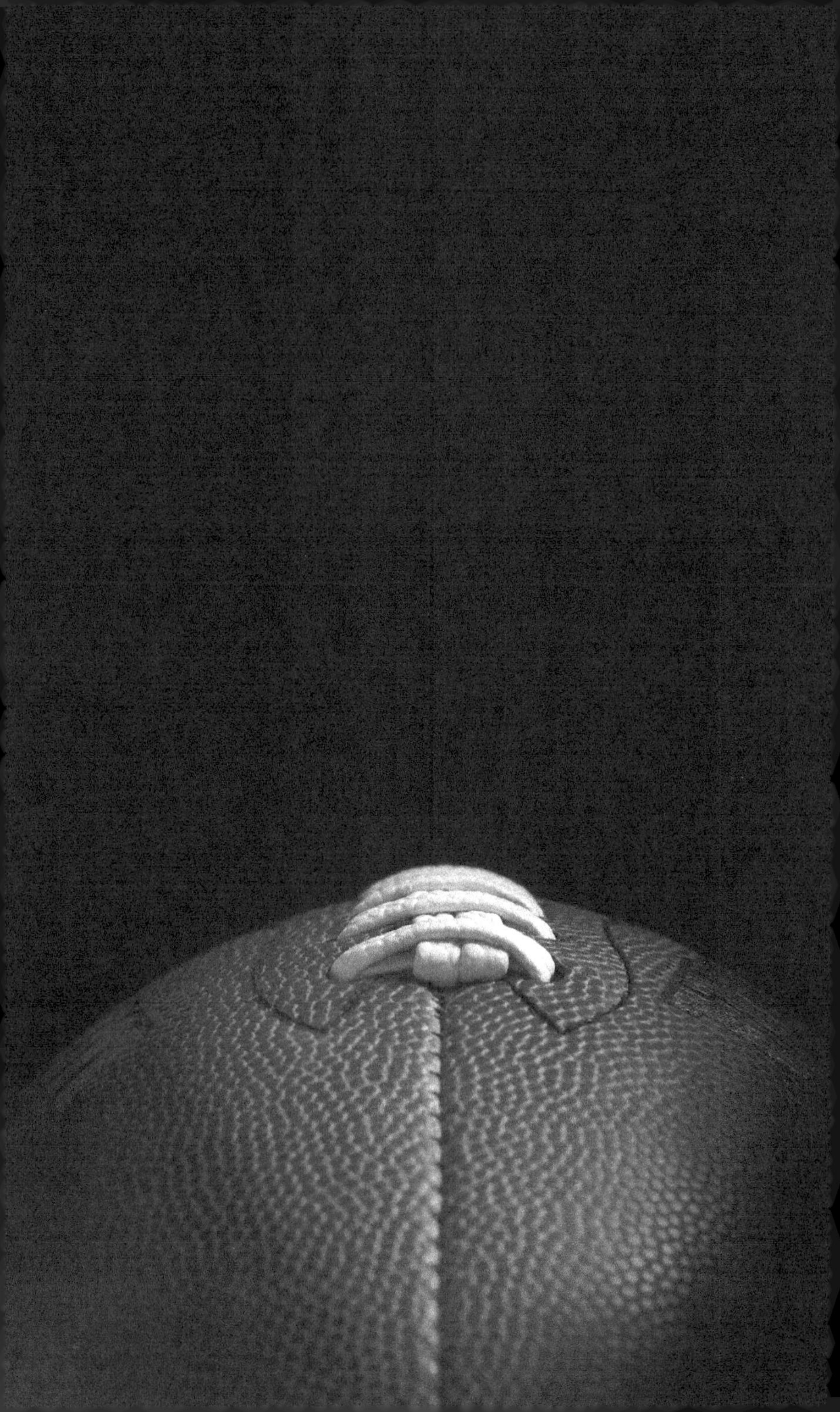

SEVEN
FORD

MY DICK ACHED as I crawled out of bed and headed to the shower. Last night was the first night I'd stayed the night at my house in two weeks. I still made them dinner and breakfast each day, but other than that, I was gone. Mostly at Xander's house. Except last night he said we both needed to get some sleep since today was the first day of class. What he didn't say was he was ending it. I knew it was going to happen. I wasn't blind to how his demeanor changed each time I mentioned school or football practice. It was a reminder to him that what we were doing was wrong in his eyes. I wouldn't be surprised if the next time I showed up on his doorstep, he told me to go home—because there was going to be a next time. I was addicted to Xander.

Stepping into the steaming hot water, I let it rain down on me, loosening my tight muscles. Each and every day, I gave my all at practice, exhausting my body in the hopes it would exhaust my mind as well. When that didn't work, I fucked Xander until neither one of us could come again. Only then could I sleep for a few hours before the nightmares woke me up.

I lathered my hands with soap and ran them over my body until I reached my still hard cock. It wasn't going away, especially when I woke up from a dream of Xander's lips wrapped around the tip of my dick.

Fucking alarm clock. Fucking classes.

Why couldn't I have a few minutes more to finish my dream? It didn't matter because I was going to finish it now.

Wrapping my hand around my shaft, I fucked my hand as fiercely as I would fuck Xander's ass or mouth. I never held back with him as I tried to rid my demons one orgasm at a time.

Picking up my pace, I imagined Xander's dark skin glistening with sweat as I slammed into him from behind. The way his muscles rippled as he pushed back against me, wanting more, his kind eyes fueled by lust as he panted my name.

I tightened my grip, squeezing the tip when I reached the top, trying to hold off my impending orgasm. It was no use as I pictured Xander stroking himself as I rammed into him and coming all over his stomach and chest.

I braced myself on the wall as pleasure shot through me. Closing my eyes, I took a breath, reality slowly seeping back in.

My mom was dead. She'd lied to me and everyone else. My brother and sister refused to speak to me, and there was no way I could travel to see them and make them understand. At least not until the football season was over or I had a break in my schedule.

With the real world staring back at me in the mirror, I quickly dried off and got dressed in order for me to cook breakfast and once again forget everything for only a few minutes. The moments when I could push down all my problems were what got me out of bed. Usually, I only got a handful of hours of sleep each night. Nightmares plagued me. I never used to want to get out of bed, but now I resented my bed and what would follow.

Lo watched me from the dining room table as I set down their breakfast. I grabbed the sausage burrito I made, along with my backpack. "Good luck with your classes. I'll see you tonight." I knew she was nervous about finally getting back into the classroom after a year of classes online.

"Thanks. You're not eating breakfast with us?" She eyed my hand on my backpack strap.

"I need to pick up my new schedule and see what classes I have."

Lo smiled at me, hurt feelings over me not talking to her forgotten. "I'm proud of you for getting into the culinary program. You're going to make one hell of a chef one day."

"One day?" West laughed as he sat down at the table. "Ford is a rock star now. In ten years when he's a famous chef, we'll all be saying how he used to cook for us every day."

I wasn't sure how to take their praise. It didn't feel warranted. I didn't deserve their kindness or this life. Not when I couldn't even save my mother.

A weak smile tipped my lips. "Thanks, guys. Have a good day."

"You too," they both said at the same time.

Giving them a brief wave, I stepped outside and felt my fake smile fall. I was trying not to be an asshole when I was at home, but it was difficult when I knew they all wanted me to talk.

I was unprepared for my first day of classes, and it sucked balls. I'd only been accepted into the program two days ago, and on both of those days, we'd had two-a-day practices. I didn't have the time or energy to even look at the information I was given about my classes. Now I wished I had. I needed a set of knives I couldn't afford. I was supposed to have a week's worth of meals planned out with all of their nutritional information. I'd barely started, and I was already in the hole. Tonight, when I got home, I was going to finish going through the rest of my classes to make sure I was prepared for tomorrow. Luckily, this was my last class for the day. I took the steps two at a time as I climbed to the top of the classroom. I already knew Econ wasn't going to be my strong suit, and I wanted to be as far from the teacher as possible. Maybe if I was all the way at the top, whoever was teaching the class wouldn't call on me.

Pulling out my notebook and pen, I sat back, ready for class to start, so it could hopefully be over quickly. Maybe the teacher would go over the syllabus and let class out if I was lucky. I guess I should be thanking my lucky stars that I didn't have to take Stats. It was a class I would surely flunk. I understood they wanted us to be prepared for the world, but these business classes weren't my jam.

I ignored everyone who sat around me. Scrolling through my phone as I looked up recipes and nutritional information, I heard the room get quiet and then a steady flow of excited whispers.

"Good afternoon, class. I'm Professor Lawrence, and I'll be your teacher for Econ 101." My head whipped up to find Xander standing down at the bottom of the classroom with a piece of paper in his hands. "This will be your seat for the remainder of the semester unless you talk to me and I approve you moving. I'm going to do roll call, and then we'll get started."

I held my breath as each name was called out. I knew Xander was going to freak out when he saw me, and it wouldn't be long since he was going in alphabetical order from A to Z. Ford Fitzgerald was always close to the front, something I'd always hated since I was a young kid when teachers did activities alphabetically.

"Ford Fitzgerald," Xander called out without looking up. When I didn't answer, his gaze swung up and searched the room until his eyes landed on me. His voice was tight as he said my name again.

"Here," I called out and then had to clear my throat.

What were the odds he'd be my professor? I

pulled out my schedule and searched for the class and teacher, only to find the teacher's name blank.

Fuck my life.

Xander's jaw flexed before he went back to calling roll. Before he walked into the room, I planned to keep my head down and be as invisible as possible. Now, I couldn't take my eyes off of my teacher. Econ suddenly just got very interesting.

He was never going to let me inside his house or in his body ever again.

My eyes never left Xander as he introduced what we would be doing throughout the semester, while he did everything in his power not to look at me. I was almost tempted to wave my hand in the air or ask a question to get his attention back on me. Was Xander going to try and ignore me like this every day?

It was interesting to see and hear all the girls whispering about him, talking about the hot professor. I even overheard one say she wondered if she could do a little extra credit with him to get a better grade. I'd never thought about women finding Xander attractive. We hadn't spoken about our sexuality, but I didn't think he was bi like me. Xander was strictly dickly as far as I was concerned.

Maybe it was in my best interest to try and find a

new fuck buddy, especially since fucking my teacher wasn't going to work. I could easily find some girl to suck my dick and let me dominate her for a short while. There had been a few during my time at Willow Bay U, but none had held my interest for long.

Class ended with twenty minutes left. I hung back, waiting until the room had cleared before I made my way down the stairs and stood in front of Xander's desk. He didn't bother to look up at me as he spoke.

"My office hours are Tuesdays at three and Wednesdays at two." His voice was matter of fact like we'd never spoken before.

Bracing my hands on his desk, I leaned down and waited for him to look up and meet my gaze. A slow smirk spread across my face. "Are you saying you don't have time to talk to me now, Professor?"

"That's exactly what I'm saying." He looked back down and went back to writing. "If you need to talk to me, come see me during my office hours."

We'd see if he had the same stance when I showed up on his doorstep tonight.

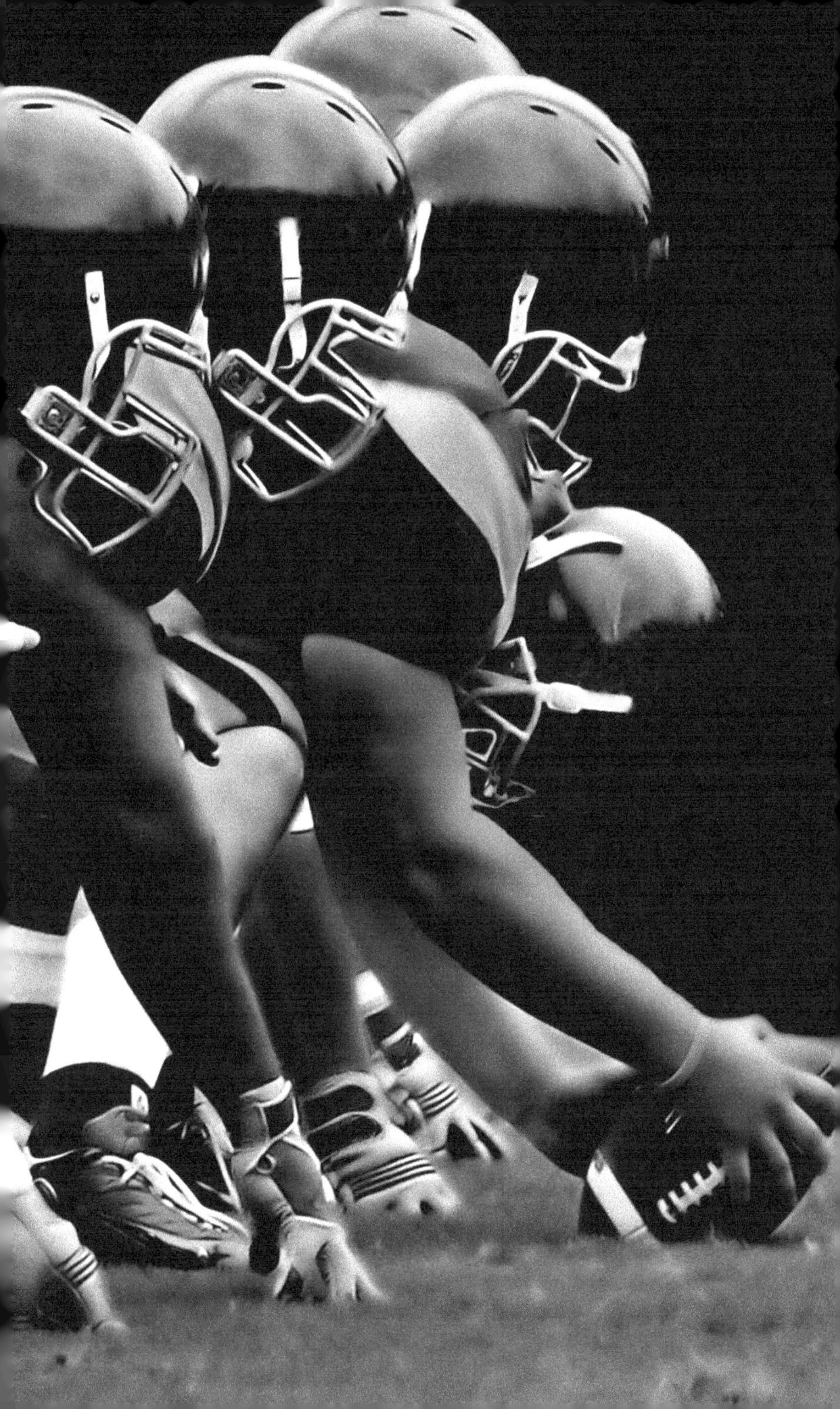

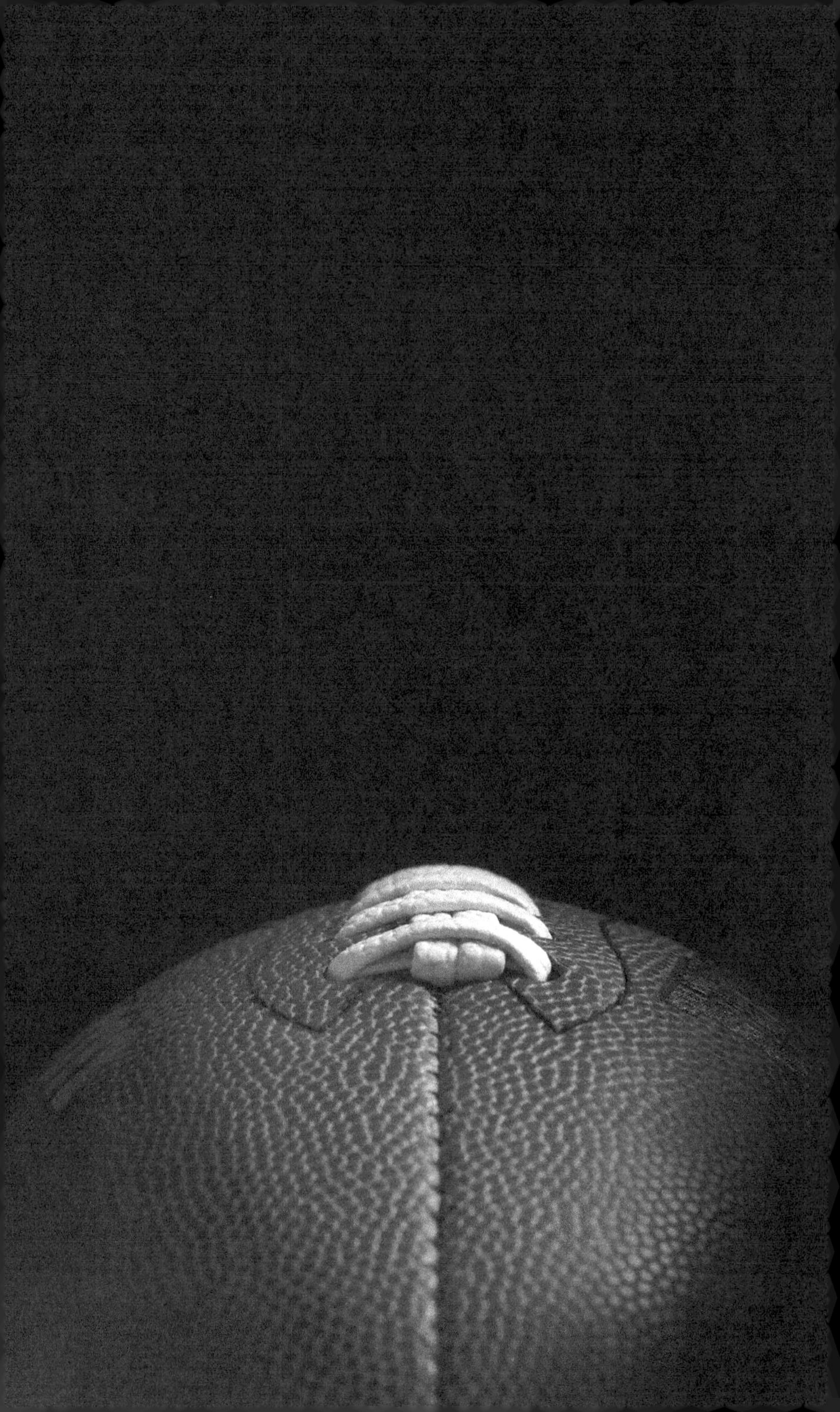

EIGHT
XANDER

AT TEN O'CLOCK on the dot, I was startled when a loud knock sounded on my front door. I shouldn't have been. I knew Ford would likely show up after I refused to speak to him after class, but why did he wait until so late? Maybe he knew the chances of me opening the door were greater the later it was. While I didn't want to disrupt my neighbors, I also didn't plan to let him inside.

"I know you're inside, so open up," Ford pounded on the door again.

Resting my forehead on the door, I closed my eyes as I spoke. "Go home, Ford, and get some rest. We both have classes tomorrow."

"I'm well aware, but if I can make it to early

football practices, I can make it to a ten o'clock class after being inside of you all night."

I gritted my teeth at what I was about to say. "There won't be any more nights of you fucking me. It's over."

"Stop being so fucking lame. You know you love the way I fuck you. Now, let me the fuck in."

Did he really think talking to me like that would change my mind? I scoffed.

"Leave Ford. Nothing you say is going to convince me to let you in. I can't do this any longer. You're my student."

"Why? Are you planning to give me all A's or F's because we're fucking?" With each word he spoke, his voice grew louder.

I turned, rolling my head against the hard wood of the door. "I would never do that."

"I didn't think you would, so I don't see what the problem is." He slammed something against the door. I couldn't tell if it was his hand or his head. There was a long pause before he spoke again. This time, he was quieter, the tone of his voice almost begging. "Let me in, and I'll give you the best damn orgasm of your life."

"I'm sure you would, but I can't, Ford. I'm sorry," I choked on the last word. "Keeping my job is more important." I knew the second I said those words that they were the wrong ones to say. I meant them, but Ford was in such a fragile state I shouldn't make him feel unimportant.

"Yeah, I see how it is." He slammed something hard against my door again. This time it sounded like his whole body. "I was good enough for a screw, but nothing more. Now you'll find someone else to fuck your brains out."

He was so angry and hurt, and this time it was me who had done this to him. I couldn't tell him there would never be another man to fuck me the way he had, even if it were true.

"Ford," I sighed out his name. "If your coach found out, you wouldn't be able to play football any longer. How would that make you feel?"

There were a few muffled sounds before he spoke again. "If the choice were fucking you or football, I'd choose you. Let's be real here. I'm not going pro." There was a pregnant pause. "Just let me in, Xander. Why are we talking like this?"

Because I knew if I let him in, it would lead to him in my bed, and I could let it happen again. If I did, I wasn't sure I'd be able to stop him again.

"Listen, Ford." I slid down the door and sat on the floor with my back pressed against the cool wood. "You're young, insanely good-looking, and fit. You can have anyone you want. You don't need a man who is fifteen years older than you when you can have someone your own age. Someone there won't be consequences for being with."

Ford let out a deep and dark laugh that sent chills down my spine. I knew immediately I wouldn't like what he was about to say. "Are you saying it won't bother you to know I'll be out fucking someone else? Or multiple someones?"

I couldn't say that because deep down, I knew it would, but I'd have to get over it. This was what was best for both of us.

"No, it won't bother me," I struggled to get out. The thought twisted my stomach into knots even though I had no claim on Ford. None whatsoever.

"And why don't I believe you?" he laughed bitterly.

"You can choose to believe me or not. That's up to you, but I am not going to let you into my house or my bed. I'm not going to let you fuck up my life for a quick roll in the hay."

"I see. Well, thanks for using me to get your rocks off. Tomorrow I'll transfer to another Econ class, so you won't be reminded every time I'm in your class what a mistake you made being with me."

I didn't have the heart to tell him I was the only one teaching that class.

"You're not a mistake, Ford. You're just a complication I can't continue to have in my life."

"Yeah, fuck you too." There was a loud slam on the door right where I was resting my head. I felt the reverberation through my body and where it settled deep down in my soul.

I sat there and listened as Ford cursed his way back to his car and peeled out as he left my driveway. Half the street was probably up and looking out their windows, wondering who the hell was disrupting their early bedtime. They'd be glaring at me and whispering about me for the next two months, if not more. Nothing happened in my sleepy neighborhood, and Ford just gave them the show of a lifetime.

My body was stiff as I pulled myself off the floor and up the stairs to my bedroom. Even though I was emotionally drained, I stepped under the steamy spray of my shower and tried to let the hot water ease some of the tension in my muscles. My dick was angry at me, jutting up and laying against my stomach, cursing me for sending Ford away before he got me off one last time. I was going to miss the way he knew how to make me cum with little effort. Ford was an aphrodisiac all to himself.

I crawled into bed still wet and pulled the blanket up, trying to chase away the hurt in Ford's voice as I lied to him. It wouldn't have done either one of us any good if I'd told him the truth. We'd both be better off in the long run. At least that's what I was telling myself. It didn't help, though. I tossed and turned the entire night, barely getting any sleep. If it weren't for the pot of coffee in my system, I wouldn't have been able to keep my eyes open the next day during my classes.

You would have thought I would have been able to sleep the next night, but that wasn't the case. My mind kept replaying Ford outside my door, each of his words digging deeper and deeper, making me want to rewind time and let him in. Maybe I would have been strong and not have given into temptation, but I knew I would have. That's why I hurt him—to protect us both.

STEPPING into my classroom bleary-eyed since I hadn't slept in two days, I caught Ford's dark eyes staring daggers at me. I wanted to say fuck you too since he'd been the reason I hadn't slept. Instead, I gave him a tight-lipped smile and moved behind my desk. I set my briefcase down, got out my materials for the class, and sat on the edge of my desk.

I went on autopilot as I tried not to look in Ford's direction. Was I successful one hundred percent of the time? No, but I sure as hell did my best not to meet his penetrating gaze. Maybe I should have said there were no other Econ classes, so he would have been prepared, but I knew it would have only set him off further.

With the scathing looks he was giving me, I had a feeling I should expect him to be beating on my door tonight.

I kept myself busy once class ended, speaking with other students as Ford tried to stick around. The girls were hungry for my attention, and I knew it would only increase how pissed off he was. Little did they know, I had zero interest in women, no matter how much they fluttered their eyelashes at me. I didn't notice Ford leaving until I heard the door slam behind him.

I knew then I'd be expecting my midnight visitor.

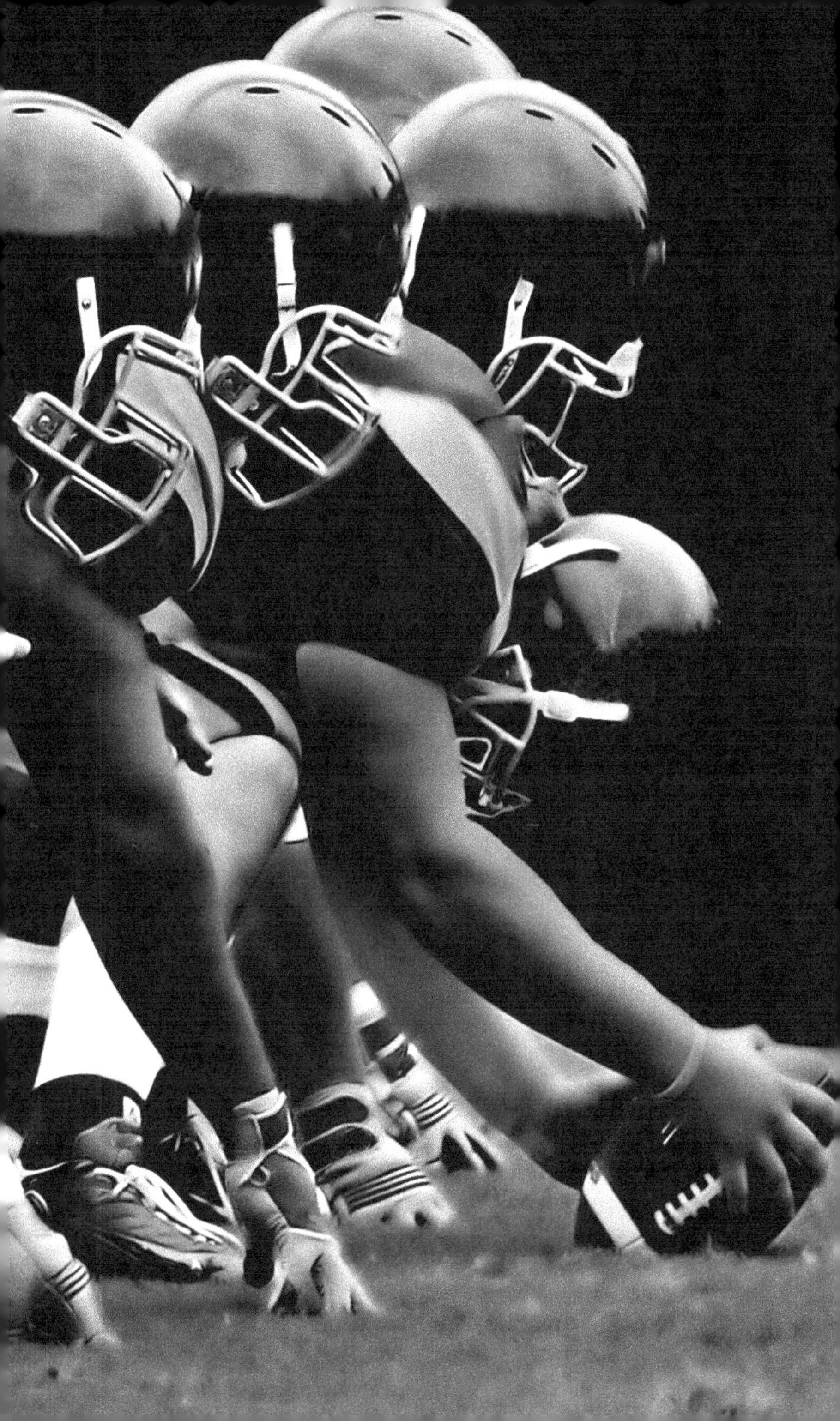

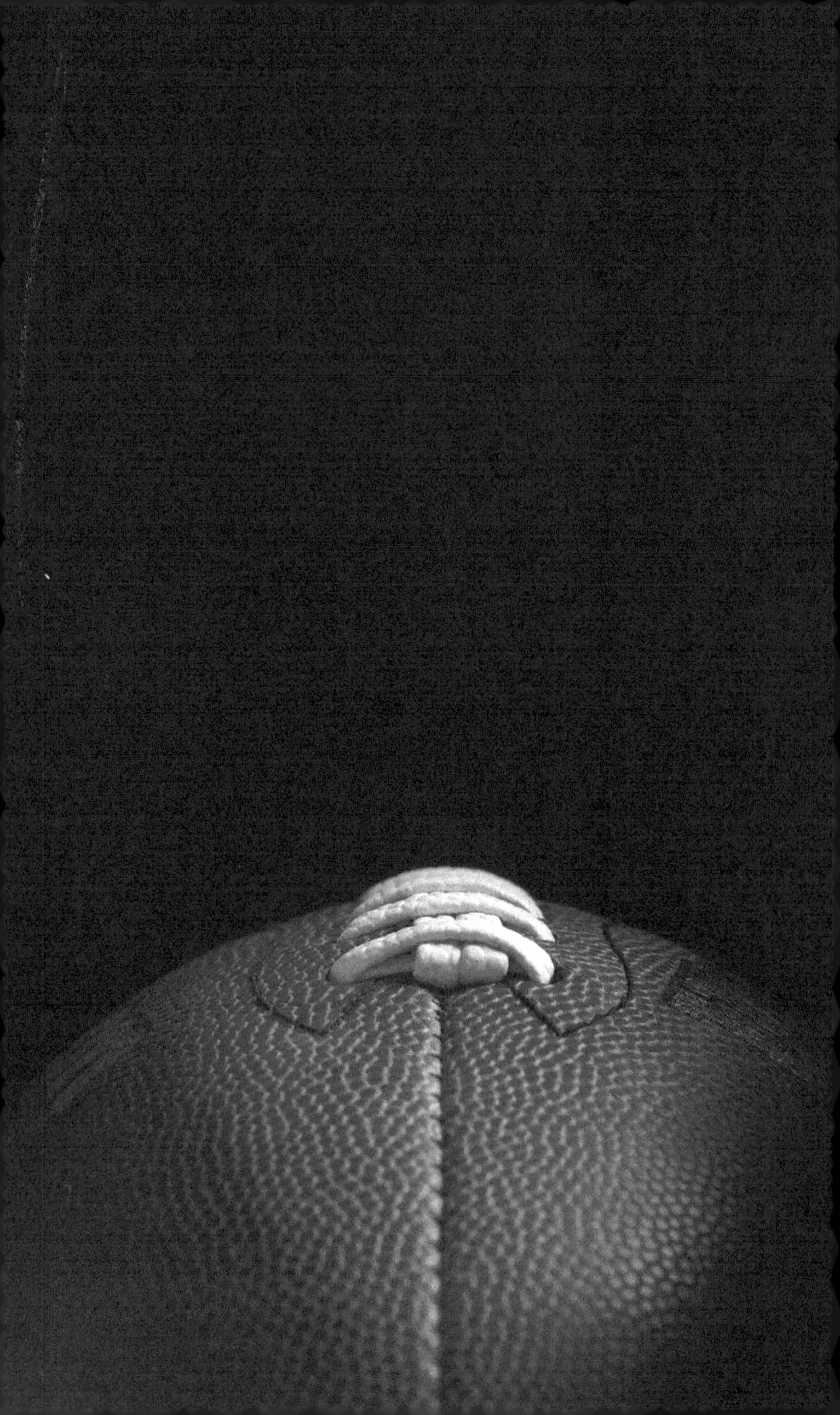

NINE
FORD

ALMOST SEVEN HOURS LATER, my blood was still boiling. There wasn't even a level to how livid I was. If I didn't do something to eliminate the riot of emotions circling inside of me, I was going to do something stupid. My roommates were all sticking to their rooms to keep some distance from me. Even Fin and that was saying something.

I was itching for a fight or release.

Jumping in my car, I headed to the one place I knew I could vent my overwhelming frustrations. That was *if* he let me in. Even if he didn't, Xander was going to hear what I had to say to him. Even if I had to do it from outside his door with his entire street listening, it was up to him if they knew all of his business or not.

Slamming the brakes in front of his house, I slowly got out of my car, barely able to contain my rage now that I was here. The loud bang of my car door closing should have been an indicator to everyone in the vicinity of how this was going to go down.

I moved slowly, taking in Xander's perfect house. Why did he get to have everything he wanted, and I got nothing? I had no home to go to once college was over. No family to speak of since my brother and sister still refused to speak to me. Didn't they see they were better off at Aunt Celicia's than homeless with me? Our aunt could give them the life they deserved. While Xander had it all, he didn't appreciate how easy his life was. I was a nuisance he couldn't afford in his precious little world.

Before I could hit the first step, his deep voice rose from the shadows. "What are you doing here, Ford?"

I scoffed. He knew exactly what I was doing. Otherwise, he wouldn't be out here waiting for me in the dark. "Don't act like you don't know. Let's not pretend you're stupid. If you were, you wouldn't be a professor at the university."

There was a long moment of silence before he let out a harsh breath. "Maybe I'm just stupid when it comes to you."

Maybe we both were.

I gritted my teeth together so hard I was sure a layer of enamel came off before I spoke again. "Why didn't you tell me I couldn't get out of your class?"

His shadow leaned forward. "Would you have listened?"

No.

"You would have tried no matter what, and at the time, I didn't want to pour more gasoline on the fire."

"So, you decided to let some poor innocent women do the pouring for you?" I chuckled darkly. "Now I'm at a Hiroshima nuclear level, so good job. I'm stuck in your stupid class where I have to listen to you for a fucking hour and then watch as you let your students paw all over you. Don't you have any self-respect?"

"I can assure you I feel fine about myself. You're not the only student who gets my time."

"Oh, so was it all a lie then? Are you fucking your other students? Was I just the one to get you through the summer?" I was shouting now. I couldn't hold back.

Xander stood quickly in the darkness. I could barely make out his form until he opened his front door and started to slip in. He tried to close the door before I got there, but he didn't account for my speed. He underestimated me again.

I moved inside, grabbed Xander by the shoulders, and pushed him against the door, crashing the door closed with his body weight.

His face was stoic as he narrowed his eyes at me. "You need to leave. Now," he bit out.

"Not happening. We both know you want me here. I can feel how hard you are for me."

Even as I said the words, his length grew longer against my thigh.

"Just because my dick wants you doesn't mean the rest of me does. Did you not hear me when I said this was over?"

"Oh, I heard loud and clear. What you failed to realize is I don't care. I have nothing to lose. My life has already gone down the drain, and I can make sure yours does the same if you keep denying me."

"You wouldn't," he stuttered as his body leaned into mine. He wanted me so damn bad even his body betrayed him.

"Why not? I can say you took advantage of me. I'm just a poor college student who got drunk in a bar and had an older man seduce me into experimenting with him."

Xander's eyes flared. "You can't do that."

"But I can. Even if they don't fully believe me, it will plant a seed of doubt against you, and most likely, you'll get fired."

He shook his head franticly. "I understand you're angry at the world, but don't do this, Ford. You're not the victim in this scenario."

"And you are?" My hand dipped inside the band of his sweatpants and gripped his thick shaft. Xander shuddered against me, his eyes changing from angry to full of lust in ten seconds flat. "You want me just as badly as I want you. If you let me inside that tight little hole of yours, I'll keep quiet."

His deep chocolate eyes met mine as harsh breaths left his plush lips. "Are you blackmailing me?"

"If that will get you to stop fighting me, then yes, I am." I wasn't sure why he was fighting me on this.

His jaw ticked as he spoke. "You're going to regret this one day."

Was I? There were plenty of things I regretted in my life. The first was not seeing the signs of my mother's illness. Fucking Xander would be the last thing I'd feel guilty about.

Before I could say another word, Xander's deft hands had my shorts on the ground and started to stroke my already maddeningly hard dick.

I couldn't wait another second to be inside of him. It had only been a few days, but it felt like forever. I pushed him off me and ground out the words. "Turn around."

Dipping down, I pulled out the condom and lube I had in my pocket. See, we both knew how tonight was going to end. With me balls deep inside Xander's ass.

Xander only fumbled for a second before he turned around.

Sheathing myself with the condom, I smeared the lube on with one hand while I pulled his sweatpants down with the other. His pert ass was waiting for me. I wanted to slap it, but the need to feel him around my dick was all-consuming. I'd punish him later for putting us through this unnecessary torture.

I rubbed my slick fingers around his hole before I lined the tip of my cock to his entrance and pushed inside.

Xander let out a cry, his hands scrambling for purchase on the door. I pulled out and slammed back inside until my pelvis was flush with his ass. "The next time I come over, you're going to let me in. There won't be a fight." I punctuated my words with another hard thrust that had my balls slapping against his.

"If you try to end us, I'll go to the Dean and tell him you pursued me until I gave in." The words felt bitter on my tongue, but I had to do something so that he wouldn't end what we had going.

"He won't believe you," he gritted out as he pushed back against me for more.

One hand went to the nape of his neck, pressing his face against the door. I panted as I spoke, thrusting faster. "I think he will, but do you really want to risk your career on the chance?"

He stopped moving and looked at me over his shoulder. "This isn't you, Ford. Can't you see that?"

Leaning forward, I licked up the side of his neck. "I don't know who I am anymore except for the man fucking you into oblivion."

His body shook, and I knew he was close to coming. I moved closer, pressing my front to his back as I pumped frantically. The way he clamped around my cock had me close to coming, but I held off, wanting to enjoy the moment I'd been dreaming about for the last three days.

Reaching my hand around, I gripped his weeping dick and started to stroke in time with my thrusts. Once, twice, three times, and then Xander was shooting all over my hand and his door. A wicked sense of satisfaction settled over me. Every time he saw his front door, he'd think of me and this moment.

Rearing back, I slapped his ass hard and slammed inside. I stilled as my dick jerked and pulsed as I came in long bursts. I moaned and then sagged against his frame and pressed my forehead to his shoulder.

I turned my head, brushing my nose against the nape of his neck. "Don't deny me again."

I slipped out, pulled off the condom, and pulled up my shorts. Xander still stood with his body plastered to the door, panting. I slapped his ass lightly, making him jump back.

"I'll see you tomorrow night," I mumbled as I moved to open the front door.

"Wait!" He called out, sounding almost frantic. "You're leaving?"

I turned to look at him. He was perfection standing there with only his t-shirt on. His dark, muscular thighs flexed as his semi-erect cock hung heavy between his legs. His biceps and pecs bulged as he crossed his arms over his chest. What I wouldn't give to strip him down and fuck him again, but that would have to wait another night. Tonight he needed to learn not to deny me.

"I'm leaving." I cocked my head to the side and smirked. "Isn't that what you wanted?"

"Yes, that's what I wanted, but I thought—"

"That's not what this is. If you want me to stay, you'll have to be more inviting on my next visit." I opened the door and looked back at him. "Have a good night, Professor."

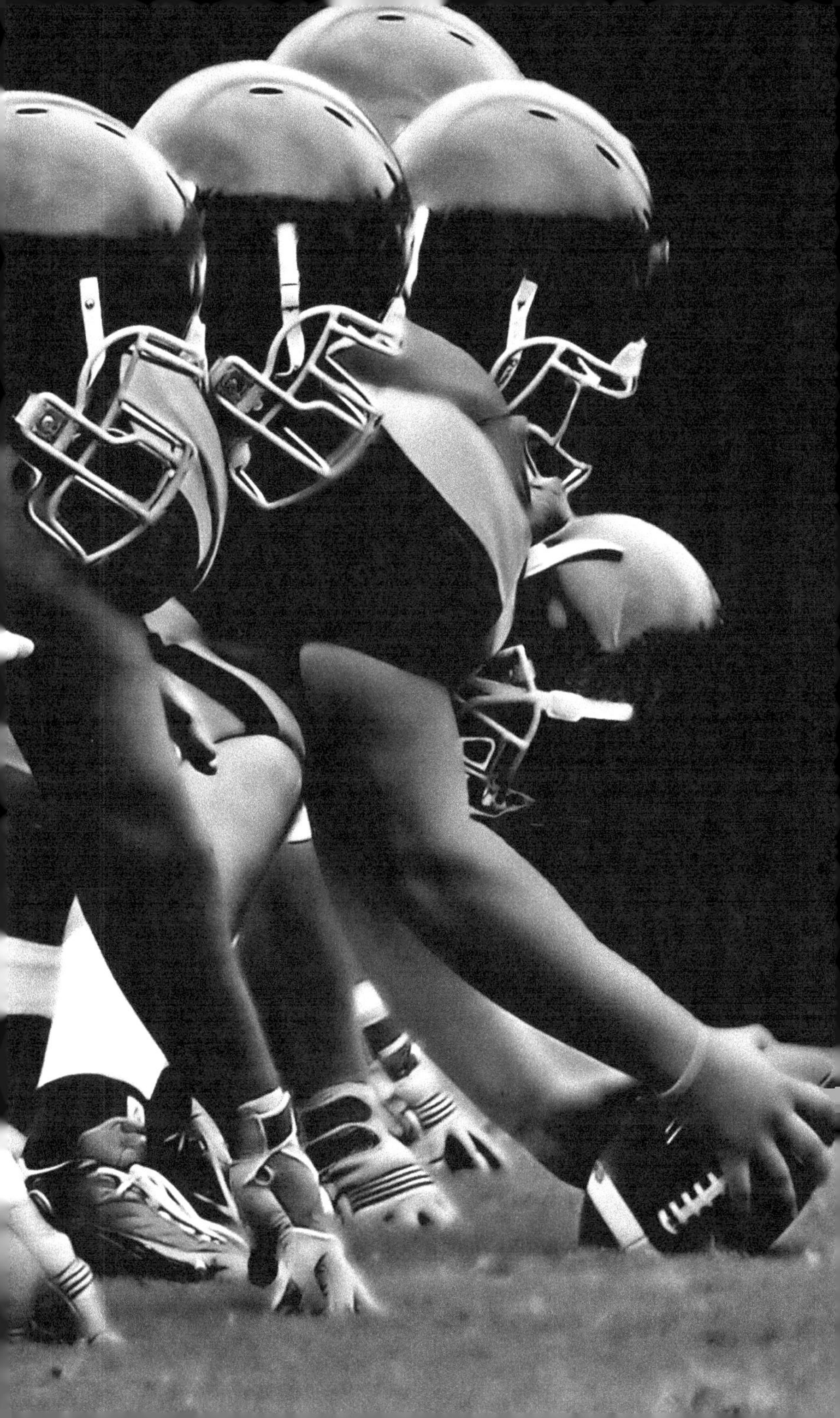

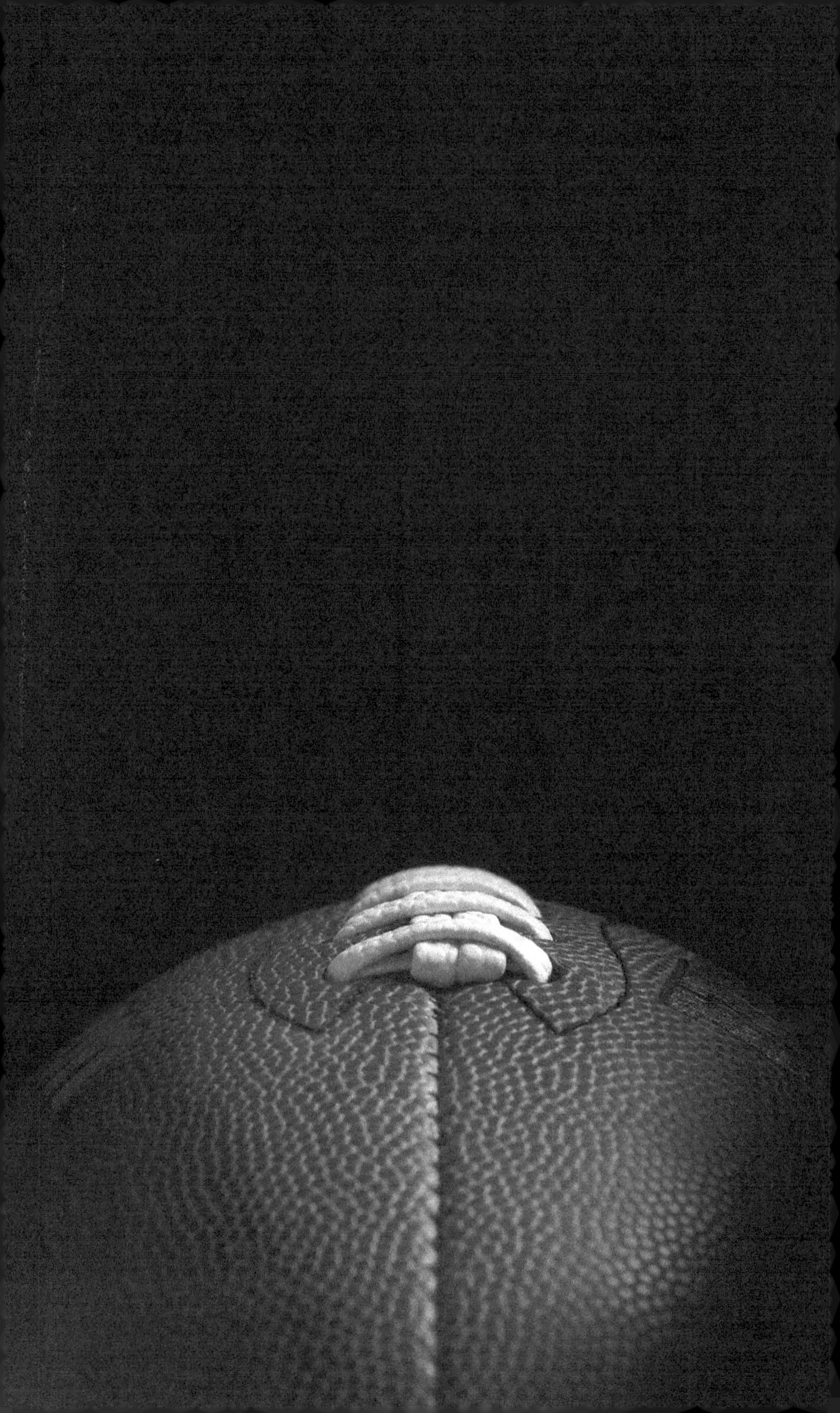

TEN
XANDER

I LOOKED DOWN at the time on my phone and wondered if Ford was at my house. Was he banging on my front door, or was he sitting in his car stewing as he waited for me to come home? I shut off my computer, knowing I couldn't hide forever in my office to avoid Ford. Plus, I didn't have a couch to sleep on here. It would be pathetic to sleep here just to avoid Ford's wrath.

How had I let some twenty-one-year-old boy dictate my life? I had no idea. Well, I did. He was a beast in bed, and no matter how I tried to deny it, my body was addicted to him. Then there was how much he was hurting. I didn't think Ford was a bad guy. He was just grieving and didn't know any other way to accomplish it than by being angry. It was one of the seven stages of grief.

Flipping off my light, I shook my head at what my life had come down to as I walked out to my car. I thought I'd be in a long-term relationship and maybe have a dog. Instead, I was hiding from one of my students.

It was late, and I was the last person in the building besides the cleaning crew. As I pushed open the door, I decided I needed to take back my life no matter how difficult it was going to be. Even though Ford was hurting, I couldn't let him jeopardize my life and career. He was fixated on me, but he'd find someone better suited to his needs and his own age.

Pulling my keys out of my pocket, I was startled when I heard a voice ring out from behind me. "It's good to see you tonight, Professor." Whirling around, I nearly dropped my keys when I saw Ford sitting with his back against the brick building.

With my hand to my chest, I tried to slow down my rapidly beating heart. I wasn't sure if it was from being shocked or Ford being near and unsure what he'd do. "What are you doing here?"

"Looking for you," he said as he stood up. "I believe I said I'd see you tonight, and yet when I showed up at your house, you weren't there. Imagine my surprise." He wasn't surprised. Ford was annoyed, and going by the way he growled out his words, he wanted to take it out on me.

"But how did you find me here?"

"After I went by your house and waited for over an hour, I went to the bar, and when you weren't there, I tried here." He tilted his head to the side. "There aren't many places to go in Willow Bay. I drove by and saw your car and decided to wait for you."

"You didn't need to do that." My words came out soft and shaky.

"But I thought you wanted me to come by. Didn't you want me to stay and fuck you all night?" A wicked smirk spread across his face.

"That's not what I said." I shot back, backing away from him and closer to my car.

"Oh, I think it was. You were hurt when I didn't stay the night last night even though you're worried about your precious job."

"I have the right to change my mind. I didn't like the way last night went down, so I chose to remove myself from the situation." I wanted to say like an adult, but right now, I wasn't feeling like an adult. Ford had a way of making me feel like I was the same age as he was. Maybe that was part of the draw. It was nice to feel young and carefree again.

"And yet here I am. Maybe you should show me that office of yours you wanted me to see the other day."

"I don't want you to see my office. I was merely stating if you wanted to speak to me, it needed to be during office hours. This is not my office hours."

"Hmmm." His brows drew down. "I think you can make an exception just this once. We can pretend it's not late at night, and instead, during one of those times that you said I could come by."

I wanted to yell. Why did he have to twist every word I said around?

"I don't think that's a good idea. Why don't we both go home, and I'll see you tomorrow during class?"

"Yeah, I had other plans in mind for you. Why don't you give me a tour of your office, and then if you're lucky, I'll bend you over your desk and fuck that sweet ass of yours?"

"We can't," I choked out. There was no way in hell I was going to fall down that rabbit hole. I knew once I let him inside my office, Ford would think of it as an open invitation to stop by whenever he wanted. There needed to be boundaries.

"Really, that's strange because I'm pretty sure we can." Stalking toward me in two large strides, Ford clamped his hand around my wrist and pulled me to the door I had just come out of. "Don't make a scene because it will only end badly for you."

"What are you going to do when we're caught? I'll be gone, and you'll have no one to take out all your sadness and anger on." I said as I unlocked my office door and watched from out in the hall as Ford stepped inside.

Maybe I should go to the Dean and tell him how I had a student who was obsessed with me? I could get Ford kicked out of school, and I'd be in the clear. Last year, there was a teacher who was fucking his student, and when they were caught, he was blacklisted from teaching at any school in all of California. Last I heard, he'd found a job teaching at a high school in Colorado. I didn't want to end up with the same fate as him.

"Close and lock the door," Ford ordered.

I followed his demand like a lost sheep. I was so far gone when it came to Ford. Turning around, I leaned against the door, giving us as much space as possible. My office wasn't large. It didn't need to be since I didn't spend much time here. Mostly, I used the office I had set up at my house. This space was only used to meet students and was bare of anything personal. It was all white walls and a plain desk with a computer setup.

"Tell me what you pictured us doing in here when you invited me."

Was he deranged? It wasn't an open invitation for sex.

"That's not why I gave you my hours, and you know it. Don't pretend this is something it's not. If you hadn't threatened me, I wouldn't be in here with you."

"I think we both know that's not true. My threat is just the incentive you need to give in to do what you really want to do." He moved to sit on the edge of the desk and started to undo the fly of his jeans. "Tell me the truth. If I wasn't a student here, would you have a problem with me fucking you?"

We both knew I wouldn't, but I didn't want to tell him the truth. Ford would only take advantage once it was out there. I guess now I understood why he hadn't wanted to talk about his mom. Once you put those words out into the universe, there was no going back.

Instead of answering, I watched as he slowly started to stroke his magnificent cock. My mouth watered at the thought of how it always felt as he pounded into me from behind.

With half-lidded eyes, Ford licked his lips as he continued to touch himself in a lazy manner. "I can see how hungry you are for my dick. Would you like to suck it? I can't say I'd be opposed to having it down your throat and you choking on my length. Or would you like me to bend you over this fine desk here? It's a shame you keep such a tidy space. I would have liked to have thrown your papers all over the floor as I pressed you down on the cold, hard surface. What do you say, Professor?"

How could I tell him I wanted it all? It was taking everything in me not to kneel down in front of him and take his cock into my mouth. How did Ford have this much control over my desires? Never before had I wanted a man so desperately. I wasn't sure I'd ever get enough of him. He was right. By threatening me, I was giving in to what I wanted and pushing away the guilt.

Standing, Ford moved quickly to stand in front of me. He was peeling off my clothes before I had a chance to register what he was doing. I let him strip me of every piece until I was standing bare before him. The way he looked at me pulled my body into his magnetic force. It wasn't a secret Ford wanted me just as badly as I wanted him. The feel of his pre-cum smearing against my stomach had my body overheating and frantically removing his clothes to feel all of his body against mine. Skin to skin.

"You don't have to do this," I panted.

"Says the one who has both of our cocks in his hands." He bent to nip along the column of my neck. "Your mouth says one thing, but your body says another."

He wasn't lying. My brain was telling me one thing while my body rubbed up against his like a cat in heat. It was embarrassing how easily my body betrayed me. I was beginning to hate the riot of emotions Ford brought out in me. The only thing that would come from all of this was self-destruction.

Breaking apart from me, Ford dipped down and pulled out a packet of lube and a condom. He was always ready. It made me wonder if I was the only person he was fucking. I didn't think he had the time for others, but it wouldn't surprise me. I was just another hole to put his dick into.

"Stand behind your desk," he grunted out as he put the condom on. He watched me with hooded eyes as I made my way around to the other side of my desk.

I couldn't say I hadn't fantasized about having

sex in my office, but I never pictured it like this. I should have been the one fucking the man I was in a relationship with. How had I become the submissive bottom in this fucked up thing I had with Ford?

"You're so ready for me." Ford lined up behind me and smoothed his hand over the globes of my ass. "You've already got your back arched and your ass out for me to slide inside." Running one hand down from the nape of my neck to the base of my spine, he slid it around to grip my hip while he lined himself up with the other. As he started to push through my tight ring of muscle, his other hand left my hip and splayed out between my shoulder blades. The deeper he was inside of me, the harder he pressed me down until he was fully inside of me, and I was flat against my desk with my head turned to the side, watching his face turn from stoic to one filled with pleasure.

"Your body was made for taking my dick deep inside of you." His eyes were focused on watching as he slid in and out of my ass. Tonight wasn't as rough as he usually was. It was as if he was trying to savor the moment. Maybe tonight would be the last night he'd visit me, and he'd let me go in peace. Then he'd only be my student after this.

Why did the thought of not having Ford's nightly visits make my heart drop into the pit of my stomach even as it raced from the pleasure he had mounting in my body?

Ford pulled out, causing me to whine from losing our connection. He pulled my office chair around and sat down in it. "Come sit on my dick and bounce." He spread his legs wide and tapped his thigh, welcoming me like I was a child to sit on his lap.

He held his cock as I lowered myself down, using the arms of the chair as leverage. It wasn't easy. I wasn't a small man. I let out a low moan once I was sitting on his lap with his cock deep inside of me. At this angle, Ford felt so much bigger, which I didn't think was possible.

Using the tips of my toes and my arms, I started to rise and fall, sliding up and down his thick shaft. I'd barely started to move, and I already knew I wouldn't last long in this position. When Ford gripped my length and started stroking me in long, hard movements, I nearly lost it right then. His other hand ran up my chest and gripped me by the throat. A jolt of excitement shot down from where he held me, straight to my cock he held in his other hand.

Ford started to peg me from the bottom. Each thrust up hit my prostate and made it nearly impossible to hold out. As wrong as this was, I didn't want it to end. The man controlling my body knew exactly what to do to make me consumed by every touch he gave me, no matter how soft or rough they were.

His movements became erratic the quicker he plunged deep inside of me. "Come now," he demanded, and like he had a direct line to my body, it obeyed. White-hot jets of cum coated his hand, my legs, and my stomach as he pounded into me from underneath. The feel of him growing harder and coming inside of me had my orgasm reigniting—hot pleasure coursed through my entire body until I was spent. I leaned back against Ford's slick chest and turned my head to look at him.

He had his eyes closed, and for the moment, he seemed at peace with himself. I knew it wouldn't last, and I also knew he'd be back. Ford craved the moments all of his problems floated away, and being inside of me was one of them.

I closed my eyes and took in the moment with him, knowing it wouldn't last. And I was right. A couple of minutes later, Ford twitched underneath me before he patted the side of my leg.

His hot breath soaked into my skin as he spoke. "I need to get going."

"You can come back to my place if you want." I

wasn't sure why I said it. I needed to stop being weak where Ford was concerned. No wonder he didn't take no for an answer when later I was almost begging for him to be in my bed.

He pushed me up and started to stand. He slipped out of me and caused me to wince. He pulled off the condom and threw it in the trash like we were anyplace but my office. I scrambled to pull it out of the trash. I couldn't let anyone find a used condom in my office.

"Maybe you should have thought about that before you tried to hide from me." He stepped into his shorts and pulled on his t-shirt while I stood there with my cum drying on my skin, a used condom in my hand, and my pride thrown to the floor.

Tonight would be the last night I asked him into my bed.

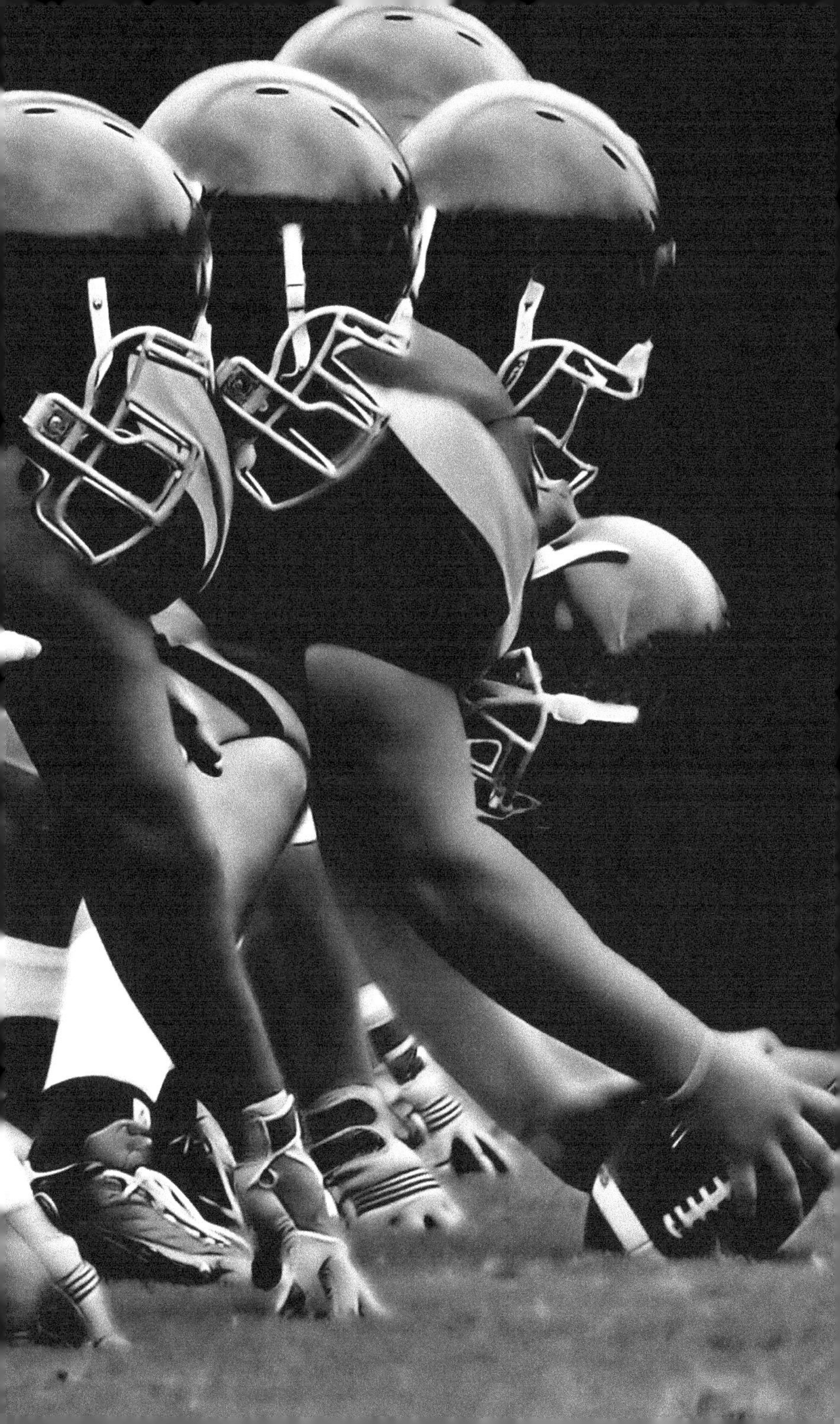

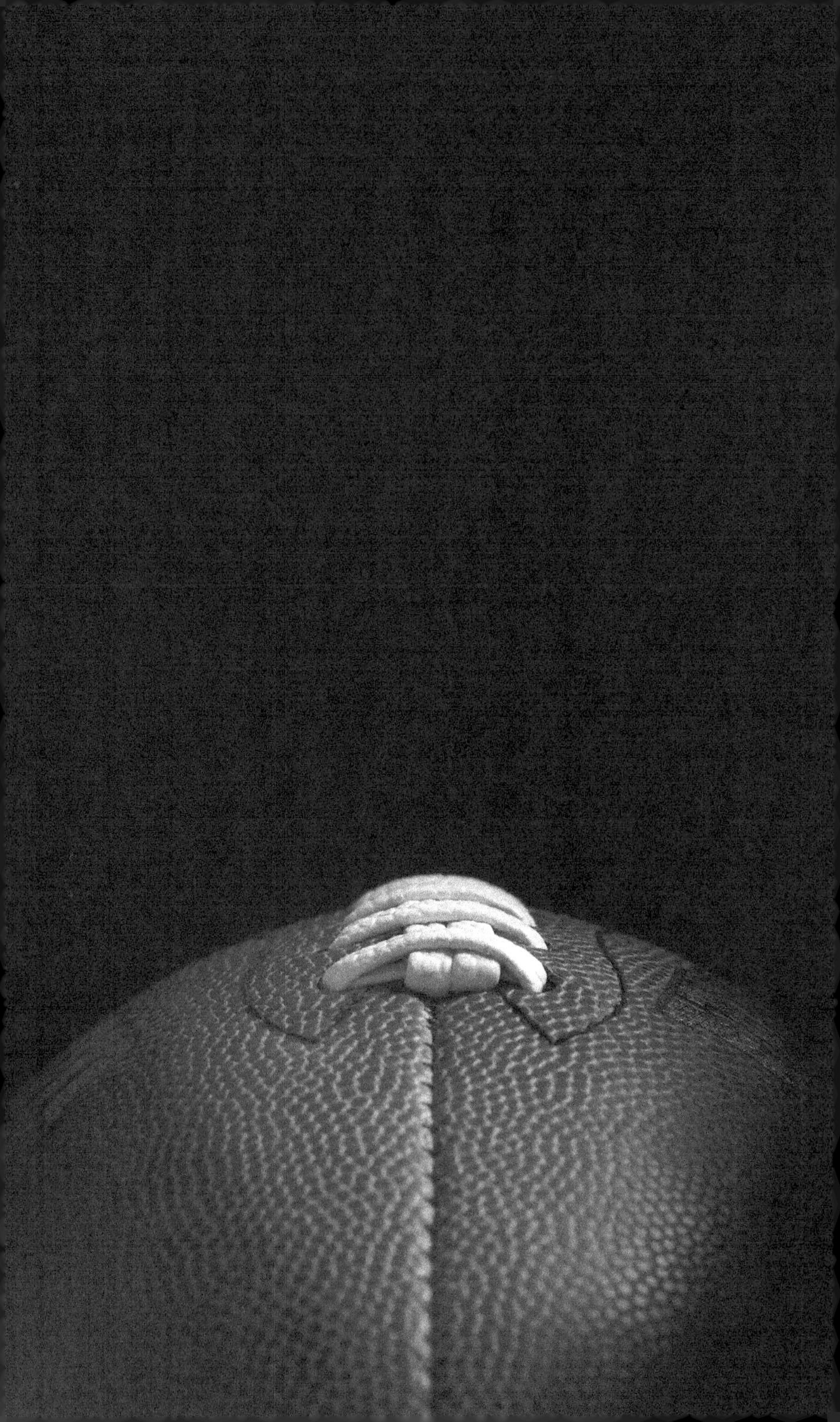

ELEVEN
FORD

WIPING a drop of water off my face, I ran the towel through my hair, drying it as best as I could. The school didn't provide us with the most absorbent of towels in the locker room, but I made do. I walked past Fin, who was scowling at his phone and made sure to keep a wide berth between us. While the house had been giving me time to talk, I saw the annoyance on Fin's face every day that I hadn't opened up to the others. He didn't care that I wasn't talking to him. No, Fin cared that West and Lo were concerned about me and that I hadn't spilled my deepest, darkest secrets to them.

I'd only made it a few steps when Fin's cold, dark eyes landed on me. "Have you seen this shit?"

My brows furrowed as I tried to read his phone

from a few feet away. Moving closer, my blood ran cold. On Fin's phone was an article about how Alpha Mu was back to living in their fraternity house.

I looked to see if West was anywhere around before I spoke quietly. "What the fuck?"

"No fucking clue, but it's bullshit. They didn't even contact West to inform him. How the fuck did they get back into their house?" He gritted out.

"I don't know, but I don't trust it." I saw what they'd done to West all because of him being gay. They drugged him and then beat him up after failing to get him to have sex with some girl they thought could fuck the gay out of him. I could feel the fury rolling off Fin in waves. He was going to do something stupid. I just knew it. It was only a matter of when.

Putting his phone in his back pocket, Fin leaned closer so only I would hear him. "What do you say we let you off cooking duty tonight, and me and you go pick up some dinner?"

I knew this was code for want to go fuck up some Alpha Mu dudes tonight while everyone thinks we're out getting food.

I nodded even as I spoke. "Won't you be the first suspect if anything happens?"

A slow, evil smirk tipped the corners of his

mouth. "Probably, but if there's no evidence, what can they do? Let's not talk about it here, though. There are too many innocent ears around. We'll talk at home."

My fists connecting to a few jaws at Alpha Mu sounded like the perfect plan to rid myself of some of the anger brewing inside of me. Now that practice was over, and my body was slowly coming back from its exhausted state, my mind kept flashing back to finding my mother's lifeless body. It was a nightmare I couldn't wake up from, no matter how hard I tried. I knew it was time to get some professional help if I ever wanted for my life to be anywhere near what it was before. I couldn't live the rest of my life with daily flashbacks of finding my mom.

I rushed to my locker to get dressed. I knew the guys were waiting for me to get home. Stepping out of the locker room, I found Fin, West, and Oz arguing. West and Oz stood side by side with red faces as they whisper-yelled at Fin.

The second Fin's gaze landed on me, he pushed off the wall and strode toward his car. "Let's get the hell out of here."

Oz and West looked at me with worried expressions marring their faces. Oz fell into step with me, keeping his words low. "Did he talk to you?"

"About?" I played it off like I didn't know what he was talking about. I had a feeling neither West nor Oz would want any action taken. Okay, maybe they'd want something done, but not by us. If we got caught, we'd be thrown off the football team at the very least.

"Alpha Mu is back, and Fin wants to annihilate them for what they did to West."

As far as I knew, West didn't remember who drugged him or who threw punches at him. What we did know was who was in the room when Fin found West face-first on the floor, barely knowing his own name. That could easily have been Fin or me, except no one knew our proclivities to men then. No one but the people I lived with knew I was bi now, but everyone knew Fin and West were a couple. The only reason no one gave them any shit was because they were all scared of Fin. While Alpha Mu was no more for the last year and a half, that isn't to say they haven't been around. They were still on campus in classes. Whenever we passed by them in the halls or anywhere on campus, they were always speaking in hushed whispers as if they were plotting our takedown. Maybe they were, and this was the first step. I didn't know. The only thing I knew was Fin would be the prime suspect if anything happened at Alpha Mu or to any one of their guys.

Keeping my gaze forward, I ground my molars as images from that night flashed through my head. West was one of the nicest guys I'd ever met. He didn't deserve to be targeted. "Do you blame him? What they did to West wasn't just a prank. They could have killed him or at the very least scarred him for life."

Oz stopped walking. A deep scowl sat heavily on his face. "I'm not saying they don't deserve to have anything bad happen to them. They've probably been planning Fin's demise since he walked into that bedroom and saved West, but *if* he got caught, Fin would likely be thrown out of school. Where would his life be then?"

"Then the objective is to not get caught. Leave no evidence of ever being there." When had Fin fallen back?

Oz let out a weary sigh. "Listen, you can't do anything today. Won't it look suspect if you do something the day it's announced those douchebags are back to being a fraternity again?"

"He does have a point," I agreed. "Maybe, for now, we make a foolproof plan. We're bound to make a mistake if we go in guns blazing without any plan in place."

"I don't want those assholes to be in that house again for one single day," Fin gritted out.

"What are you going to do, burn the house down?" Oz laughed for a second before sobering. "No, you can't burn down their house. Arson is so much worse than kicking someone's ass. You'll go to prison if you're caught."

"That's why we make a plan like Ford suggested. Do you have a better idea?"

"Not right now, but if you give me time, I'm sure I can come up with something better." Oz would stall until he couldn't stall any longer, leaving Fin to do something rash and spur of the moment.

"Let's get home, so the whole fucking team doesn't overhear us bickering like little old ladies." Fin turned to me. "Do you want to cook tonight, or should we get something out?"

This was Fin's way of asking if I was still in for fucking up Alpha Mu tonight. If I didn't agree, would he go without me and likely get caught? I understood why Fin wanted to do it tonight, but we needed to be smart.

"Let's go back home and figure out what everyone wants to eat, and then we can go pick something up. How does that sound?" I wasn't sure if he got my meaning. Let's come up with a plan and then go.

"Yeah," he nodded along with me. "Let's see what Lo would like."

Oz looked back and forth between us. "Why are we eating out? It's the middle of the week, and we have a game on Saturday. Wouldn't it make more sense to do it after we win?"

Yes, it would, but Fin wouldn't wait forever.

Fin nodded to me. "Look at Ford. He looks wiped. Let's give him a night off from cooking. I'm sure we can still get something on the plan if we go to Loganville or something like that."

"Whatever," Oz sighed and started toward the car. "Let's get home. I want to see how Lo did on her test."

Crisis averted.

"West and Oz can't know until after the fact. Got it?" Fin asked out of the side of his mouth.

"Loud and clear. I won't say a word. I'm just a tired cook in need of a break. We'll definitely have to go to Loganville to get something to eat."

"Agreed. It's going to have to be quick, so we don't rouse any suspicions."

I wasn't sure how we could do anything quickly

and effectively. Hopefully, Fin had an idea because I had nothing.

"Do you think they know?" Fin asked as he drove us toward fraternity row.

"Do they know? No, but they think we're up to something. Maybe you should get West some flowers or something on the way back, so he'll think you just wanted to be romantic and not ruin the people who attacked him."

"I'm not the kind of guy who brings home flowers. He'd know something was up if I did," he chuckled lowly in the dark of the car's cabin.

I turned to look at Fin. He was so calm as we discussed burning down a building. "Are you going to tell him what we're about to do?"

Fin closed his eyes for a second. When he opened them, he let out a harsh exhale. "I'll tell him. Nothing good comes from secrets."

"Is this where I tell you mine?" I asked bitterly.

"You don't have to tell me shit if you're not ready. I know what it's like to have something you don't want to acknowledge. I *can* promise you I won't judge you."

I wasn't worried about that. It wasn't as if I'd killed my mom. Still, it was too painful to talk about. Although maybe talking about it instead of keeping it bottled up inside would lessen the pain.

Looking out the windshield, I stared out at the darkness as I spoke. "Two weeks before I came back to Willow Bay, my mom killed herself."

Fin jerked the car to the side of the road and put it into park. "Fuck, Ford, I had no idea."

"I didn't expect you to."

"I'm…" Fin cleared his throat and started again. "I'm sorry."

"I didn't tell you for you to feel sorry for me. I thought if I told you, it might ease some of the pain, but I was wrong. It still feels as strong as ever." My chest felt like someone was stabbing it repeatedly with a knife.

"I'm not good at this type of thing." Fin leaned forward on the steering wheel and penetrated me with his fierce gaze. "But if you want to talk about it, I'll listen."

"Thanks. Maybe not today when we have more pressing matters at hand."

"Hey," he moved, placing one of his hands on my arm. "While I'd love to end Alpha Mu tonight, what you're going through is more important."

It was touching Fin cared, but I couldn't go any further tonight.

"I prefer not to think about it, and fucking with Alpha Mu is the perfect distraction."

"Is that where you go every night? To get distracted?" The concern in his eyes had me feeling uncomfortable. Fin didn't show many emotions except to West.

"Cooking, practice, and fucking are the best remedies." I wasn't going to say I was nailing one of our teachers almost nightly.

He lifted a knowing brow. "And are you visiting Mr. Lawrence?"

I shook my head. "Let's get moving. We can't be gone for too long." We didn't even have a real plan. We had no idea what we'd be walking into.

"Fine. Let's go kick some ass. You can tell me about fucking your teacher later."

"How did you know he's my teacher?"

"I didn't. You just confirmed it for me," Fin laughed.

Fuck, he'd played me. But I knew he wouldn't tell anyone except West.

"No one can know."

"I agree. I can't believe he's stupid enough to keep fucking you."

"I'm the one doing the fucking, and let's just put it this way. I didn't give him any choice."

"You sound more and more like me every day. I kind of love it." Fin laughed as he put the car into park, and we headed to Alpha Mu's demise.

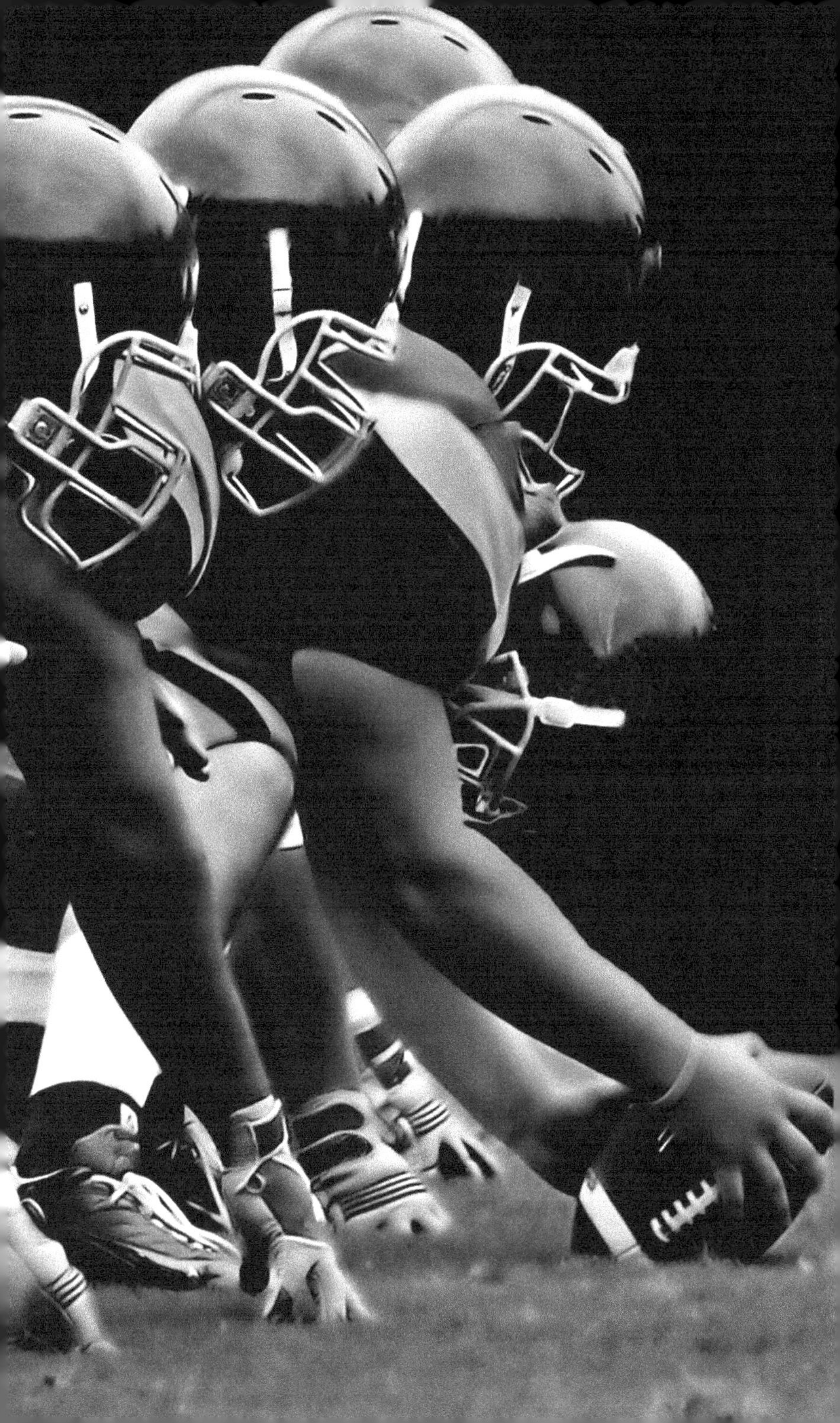

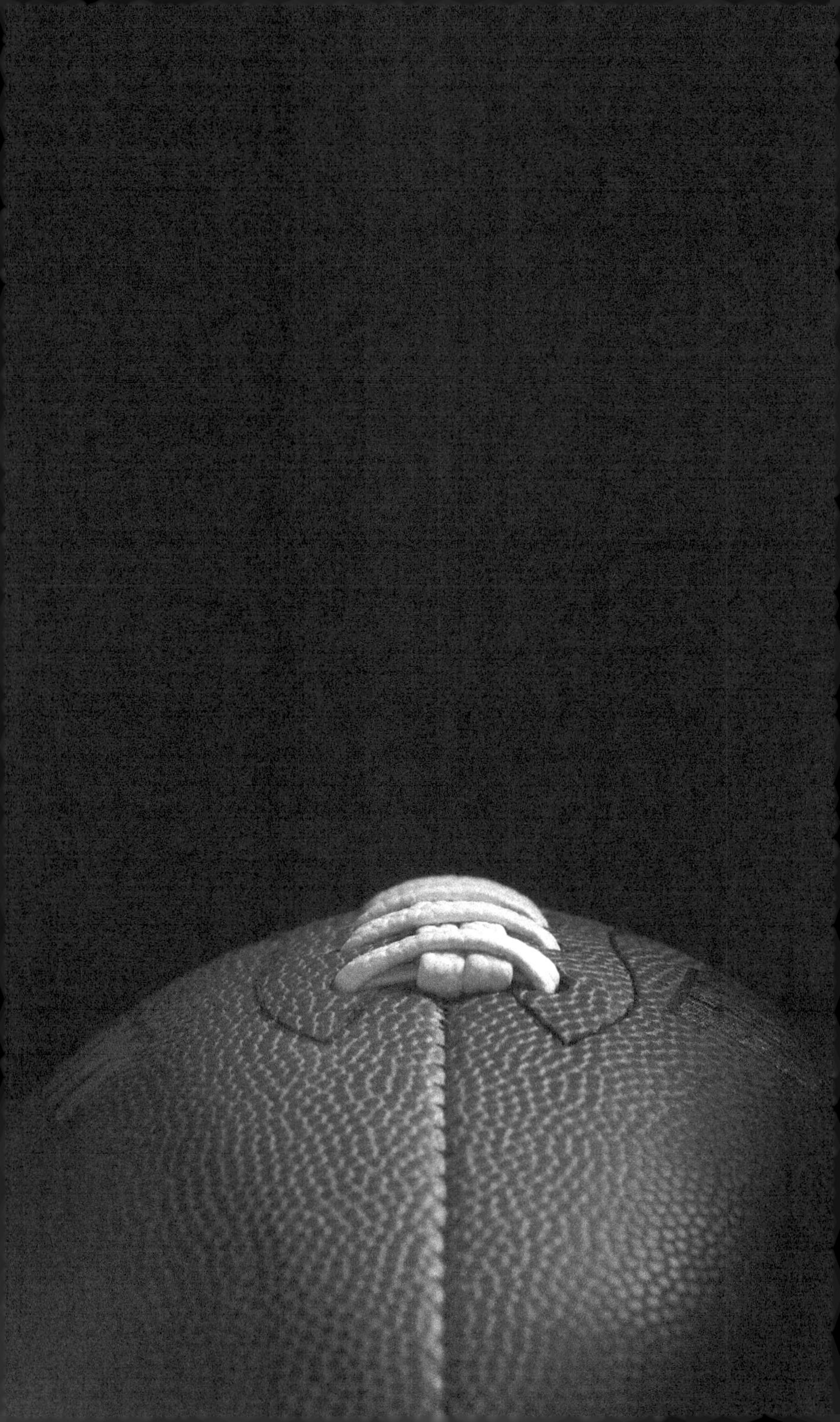

TWELVE
FORD

WE'D BARELY STEPPED inside the house when West and Oz came rushing toward us. "What the fuck did you do?" West shouted as he circled around Fin like a dog in heat.

"We went and picked up dinner. The... car broke down on the way, but eventually, we got it going again," Fin lied through his teeth.

"Do you really expect me to believe that shit?" West stopped in front of his boyfriend and stared him down. It made me happy I didn't have to be accountable to anyone. "You smell like smoke, and you've got dirt all over you. I'd be more apt to believe you two wrestled a pig than that bullshit you just spouted."

Oz's blue eyes sent daggers both our ways. "Why didn't you ask me to help?"

"Maybe because you can't afford to get in trouble, and Lo would never forgive me if you did," Fin pushed past them as he sat the food on the table.

"You're a real piece of work, you know that? I've been your accomplice since elementary, and today you decide to bring Ford into the mix." Oz glanced at me with a deep frown. "No offense."

"Oh, none taken," I laughed with my hands up at how absurd this conversation was. Oz wasn't mad we'd done something. No, he was mad he wasn't involved.

"Tell us what you did. Now," West growled out.

"It's probably best you didn't know that way you can't get into any trouble." Fin mumbled as he pulled out the food from the bag as if this were any other day.

"I want to know now, Fin. I'm not kidding. If you don't tell me, I'll leave." That had both of us stopping dead in our tracks. West was always laid back, the yin to Fin's yang.

"You can't be serious," Fin shouted, his arms flying up to the side. "If you don't know, you can't get into any trouble. It's plain and simple."

West's green eyes narrowed into slits as he took in

Fin's defensive posture. "What's plain and simple is if you don't tell me what dumbass thing you did that could jeopardize your future, I'm leaving. I'll ask Coach to let me stay at the football house."

"Fine, you want to know what happened?" Fin yelled. The sound reverberated off the walls and made us all cringe. "We were going to burn down their house until we saw they were already living in the house. There was no way we could do that with people inside."

West slumped down and sat on the floor, looking up at Fin and waiting for him to continue. His eyes were wide, and this mouth turned down in a grimace.

"While we were casing out their house, a couple of the guys from the room that night stepped outside laughing. They were laughing about how easy it was to get their house back. How the school has forgotten all about how they drugged you and beat you up." Fin's jaw ticked as he glared down at West. He wasn't mad at West, though. He was fuming at what we learned from the shadows.

West stood and moved closer to Fin, who was now moving around like a caged animal. "They admitted it?"

"I got most of it on video," I announced from the sidelines, holding up my phone.

West looked us both up and down. Nonplussed by what he'd just learned, or so it seemed at that moment. "That doesn't explain why you smell of smoke and are all dirty."

"I had no idea Ford was recording what they were saying. My vision became redder and redder with each word they spoke. I couldn't just sit back and do nothing. It brought the entire night back in vivid detail. I couldn't let them think they got away with what they did to you."

"So, you didn't burn down their house?"

"No," Fin's brows puckered. "I already told you I didn't. They already moved in. Once they were finished talking shit about you and what they'd done, I kicked their asses." Fin looked in my direction. "With Ford's help. Once they were on the ground begging for us to stop, we quietly left."

Now it was Oz's turn as he leveled us with a glare. He rounded on Fin, placing his hands on his shoulders. "And you think they won't go to Coach or the Dean and tell them how you kicked their asses? How fucking stupid are you? You might as well start packing now."

Fin pushed Oz off him and went to stand by West. "They have no idea it was us. We didn't talk the entire time, and we were wearing masks. There are probably at least a dozen people on campus who want to kick their ass, so how are they going to pinpoint it was us?"

Oz looked at me with a raised brow.

"What? I just went along to make sure he didn't do anything stupid."

"It sounds like you failed," Oz gritted out.

"Everything Fin said is the truth. There's no way in hell those douchebags will ever know it was us. They didn't even get one punch in. We're unscathed except for being dirty. Once we take a shower, it will be like nothing ever happened."

They should be thankful Fin didn't burn down their house because he was bound and determined to do so when we first set out.

Lo stepped into the room and quietly spoke as she looked at each one of us. "You need to send the Dean that recording. It will get their house shut down for good this time."

"Anonymously. Otherwise, they'll know it was you who beat them up," West said from across the room. He wasn't looking at me, though. He only had eyes for Fin in that moment. With their fingers laced together, they left the room and went straight to their bedroom.

Oz slapped me on the back. "You should probably take a shower, too. Then we can eat and figure out how to get the Dean the footage."

"Good idea." I headed toward the bathroom I shared with Oz and Lo. It looked like I wouldn't be making an appearance at Xander's house tonight. I wondered if he'd be relieved I didn't show up. It didn't matter because tomorrow I'd be there, ready to knock down his door.

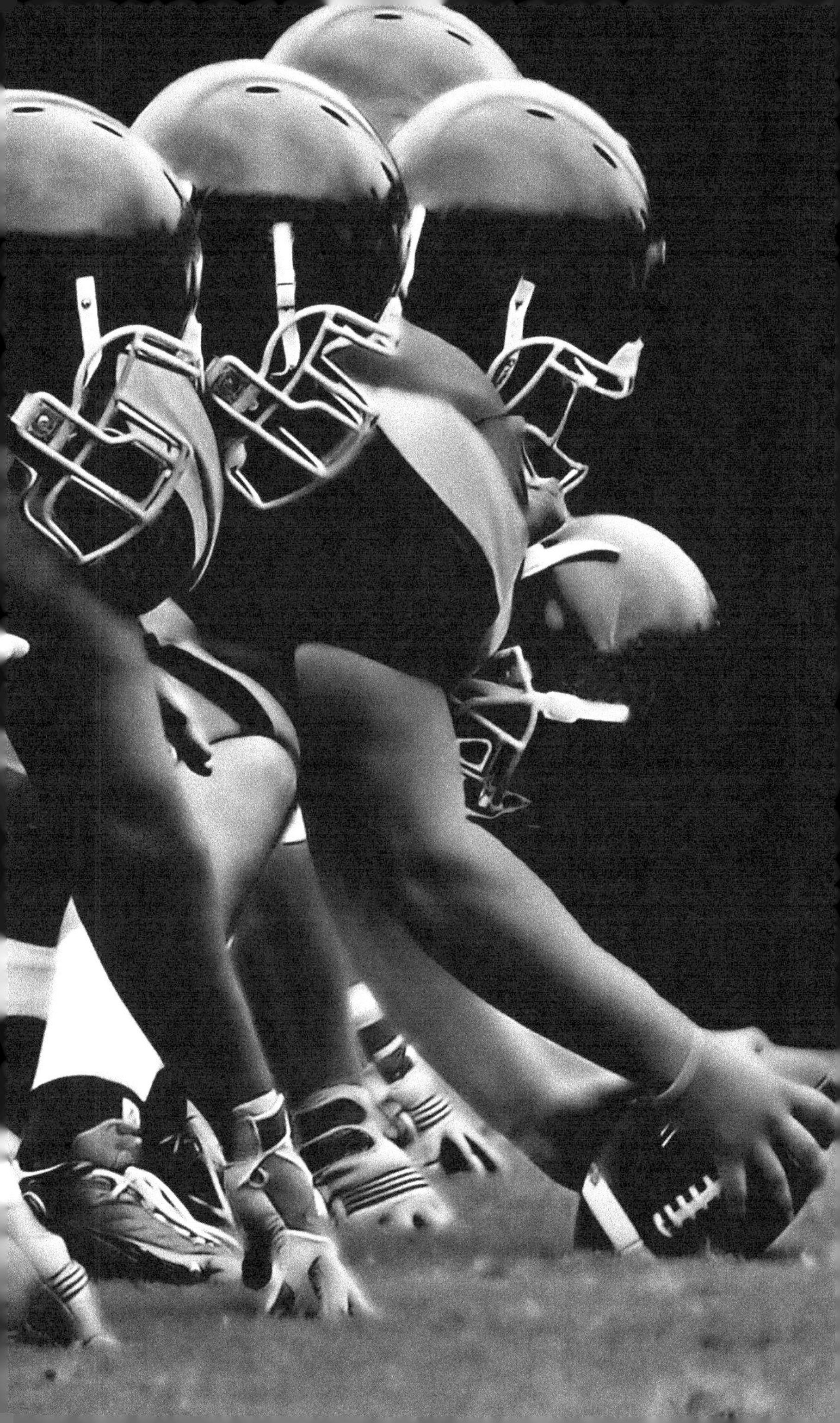

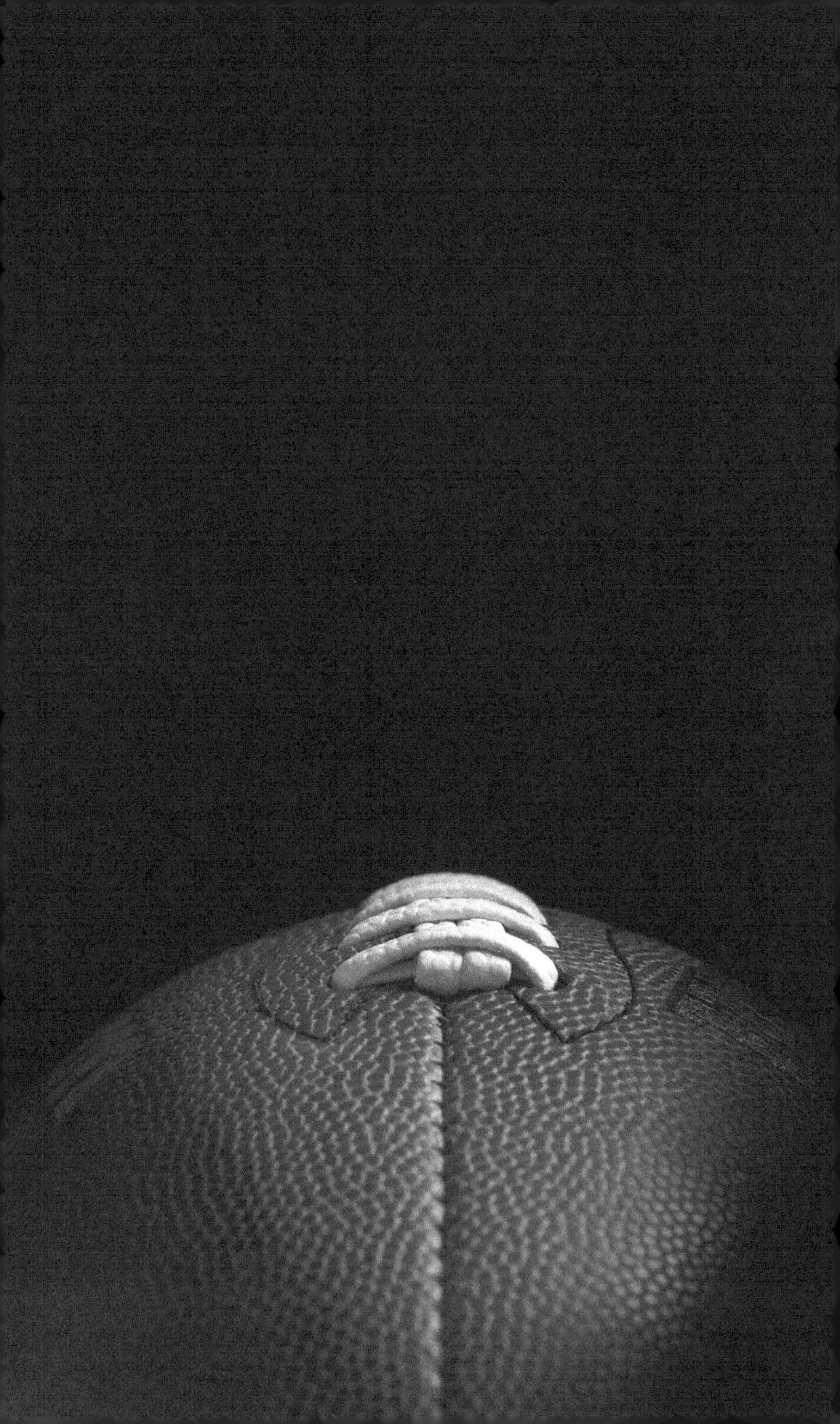

THIRTEEN
XANDER

WHY DID I agree to this date? Oh, I know. It's because the person I'd rather be with but can't be, ghosted me last night. I waited up for him until one in the morning, only for him to never knock on my door or window or anything at all. While I should be happy that Ford came to his senses and was going to leave me alone, I wasn't. When Courtney, one of my fellow teachers, brought up her dear gay friend again, with who she thought I'd be perfect, I finally said yes. I wasn't sure if it was to get her to stop asking finally or to get Ford out of my head.

I plastered on my fake smile as he babbled on and on about his job as an accountant. How busy he was during tax season and how I wouldn't see much of him then. As if spending twenty minutes with me in a restaurant proclaimed us a couple. He'd be lucky if I ever saw him again on the street without going the other way. Greg was boring as hell and a clinger. I could already tell by him claiming us as a couple.

And I was never letting Courtney set me up on another date as long as I lived. I didn't care if I ended up alone if this was the type of guy she thought I should be with. While I taught a whole host of what college students deemed boring classes, I didn't consider myself a bore. I liked to be outdoors as much as possible. I liked to go hiking, camping, ride my bike and work out. Okay, maybe I was boring, but who wasn't when all of their friends lived all over the country, were married or in a relationship, and you were the single one?

Maybe Ford and I could go camping? No, that would only end badly. Plus, he was done with me.

So, why wasn't I done with him?

I signaled for the check, unable to sit here longer than necessary. I would rather have been home grading homework than listening to how important Greg thought he was. You're an accountant, dude. You're not out saving lives every day. I already had my card out and handed it over to our waitress the second she stepped close enough to take it from me.

"So, what's next? Dessert?" Greg lifted a sand-colored eyebrow at me. "Maybe a walk on the beach?" His whiny tone grated on my nerves. It wasn't his fault his voice sounded like that, but it would be all on me if I chose to be around him another second more than necessary.

Maybe I should have suggested we go Dutch. Then he wouldn't think I was paying because I enjoyed his time instead of the real reason of needing to get the hell away from him before I gouged ears out, so I wouldn't have to hear another word coming out of his mouth.

"I…" Shit, I wasn't used to coming up with lame excuses as to why I needed to end a date. "I have to cut our date short. I have a two-inch stack of papers to grade before I go to bed tonight."

Greg's face fell, and for a second, I felt bad. That was until he opened his mouth again. "Oh, I'll be like that soon enough come January. I'm buried under paperwork until April comes around. What day works for you this weekend to go out again?"

Was this man delusional? I'd barely spoken, so I don't know why he was interested in me? Well, besides my looks.

"I can't. I've got a lot to grade and have them entered into the computer for mid-quarter grades. Plus, I have to write out their tests." What was I saying? I was just coming up with bullshit excuses instead of being honest with the guy.

"Oh," his face fell but then lit back up. "When you do have some free time, call me, and we can go out again. I had fun tonight and look forward to doing it again."

I was going to need to either start lying to Courtney about having a boyfriend or say I wasn't ready to date because *this* was not happening ever again.

Giving him a tight-lipped smile, I stood from my seat. "Have a good rest of your night, Greg." I didn't wait for him to stand or walk out with me. I shoved my credit card back in my wallet as I walked out to my car. My head was down, not paying attention to my surroundings, happy to get the hell out of there.

"What the hell do you think you're doing?" Ford growled.

Looking up, I found him leaning against my car with one ankle crossed over the other. His face was closed off as he watched me walk toward him. "I was having dinner."

"You were on a date." His words were thrown at me like an accusation.

"And so what if I was?" I shot back. It wasn't as if we could go out on dates.

"I don't like it. It needs to stop."

I stopped a couple of feet in front of him and laughed. "It's cute that you think you have that type of control over me, but for your information, you do not get to dictate who I do and don't date. You're just the guy blackmailing me into letting him stick his dick in me."

"Ah," he uncrossed his ankles. "So, you do remember. Then let me remind you, I can just as easily go to the Dean if you keep seeing that guy."

While I didn't plan to ever see Greg again, Ford didn't need to know that. He couldn't control every aspect of my life.

"You're not going to go to the Dean just because you don't like that I might be out on a date or fucking someone else."

Ford stood from my car and stalked toward me. His eyes were blazing as he pushed his chest into mine. Okay, maybe I shouldn't have said that last part.

"You are not having sex with anyone else. Do you hear me? I will end you where you stand if I ever think you're letting someone else fuck you." He growled, pushing me back a step before I stood my ground.

"And what if I'm fucking them? Are you okay

with that?" I knew I shouldn't have said those words, but I couldn't help myself. They were out of my mouth before I had a chance to stop them. Still, I didn't back down. Ford needed to know he couldn't control every aspect of my life. In fact, he shouldn't have control over any of it.

"Are you trying to piss me off?" He hissed. "I will throw you down and fuck you on the hood of your car for everyone to see if you keep talking.

"Why do you care? You're probably fucking half the campus." I tried to push past him, but Ford wasn't letting me move.

"Is that what this is about?" He cocked his head to the side and laughed. "Are you upset at the idea of me sticking my dick into other people?"

I ground my teeth together, not wanting to answer. If Ford knew, then he'd likely use it against me. Who am I kidding? He most definitely would. Everything I gave, he used to his advantage.

A dark chuckle filled the night air. "You don't have to say anything. I already know the answer. How about we make a deal?" He lifted one dark brow at me as he smirked. "You don't fuck anyone or..." he let his words pause for several seconds as I stood in the parking lot, hanging onto his every word. "Let anyone else into your body. If you can do that, then I'll only fuck you."

The thought of me being the only one he was with sent a satisfying surge of emotion through me. Why was it that no matter how wrong I knew this was, I couldn't stay away? Ford was going to be the end of all that was good in my life.

I so desperately wanted to ask if he had been with anyone else, but I was so too scared to know the answer to the question I couldn't voice.

Ford's nostrils flared. "Fine, I'm going home. I've got better shit to do."

I wasn't sure what came over me, but I couldn't stop myself. "Do you like camping?"

He leaned back on my car with an amused smirk on his too handsome for his own good face. "I can't really say. I've only been a couple of times when my brother begged my mom." He stood still as a statue, looking at nothing for a moment. Fuck, how had I not realized his mother would most likely be involved with any camping memories he had. His body shuddered as if shaking off the memory. "She didn't know what she was doing no matter how hard she tried."

"I'm sorry. I didn't—"

"She was a single parent for the majority of my

life, and up until the end, she was the best damn mother I could have asked for. That's why..."

I nodded like I knew, but I didn't. I couldn't imagine what state of mind I'd be in if my mom had killed herself when I was Ford's age.

"Would you like to go camping with me sometime?" I wasn't sure why I asked him. It was something I enjoyed, and maybe if he was away, it would help him heal just a little bit. I had little reason to suspect he'd take me up on my offer.

"Are you hoping to get me out in the woods to kill me?" The only way I knew he was kidding was by the humor in his tone. His face was impassive as he stared at me.

"If you behave, I might let you live. What do you say?" There was no hiding the hope in my voice. I always gave too much away in regard to Ford.

Rubbing his chin with his thumb and forefinger, Ford raked his eyes over every inch of my body. Once he reached my eyes, he stood up and came to stand with only an inch separating us. I could feel the heat of his body warming mine and the touch of his minty breath as he spoke. "I happen to have a bye week this weekend, so I don't have a game on Saturday. We could go then, or it would have to wait until after the season."

"I'm sure I could pull everything together by this weekend. We can go Friday after my classes and then come home Sunday morning."

"Sure," he moved to leave. "Pick me up Friday once your classes are done."

My protest caught in my throat as Ford walked across the parking lot and slipped inside his car. If I picked him up at his place and his roommates were there, I was setting myself up for a disaster in the waiting. The more people who knew, the more likely we'd—no, *I*—would be caught.

I couldn't confront Ford in class or text him since I didn't have his number. I'd have to figure out some other way to get him to my house instead of doing what he wanted.

Did he walk away so I couldn't say no? Or was he hoping we'd be found out?

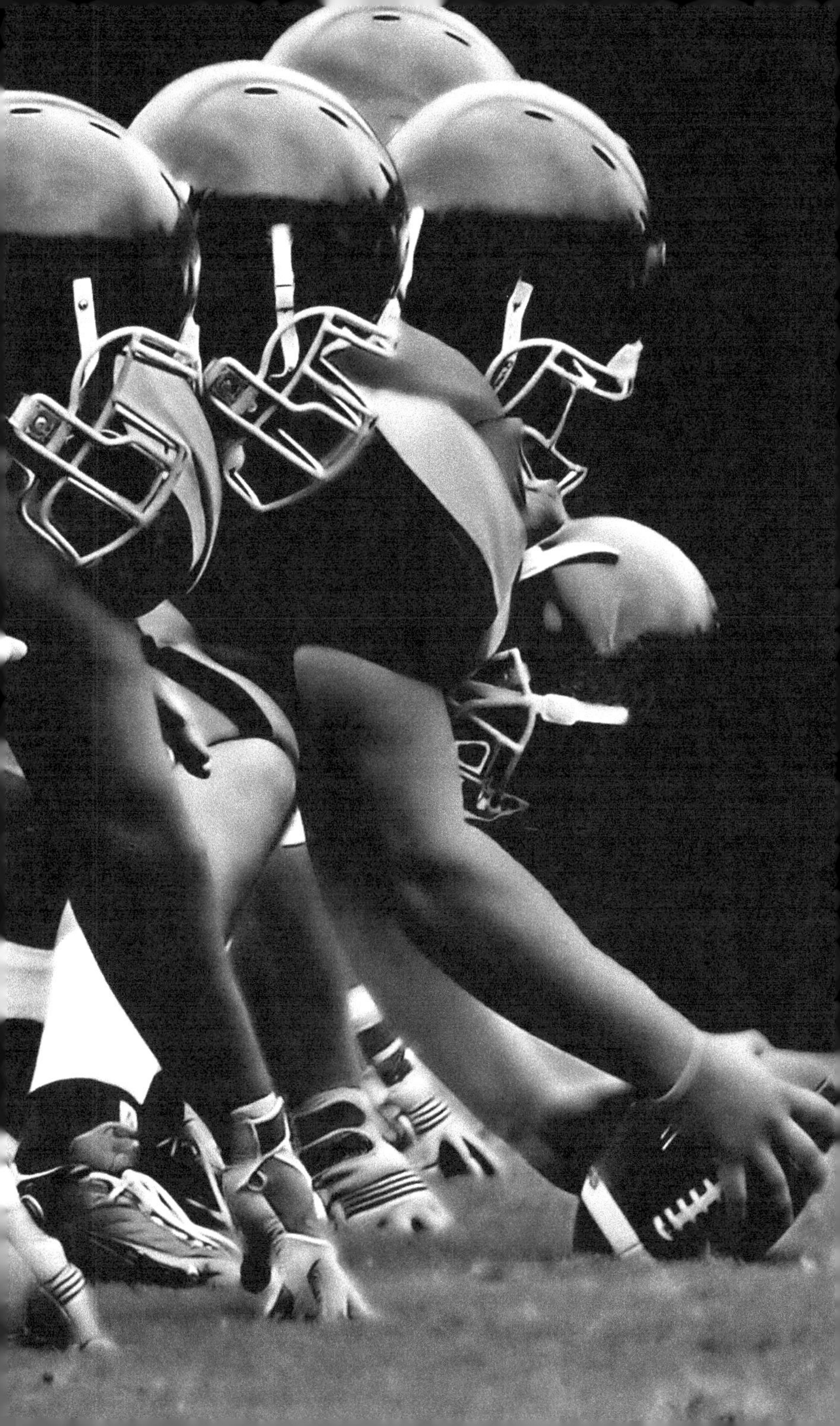

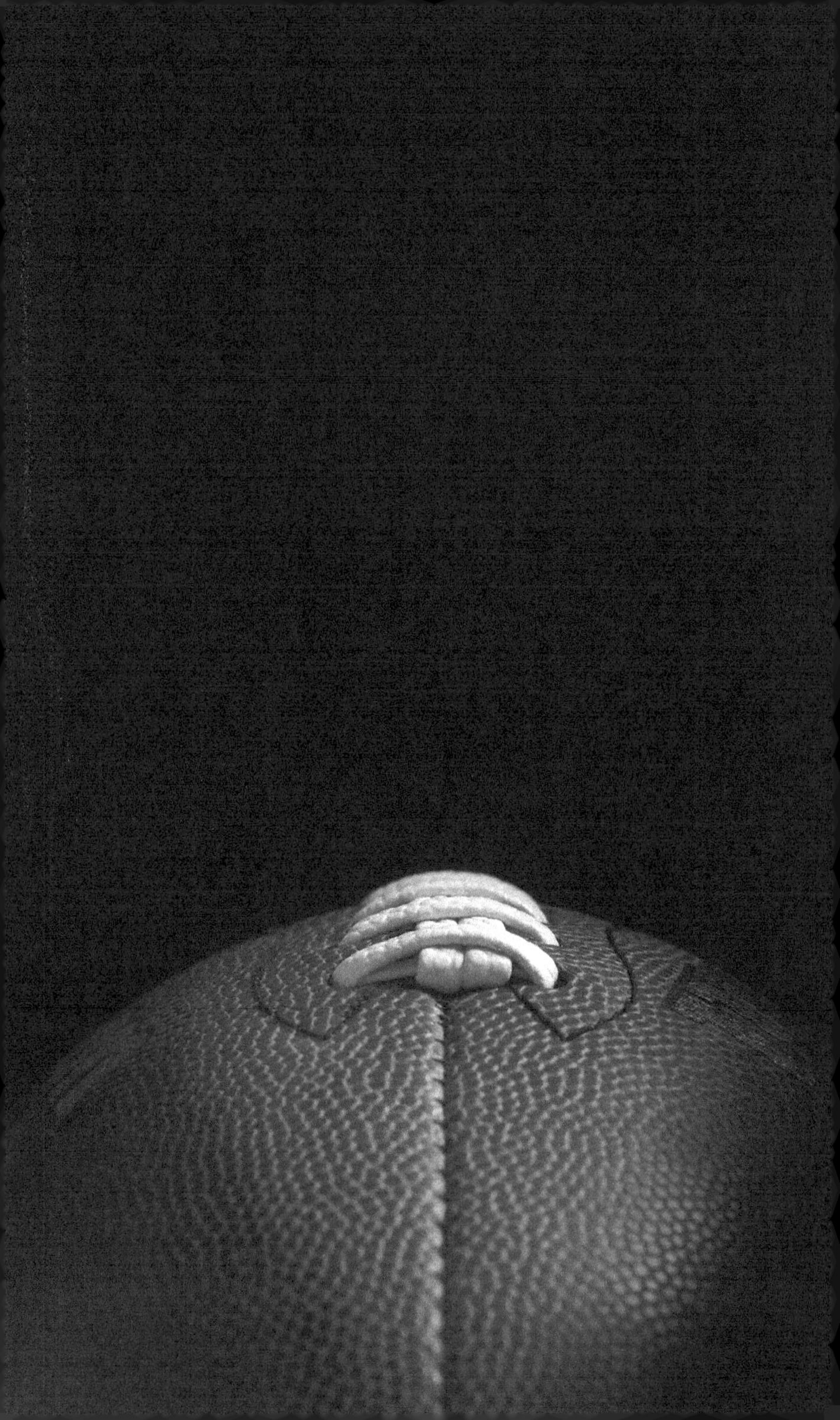

FOURTEEN
FORD

"WHERE ARE YOU OFF TO?" West eyed me from the couch where he was doing his homework.

Dropping my bag by the front door, I went to sit down in the chair across from West. Crossing my left ankle over my right knee, I stared at him for a long minute before I gave in and started talking. "I'm going camping for the weekend."

West rose one brow. "Really? You're not already spent enough from practice this week, so you thought you'd go out into the wildness and cut down a tree."

"I doubt I'll have to cut down a tree," I smirked at him. "Have you ever been camping?"

"Uh, no, and I don't ever want to. You don't exactly seem like the type to go camping either."

"I was asked, and I thought it might be nice to get away."

West leaned forward, putting his elbows on his knees. "Who are you going with? The mysterious person you've been seeing since before school started?"

"The same person," I answered vaguely.

"Okay, so you don't want us to know yet. That's your business. Are you any closer to being able to talk about what happened this summer?"

I stood and moved quickly toward the door. "And I think my ride is here."

West jumped up and ran over to me. With his hand on my arm, he pressed down as I opened the front door. "You don't have to run away, Ford. I only want you to know if you want to talk to someone I'm here. Day or night."

"Thanks. I'm not ready yet, and I'm not sure when I will be, but if I ever want to talk, I'll come to you."

Damn, why did my roommates have to be such good friends and care about me? It made me feel like shit that I wasn't talking to them to ease their concerns.

"Or your new… person. I'm not sure if it's a

female or a male. Not that I care. It's just… you know we didn't know before, you know?"

"I take no offense. I don't bring my hookups home. If I hadn't been drunk off my ass when I got here, I wouldn't have brought anyone home. Sorry. I won't do it again." I moved to step outside but was stopped again with West's hand to my shoulder.

"This is your home. You can bring whoever you want here as long as they're not a serial killer or steal our shit."

"I'll make sure they pass the test then," I laughed. I lifted my chin in the direction of West and Fin's bedroom. "Tell Fin I said thank you again for letting me off this weekend."

"You deserve breaks now and then. We made do for the summer without you, but I have to say we missed your cooking. You're damn good, and we're happy we get to reap the rewards of your fabulous cooking. One day when you're a famous chef on multiple TV shows, and everyone knows your name, I'm going to be able to say I was one of the first to sample your talents."

Damn, that felt great. For the rest of my days, I'd remember West's words.

Xander's white Bronco pulled up in front of the house and parked on the street. I knew there was no way in hell he'd get out, especially with West standing by my side.

I gave him a one-finger salute as I stepped onto the sidewalk and started for the SUV. "I'll see you sometime on Sunday."

"Yeah, alright," he shuffled his feet. "Have a good weekend."

"You too," I called over my shoulder.

The back hatch of the Bronco opened as I approached. I threw my bag in the back and opened the passenger door. Leaning down, I looked inside and smirked. "You didn't want to help me with my bag?"

Xander bit his bottom lip as the corner of his lips tugged up. Damn, did I want to take that lip between my own teeth.

"I thought you had it under control."

Slipping inside, I angled myself toward Xander. "And you didn't want anyone to see you picking me up. Am I, right?"

His face hardened. "I'm not going to lie to you. No one can know about this, whatever it is. It's not like I invited you on a weekend trip with my friends. It's just you and me. No one else can know."

I buckled my seat belt and held my hands up. "I know. You don't have to tell me. I wasn't planning on telling anyone, but if my roommates were to find out, they wouldn't say a word. They already saw you come out of my room that morning, and no one's said a word."

"Be that as it may, I can't put my trust in a bunch of twenty-something kids."

"Is that what you see me as? A kid? If so, I might as well get out now. I'm not some naïve boy who doesn't know what he's doing."

"Obviously. Innocent people don't blackmail their teachers." His jaw ticked on the last word.

"If you didn't like what I was doing, you wouldn't have invited me this weekend."

"Maybe I just see someone who needs help but won't accept it. I thought you might want to get away. Maybe being out in nature will give you some peace."

"And here I thought you invited me so I could fuck you all weekend. I bought an extra-large box of condoms to use." I swore I saw his dark skin redden just a little. It would have been cute if I were into that sort of thing.

His hands tightened on the steering wheel so hard his knuckles turned white. "What if I say no? Are you going to force me?"

"Both you and I know you'll want me to fuck you,

so why even pose the question?" I couldn't say I wouldn't fuck him because I would. Xander's no's were filled with want and need. It wasn't my fault if me fucking him made him feel guilty or ashamed of going against something in his moral code.

"I don't know. I guess it would be nice to know I have a choice in the matter in a different setting," he snapped. Hitting the power on the radio, the SUV filled with music. It wasn't music I knew, but I hadn't listened to much since I started school. Football, cooking, and homework kept me busy. Now Xander was taking up the rest of my time.

We were quiet for the rest of the drive, Xander fuming from the driver's seat. He had no reason to be pissed at me so that only left himself to blame. Why ask me to come if he planned on being celibate for the weekend?

I wasn't sure what to expect on our expedition with my small amount of knowledge of camping. I had no gear, and I hadn't asked any of the other guys since I didn't suspect they did either. Plus, I didn't want questions about what I was doing. Fin knew since I asked if they could fend for themselves while I was gone, and then West asked.

We pulled up to a secluded spot right on the edge of Big Bear Lake. It was beautiful. The trees and water were abundant, and it was like sitting on the edge of the world.

"Is this where you usually go camping?"

Xander didn't look at me when he spoke. He continued to stare out the windshield of the car. "Around here, but not at this exact location. I thought it would be best if there weren't families around our area."

"Probably a wise decision. You wouldn't want them to hear you crying out my name when you come," I chuckled. I knew he wanted my dick deep inside his ass this whole time.

Xander rolled his head on the headrest and looked at me blandly. "You don't have to keep mentioning you fucking me. I'm not sure if I should be flattered about your need to be inside of me or insulted."

I pulled my head back with my brows pinched. "Why would you be insulted? I'm just as addicted to you as you are to me. There's nothing to be ashamed about. We're both two consenting adults here."

"Are we, Ford?" He tilted his head.

"Are you not here of your own volition? All those times you've let me in your house, you chose to do so. That wasn't me."

Xander worked his jaw for a long second. "Maybe

if you weren't threatening to expose me every day, it would feel different."

"You can drive me back to Willow Bay right now if you want," I shot back. This wasn't my suggestion. If he didn't want me here, why did he ask?

His eyes lit up. "Maybe I wanted you to feel what it's like to be the one with no control."

"I can call an Uber or have some sad sack here drive me home. Don't think you can hold me hostage if I don't want to be here."

"Fine," he threw his hands up in the air. "I'm going to get my stuff out and set up the tent. You can either choose to help, or you can find another way home. Either way, it's on you."

Before I had a chance to throw a comeback at him, Xander was out of the car and unloading the back. There was no way in hell I was going to let him win, no matter how uncomfortable staying outdoors for the next two nights made me. I mean, how hard could it be?

Needing to take a piss, I walked away from where we'd be staying. I didn't want the smell of piss to be lingering the entire time we were here. I didn't stop until I could no longer see the bright white SUV.

I walked back slowly, taking in the smells of the trees and air. It was so different than in Willow Bay.

Back at home, there was always a slight hint of salt in the air. It was stronger when you were on the beach, but here it was full of pine trees or something like that. Species of trees weren't in my wheelhouse.

Xander was wrestling with a pole when I showed back up at camp. He looked me up and down as if he thought I'd fallen down or had a failed attempt to escape.

"Do you need any help?"

His shoulders slumped, and he nodded. "Yeah, the damn string inside is twisted, making it nearly impossible to connect the ends. Can you get it untwisted if I hold the pole?"

A joke was on the tip of my tongue, but I held it in. I didn't want Xander pissed at me the entire time we were here. I wanted to get away from my problems, not create new ones and fight with him.

Untwisting the string inside wasn't difficult with two people. It didn't take long until Xander had all the poles put together, and we'd laid out the tent with the opening facing the lake.

While I thought being out here might give me too much time to think, it did the opposite. Oh, there was plenty of silence to fill in my head, but there was a strange sense of peace that I hadn't felt in a long time.

Before I could think better of it, my mouth

opened. "Thank you for bringing me here. I can see why you like this place."

Xander straightened from hammering in one of the stakes to hold down the tent. He looked out at the lake and then back at me. "I'm glad you like it. I was worried you'd hate it and feel like I was holding you prisoner all weekend," he chuckled at the end.

"If I wanted to, I could find a way to leave. It's up to you to make sure I don't want to leave." I licked my dry lips as I took Xander in. He wasn't dressed to impress in only a white tank top that showcased all the muscles he usually hid underneath his clothes at school and a pair of basketball shorts and tennis shoes. He was relaxed and in his element, which was sexy as hell. Not that Xander wasn't always sexy. There was a reason I kept going back and pushing this thing between us.

"I'll see what I can do." He looked out at the lake and back at me again. "How are you at fishing?"

I'd never fished a day in my life. "I'm good at cooking them."

"Okay, how about I catch us dinner after setting up the tent, and then you cook them?"

"Sounds like a plan, but what if I want to try my hand? Maybe I'm an expert fisherman, and I don't know it."

Xander ran his tongue along his bottom lip and smiled. "You can try. Hell, maybe you are, but you still have to cook the fish."

"And what happens if we don't catch any fish? Are we going to starve to death?" If I had known he was going to go all caveman on me, I would have brought supplies. If I didn't get some sort of food in me, I'd be finding a way to the nearest place to eat or back home. I wasn't up for a round of Survivor out here.

Xander rolled his eyes, the whites of his eyes flashing in the sunlight. "I brought other food." He pointed near the fire pit where a cooler and milk crate sat. "Why don't you go check out the supplies I brought and see if they're up to your standards." I started to move away when he muttered under his breath. I didn't catch what he said, but I knew he was annoyed with me. Good, because I wasn't happy with him either.

There wasn't a lot in the crate, but Xander did have two nice pans and a Dutch oven in it that would be perfect for cooking. Why hadn't I thought to bring my own supplies? I hadn't thought about the location or how far out we'd be from civilization when I packed. If I ever did this again, I'd be more prepared.

"Stop stewing over there. There's never been a

time when I didn't catch a fish, and even if we don't, I have a couple of steaks in the cooler, along with some lunch meat for sandwiches. I'm not going to let you starve," he huffed out.

Why didn't he say so to begin with?

I opened the cooler to find more than what Xander had said. There was fruit, beer, sausage, and bacon, along with at least a dozen bottles of water.

"Now that you've seen that I'm not going to make you forage for food, do you think you can help me finish setting up the tent?" I looked up to find Xander standing there, holding a tent pole in one hand and the other hand on his hip.

I stood from my squat and walked over to him, grabbing the other end of the pole. "I thought you were an expert at this."

Xander looked away and chewed on the inside of his cheek. "I haven't used this tent before. It's one I've had but never gotten the opportunity to put together."

Now that I looked at it, the tent did seem new. Had he bought it for our camping trip? If so, why? I didn't care if the tent was ten years old. I was just happy we weren't sleeping out on the ground.

"Put the end of the pole in the shaft sticking up at the corner," he directed me.

"Did you have another tent before?"

"It was falling apart, so I thought it was time to get a new one," he answered as he moved to the other side of the tent. It wasn't large. Since the two of us were both big men, it would be close quarters once we were inside. Maybe that's what he wanted. It wasn't like I was going to let him get far, no matter how large the tent might have been.

"I wouldn't have cared if we were in a beat-up tent. I don't know the difference." I copied what I'd done on the other corner and looked down at our handy work. "It looks like a nice tent. Are you planning on going camping often?"

He shrugged and moved to put a thin cover over the top of the tent and hooked the ends at the corners. "I don't have many opportunities, but when the weather's nice, I'm going to try. Worst-case scenario, I can always grade papers out here."

"Doesn't that defeat the whole point of coming here?" I thought he wanted to get away from it all.

Xander ducked inside the tent and placed a sleeping bag and a few blankets inside. "I wouldn't come if I was going to be busy the whole time with work."

I sat down on top of the cooler and watched as Xander spread the sleeping bag and blankets out inside the tent. "You know, I would never have guessed you like camping."

"Why? Because I'm black?" He looked over his shoulder at me, his face impassive.

"I guess that's part of it, but it's more the way you dress. You're always in button-up shirts and slacks at school."

"Exactly. At school. That's what I wear to work. When you met me, I wasn't wearing my work uniform. I was in jeans and a t-shirt. Same as you." He went back to what he was doing and cleared his throat before he spoke. "You know, no one would guess the monumental asshole you are by looking at you. You look sort of… innocent."

Me innocent? I wanted to roll on the ground and laugh at the notion. Instead, I chuckled with my eyes locked on his ass. "We both know that's far from the case."

Xander sat down inside. He leaned forward with bent knees as he wrapped his arms around them. "Have you always been like this?"

"Like what? An asshole who blackmails people?" I shook my head. "You're my first."

"And hopefully your last," he muttered. I ignored what he said. I'd learned you didn't get far in life by being nice. If you wanted something, you had to do whatever was necessary to get it.

"Let's not start this old fight." My threat was the push he needed to do what he wanted. We both knew this.

"Fine," he crawled out of the tent and stood. "Let's go test your fishing skills before the sun sets. I don't feel like cleaning a fish in the dark."

I was all for cutting up a fish or any type of meat, but I didn't want to have to gut or clean it. That's where I crossed the line.

"Bring it on," I taunted as I grabbed one of the fishing poles by the tree and followed Xander down to the water.

Things were about to get interesting.

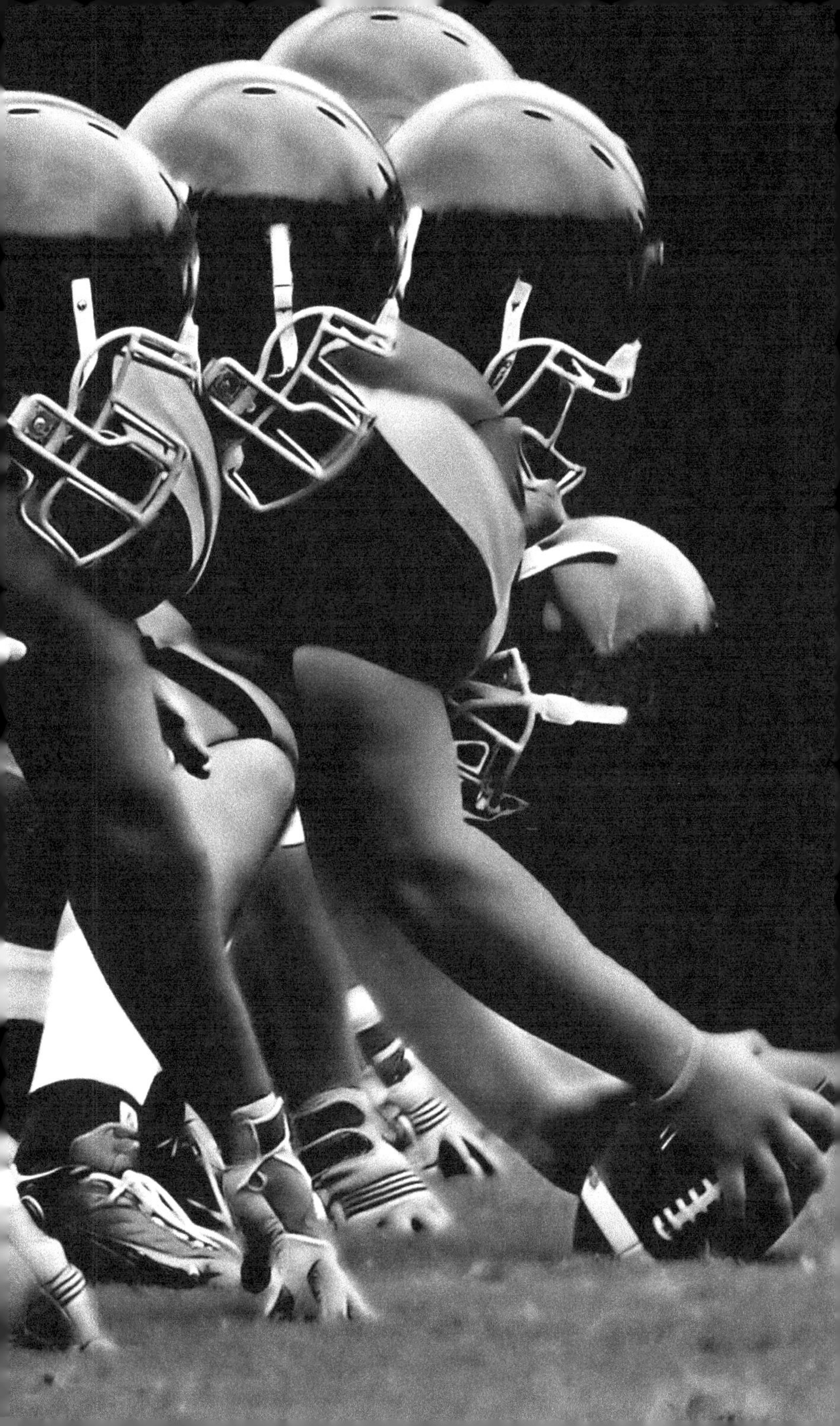

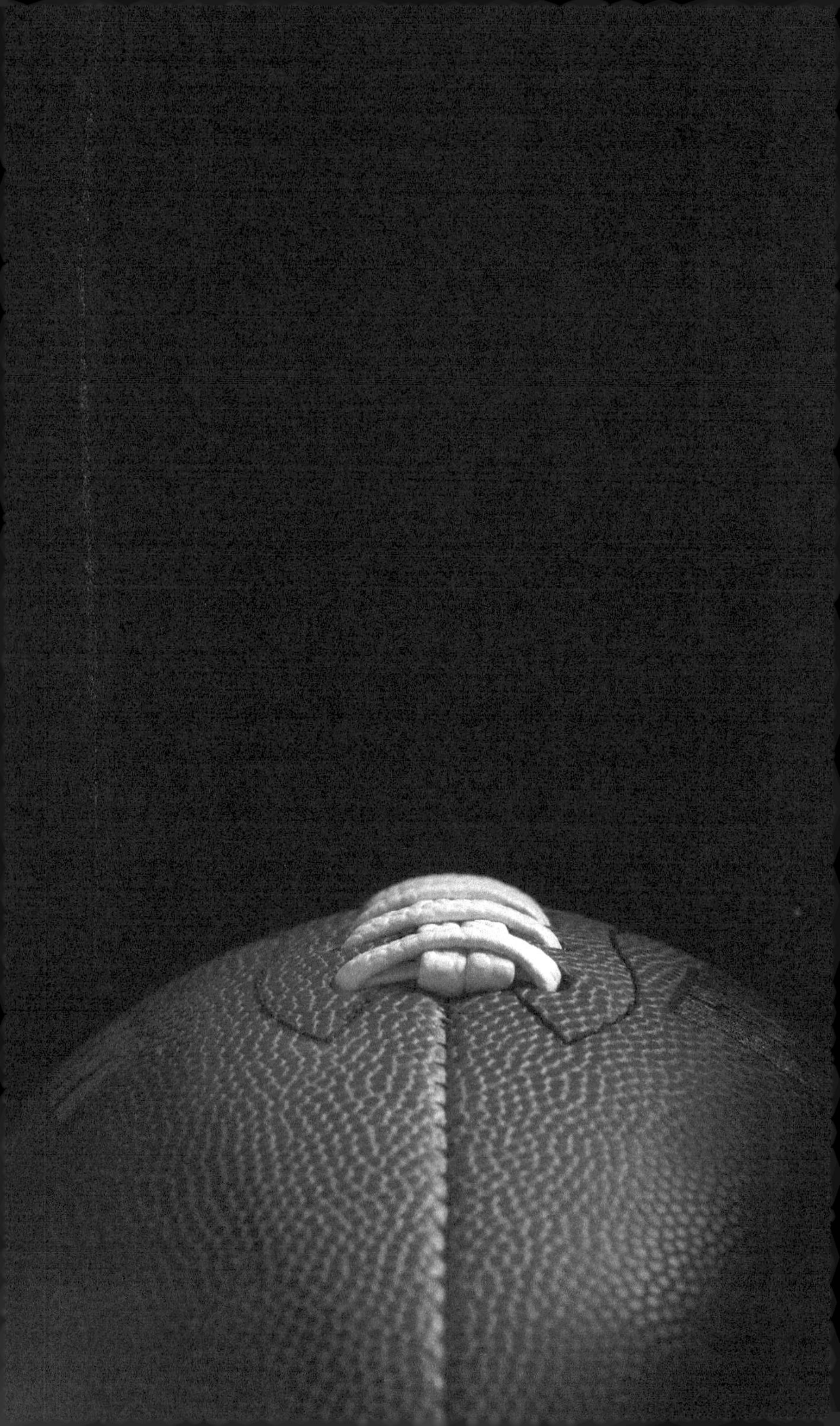

FIFTEEN
XANDER

I STOOD ONLY a few feet away from Ford as he tried to bait his hook. I could have gone easy on him, but where was the fun in that?

His eyes met mine, and he scowled. "You do this for fun?"

"It's not like I get some sick pleasure from killing worms. It's part of the process. It's how my dad taught me to fish instead of using fake ass shit."

"Now what do I do?" He looked at his pole like it was a foreign object, and I guess it was to him.

Moving behind him, I wrapped my arms around Ford and gripped the wrist he was holding the pole in. "Put your thumb on that button, but don't press on it yet." I watched as he did as instructed, and I scooted to the side behind him. "Now, pull your arm back." I guided him through the motion a couple of times and stepped back. "When you get to the top of the arc, push the button. Watch where your line lands, and after a couple of seconds, activate the reel to stop the line from dropping any further."

"And that's it?" He asked, looking at me over his shoulder.

"Then you wait to feel a fish on your line. Once you feel like one's grabbed your worm, give your pole a good yank to make sure you've got him on your hook, and then start reeling it in."

"Okay, seems simple enough." Ford shrugged and threw his line in one simple motion like he'd been fishing all of his life. It wasn't like it was rocket science, but it was still annoying he did it perfectly the first time.

I went back to my spot and cast my line. I wasn't sure why, but a strange surge of wanting to be the first to catch a fish hit me. I couldn't let someone who'd never fished before catch one before me.

After a few minutes, Ford sat in one of the chairs we'd brought down to the shoreline. "How long do we have to wait?"

"There's no time limit. It can take seconds, minutes, or hours. There's no telling. You need to keep quiet, so you don't scare the fish away."

"That sounds like bullshit right there," he mumbled, loud enough for me to hear him.

"It's the way it is. If you're not having any luck in one spot, you can always go to another location and try your luck there."

Ten minutes later, Ford was reeling in his line and picking up his chair. He didn't speak a word as he headed in the opposite direction from me. I watched until he was out of sight and then reeled my own line in. I wasn't going to move, though. I was going to stay here and try my luck now that he was gone. We didn't have long until it would be dark, and then we'd need to start a fire.

While it would have been nice to be sitting next to Ford watching the sunset, I needed to remember this, whatever it was, had a timeline. It would be over soon, so I shouldn't become attached to him or his cock. Well, the latter had already happened. There was no denying it, but I wouldn't let Ford get under my skin.

I felt the telltale sign of my line being tugged. Yanking back, I slowly reeled in my life as I felt the resistance of the fish on the other end. The fish broke the water at the same time Ford came walking back with a fish hanging from his line.

"Oh, good, you caught one. I thought I was going

to have to share this little sucker with you," he called from ten feet away. "I've already been thinking of how to cook them. Did you bring any spices with you?"

I finished bringing in my catch. "Just salt and pepper. I guess I should have mentioned bringing your own. I didn't think about how you'd want more than the bare necessities."

"I'll make do. Do you want to tell me how I'm supposed to get this guy off the hook?" He held his pole higher as if I couldn't see the fish dangling from the end with a look of innocence. It was the first time since I met Ford where he looked his age.

It was a strange dynamic for Ford to be asking me questions. He was usually so self-confident in every situation we encountered.

"You can watch me do mine and then try. It's probably easier to see it done than have it explained."

"How about I stop you right there? Why don't we strike up a deal?" I looked up from where I was kneeling on the ground, removing the hook from my catch. "You clean the fish, and I'll do the cooking."

The slight wrinkle to his nose let me know he wasn't a fan. I couldn't help but laugh. "Are you, Ford Fitzgerald, afraid of getting your hands dirty?"

Without warning, Ford tackled me to the ground

and pinned me with my hands beside my head while straddling my legs and sitting on them. "I'm not afraid of a little dirt. How about I show you how dirty I can get us both in a matter of minutes?" The last of the daylight showcased the intensity in his eyes as he held me down.

I tried to push Ford off, but he knew exactly how to keep me where he wanted me.

"Get off me, Ford. I need to clean the fish with the last of the remaining daylight." I bucked up with my hips, but it didn't faze Ford. He leaned down, putting more pressure on me.

"I like you where you are. At my mercy. Maybe I want to fuck you right here where anyone could see."

We hadn't seen a single soul since we got here, but the knowledge that it was possible for any passerby to catch us in the act had my body humming.

He leaned forward, took my bottom lip between his teeth, and bit down before letting go. "Ah, Mr. Lawrence likes the idea of being caught." Taking both my hands in one of his, Ford placed them over my head as he leaned in close enough I could smell the mint of his toothpaste on his breath. "Do you want them to see the way you completely give yourself over to me? Or the way I lose myself while pounding into you from behind?"

Both, I wanted to say but kept my mouth closed. I would never tell Ford just how much I wanted his touch and body. It would be giving him too much of myself.

In the blink of an eye, Ford rose and walked away, leaving me panting on the ground with my dick so hard I could barely think straight. I couldn't move as I watched him stride away to the fire pit. I wanted him back on top of me.

If I pulled out my cock and started stroking myself, would he come over and finish the job?

What the hell was wrong with me? I hadn't let my dick rule me since I was in high school.

After a few moments, I slowly picked myself up off the ground. Needing a little space, I took Ford's fish off the hook and found a large rock by the water where I could clean the fish and get them ready for him to cook.

Every few seconds, I'd look up to find Ford watching me with a blank expression on his face. Was he mad I didn't say yes? Surely, he had to feel how much I wanted him. He needed to learn that sometimes you had to be practical. He could fuck me all night, but I needed this light since I didn't have a lantern to use.

"Even with limited resources, you're a damn good cook. I think that's the best damn fish I've ever eaten, hands down."

Ford's gaze flicked to mine and then back to the remaining few bites I had left on my aluminum foil plate since I had forgotten paper plates when I packed.

He forked up another bite of his fish and stared blankly at me from across the fire. "You don't need to hype up my food. I'll continue to cook for you while we're here."

I wasn't sure why Ford couldn't take a compliment on his cooking. Everything he'd cooked for me was phenomenal, and he didn't seem to realize it.

"If this fish were just okay, I would have said thank you for cooking our fish. I'm never going to lie to you about your cooking or skills."

Ford cocked his head to the side. His dark eyes bore down on me. "Are you saying you'll lie to me about other things?"

"I don't plan on it." And I didn't, but I could see instances where I might have to in the future.

"So," he drew out the word. "What do people do out here once it gets dark?"

"Drink, play drinking games if you're in a group, and have sex. If it's warm, go skinny dipping." I wasn't sure what else anyone did while camping.

He nodded as he chewed. "I can get behind that."

Of course, he would. Internally, I laughed at his predictability.

"And what do we with the food?"

My brows knitted together. "What do you mean?"

Ford's eyes widened comically. "So that bears don't show up and kill us."

This time, I laughed out loud. "Do you really believe I'd bring you to a place where a bear could attack us?"

"Maybe you thought me getting eaten by a bear would be an easy way to get rid of me." He laughed, letting me know he wasn't serious.

"I promise to protect you from any big bad bears that come our way."

"That's kind of hot. What do you say we christen your tent?" He stood, balling up his aluminum foil and throwing it away in the trash bag hanging from one of the trees. I watched from my perch on the edge of my seat.

Ford unzipped the tent and moved inside on his hands and knees. He sat down and slowly removed his shirt, and then kicked off his shoes and socks.

"What are you waiting for?" He called out as he lifted up his hips and slipped his shorts down his legs.

Even with only the light of the fire, I could see his thick cock standing up and bobbing against the ridges of his eight-pack abs.

"This dick isn't going to suck itself."

No, it certainly wasn't. "What if I'm waiting for your mouth on my dick?" I adjusted my rock-hard erection through my shorts.

"I think we both want each other's mouths on our dicks. We can blow each other at the same time."

"I'm down with a little sixty-nine action." The thought of Ford gagging with my cock down his throat had me leaking in my pants.

Lying back, Ford spread his legs and watched me through the gap in his legs as he started stroking himself slowly. "Then get in here, Mr. Outdoors."

I shed my clothes as I stalked toward him and slipped inside the tent. Crawling over his long, toned body, I loved having Ford underneath me where I could control how much of me he took inside of his mouth.

Leaning down, I sucked on his tip and swirled my tongue along the underside. A guttural moan echoed through the tent seconds before Ford's hot mouth engulfed my shaft. For a brief second, I couldn't move. I was all consumed by the way his hands gripped my hips and started to rock me back and forth little by little until he swallowed me deep down his throat. It spurred me on. I bobbed up and down, hallowing out my cheeks as I massaged his balls in one hand and held myself up with the other.

Pushing me up, Ford's decadent mouth released me. I started to protest until he pulled me back down, ran the flat of his tongue from my balls to my back passage, and swirled his tongue around. Fuck, I couldn't remember the last time I had someone's tongue in my ass.

"Fucking hell," I mumbled around his cock. I didn't think Ford would let me inside him this weekend. He didn't seem like that was something he'd ever be down for, and I was okay with that. I ran my finger through the saliva that had run down his crack. Coating my finger, I pressed it to the tight ring of muscle. Lifting up, I looked at him over my shoulder. "Relax. I'm only going to do this. I want to make you feel as good as you make me feel."

His dark eyes never left mine as he gave me a slight nod. I pushed through and started to move my finger in and out in the same rhythm as I took his cock as far as I could take it.

I wasn't sure how much longer I could hold back my impending orgasm. It all felt too good, the noises Ford made and the vibrations it sent deep into my body.

We both quickened our pace, trying to outdo the other and bring the other to completion first. Ford's hips thrust up, sending his shaft deep down my throat. The moan that escaped him and the feel of the hot jets of his cum had me detonating all over his chest and abs.

Releasing his cock, I rested my forehead against his thigh and tried to catch my breath. Ford rolled out from underneath me and used the shirt he wore earlier to clean my cum off him. I watched, still on my hands and knees, as he moved to lie down beside me with his head down at my end.

Rolling to his side, Ford cupped the side of my hip and pulled me down to lie with him.

With my back to his front and his hand resting on

my stomach, I closed my eyes and breathed him in. "Give me a few minutes to recover."

I listened as Ford's breath slowed until it was shallow, indicating he was asleep. Closing my eyes, I wished we could stay like this all night, every night.

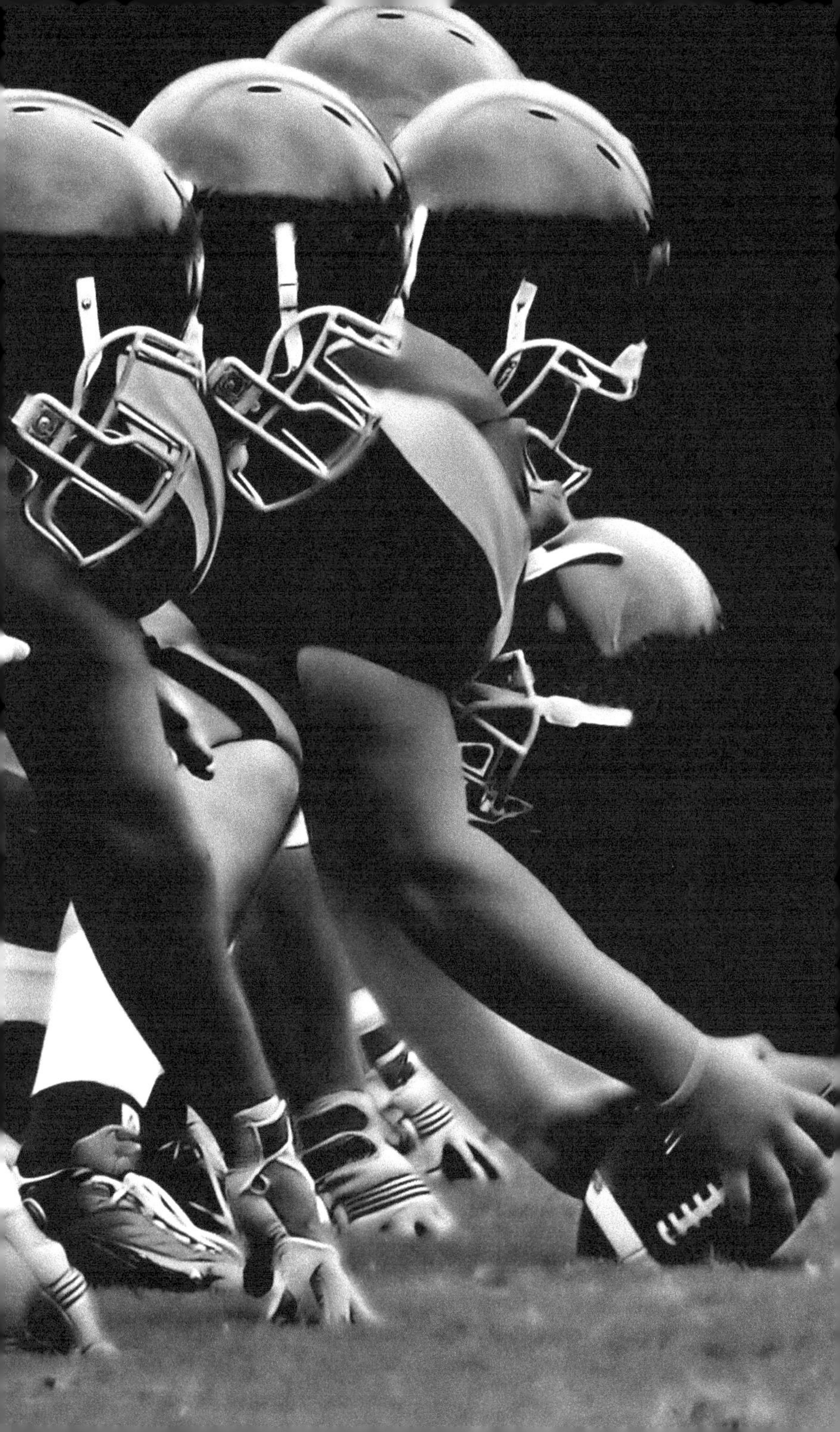

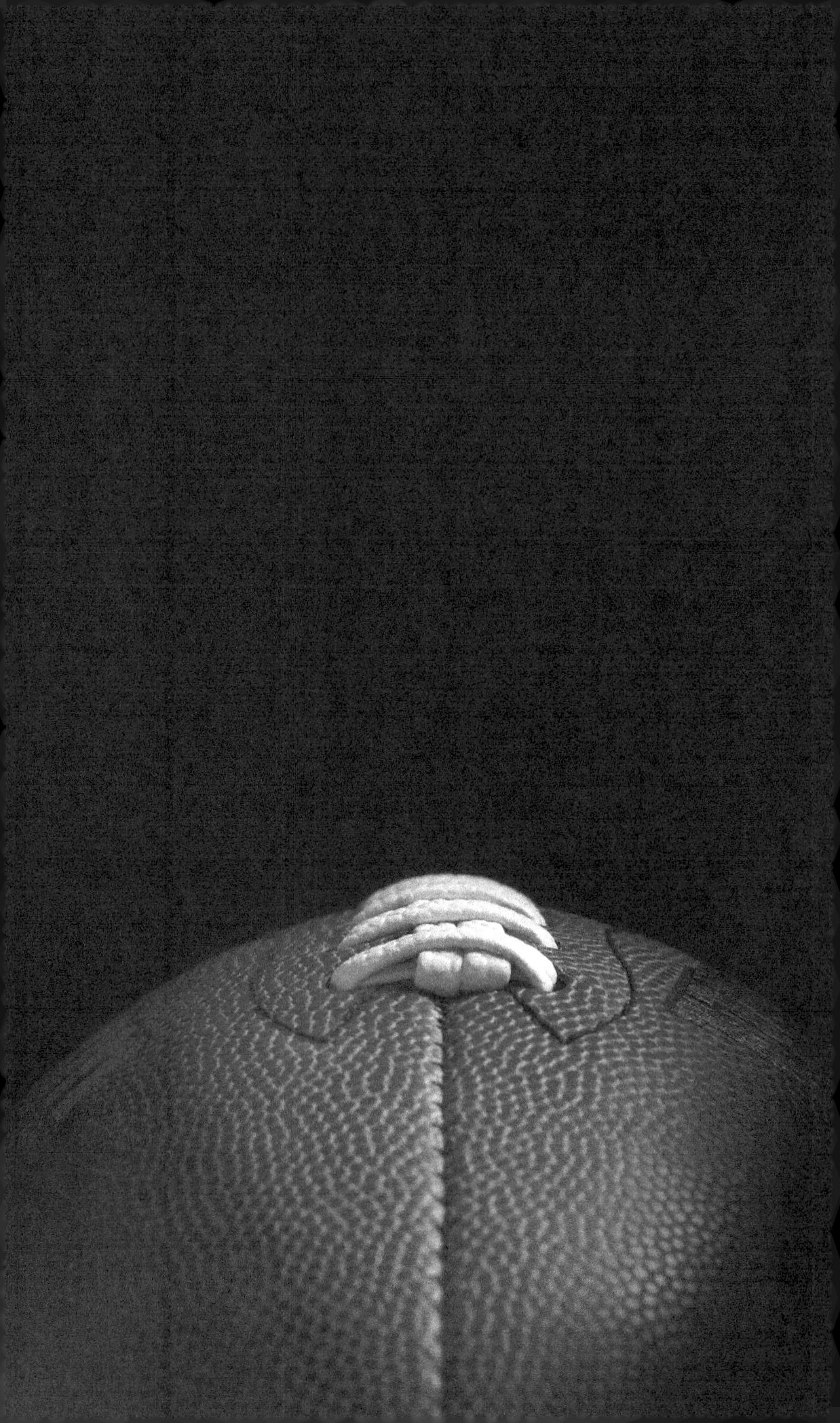

SIXTEEN
FORD

"HOW MUCH LONGER UNTIL it's time to eat?" Oz bounced impatiently on the balls of his feet as he looked over his shoulder.

I didn't look at him as I spoke. There were too many dishes cooking for me to give him my full attention. "Why are you rushing me? I told you I'd have dinner ready at two o'clock and it's one-thirty. The food isn't going to magically cook itself."

"Because Dani keeps looking in this direction like she's about to pass out from hunger." He moved closer until his shoulder pressed against mine. "Did you see her? She's wasting away. Do you think it's from being depressed about her boyfriend dumping her?"

"I don't know, Oz. I've only talked to your sister

one other time, so I can't say. Maybe you should ask her what's going on in her life." I didn't want to tell him that even though I'd only met Dani once, her appearance today was startling. She'd lost a significant amount of weight. It wasn't like she needed to lose any weight before. She was tall and toned, with an athlete's body. Now she resembled a twig. I wasn't sure how she could play soccer and not get her bones broken at every game.

"You don't think I've tried? Because I have. So has Lo, but she won't talk to us about him or soccer or pretty much anything. All she wants to talk to Lo about is our wedding plans," he hissed out under his breath. "She does realize we're not getting married until after we graduate, right?"

"Maybe she's hoping you'll change your mind. Like I said, I don't know. You and Lo are the ones that are close to her. Not me. Why don't you have Fin ask?"

Oz rested back against the counter beside me and scoffed. "Fin doesn't have any finesse. If something is wrong, he'll just make it worse."

I didn't know what to tell him. I could barely handle my own problems, let alone worry about someone else I barely knew.

"If you think it will help, I'll ask her some

questions when we all sit down and eat." I had very little confidence she'd open up when I asked the question. If she didn't want to talk, she didn't want to talk. "Alright, I need to concentrate on my food here. Let everyone know it will be ready in about twenty minutes."

Oz left, but Charlie stayed to keep me company, or he thought I was going to give him food. Probably the latter. Still, he was a good dog. Some days, he sat beside me, being my silent companion. Charlie was so attuned to everyone's feelings it was remarkable. I wasn't going to lie. There were days when all I wanted to do was bury my face in his fur and cry. I'd found nothing was better with time. My mom was still dead, and my brother and sister still didn't want to talk to me. I was going to remedy that, though. After our football game next week, I was heading to my aunt's to see them for Thanksgiving. I was going to make them sit down and listen to me. I had to make them understand why I couldn't take care of them. Hell, I could barely take care of myself, let alone two teenagers in their junior year of high school.

I snuck Charlie a piece of ham for standing his silent vigil with me before I started to take all the dishes to the dining room table. I'd barely set the first one down when everyone stood from their spot in the living room and filed into the kitchen to carry something back to the dining room. They each let out contented sighs as they took in the aromas from the meal I'd cooked.

I sat down at the table next to Dani, and she gave me a shy smile before Fin clapped me on the shoulder. "It's decided. You're stuck cooking Thanksgiving dinner for all of us for the rest of your life. Once we all graduate, we'll all meet at someone's house each year, and you're cooking."

I cracked a smile. "And I get no say in this?"

"I'll pay you handsomely once I have NFL money," West chimed in from the other end of the table. "We don't want to let this go. We're all one big happy family, and we want to keep it that way."

They didn't have to pay me. Cooking Thanksgiving and sitting around with them like this when I didn't have anyone else meant the world to me. I would never forget how hard they tried to get me to talk when I didn't want to. When I still hadn't.

"I'll take some of that NFL money," I joked. "Now, let's dig in before the food gets cold."

As if they hadn't eaten in a week, everyone grabbed a dish and started piling the food onto their plates. It made me happy that my food was part of this day. Not only did my cooking bring me solace, but it made others happy and brought them together.

Out of the corner of my eye, I watched as Dani put the smallest amounts of food on her plate. Leaning to the side, I spoke so only she could hear me. "You know you can get more food than that. I made plenty."

Dani's cheeks reddened as she put her hands in her lap. "While all of this smells and looks amazing, my coach would have my hide if I gained ten pounds over break."

Oz dropped his fork on his plate, his eyes narrowing. "Is this your coach's doing?"

"Is what his doing?" Her hands clenched together in her lap. "Me playing the best I've ever played? If so, then yes."

"I mean, you look like a fucking twig. I'm not sure how your bones aren't snapping on the field," he growled out.

Lo called Oz's name softly. His nostrils flared, but I could see the fire die inside of him as he took a moment. "I'm just worried about you, that's all. I'm allowed to do that as your brother." Oz stretched out his hand and closed his eyes when Dani took it from across the table. "You barely talk to us anymore, and then you show up looking like a completely different person."

Dani took her hand back as she looked around the table. All eyes were on her, making her squirm in her seat. "What can I say?" She shrugged. "I'm finding myself, and as for the eating part, the whole team has been put on a nutritional plan. I'm healthier and stronger than I've ever been."

"It doesn't look like it from here. You look like you might blow away in the wind if you stepped outside," Fin said in his standard monotone, bored voice.

Dani's blue eyes narrowed as she set her gaze on Fin. "I can assure you that I spend hours upon hours outside, and I've never once even been lifted off my toes from the force of the wind."

"Whatever you say." Fin leaned forward, his dark gaze leveling Dani to her spot. "Surely your coach will let you eat a real meal for Thanksgiving."

"As much as Ford's cooking is seven thousand times better than my mom's, she would be wounded if I didn't eat the mediocre meal she'll put together on Thursday."

"Thanks?" I wasn't sure if that was a compliment or if my cooking was just a step above mediocre.

"No," she grabbed my arm and looked up at me

with her blue-colored doe eyes. "Your food is great. Fin just hired you to cook until the end of time. How can you even think your food isn't some of the best we've ever eaten? I promise I'll eat some, but I'm not pigging out like the rest of you." Dani eyed our plates with her nose turned up.

The way she looked at the food screamed another thing altogether, but I wasn't going to say anything. I did my part, or at least I thought so.

Oz gave his sister a hard look. "If you don't think mom isn't going to be on your case about how skinny you are, you're deluding yourself. She's going to make you eat."

I wanted to tell Oz he might want to shut up, or his sister wasn't going to be making the family's Thanksgiving dinner.

"Well, make sure you save room for my famous pumpkin pie. If you don't eat a slice, you'll hurt my feelings."

I swore Dani's face turned green right in front of my eyes. "I'm sorry, Ford, I don't like pumpkin." With her hand still on my arm, Dani ran her hand down to my own, which was curled around my fork. "Maybe I can make it up to you later."

Fin burst out laughing. "I think you're barking up the wrong tree there, Dani. If I'm not mistaken,

Ford here is fucking one of the teachers here at school."

My gaze went to Fin's. "You don't know what you're talking about," I growled. "Who I stick my dick in is none of your concern."

Fin held his hands up and pretended to be sorry. "Maybe I should have told her you're fucking some dude. Would you have rather I said that?"

Dani's hand was off me like if she touched me a moment longer, it would catch on fire. "I didn't know you're into guys."

"And girls. I give every human an equal opportunity." I don't know why I said that. I had zero interest in Dani, and I would never go there even if I did. Not with her being Oz's sister.

"So, you're bi?" Dani leaned forward, brushing her breast against my arm.

"I am." I wasn't sure if she was hitting on me or not, but if she was, I had to nip this thing in the bud. "But Fin is right. At this time, I'm with a man."

"I bet he's hot." She fanned herself. "The thought of you and another guy is what fantasies are made of."

"Okay, I think that's more than I ever wanted to know about my sister. Why don't you keep your fantasies to yourself?"

"It seems like I can't do right by my dear brother today. Such a pity." She leaned over and whispered against my ear. "He can't stop me from picturing it in my head."

I barked out a laugh. Maybe Dani was something I needed. I couldn't remember the last time I laughed. Genuinely. "Enjoy. Just make sure I have a really big cock."

"I can hear you, assholes," Oz growled.

Dani paid no attention to her twin brother. "Why isn't your guy here?"

Because he was a professor at our school, and no one could know. I bet he would have liked what I'd cooked. He would have fought Fin, saying I would cook for him and not our friends, or maybe he would have asked if he could be part of the yearly invite to Friendsgiving.

Instead, I lied. Something I hated doing. "He's traveling to be with his family." In reality, I had no idea what Xander was doing today, tomorrow, or for the entire break. He didn't mention it, and I didn't ask because that wasn't what we were.

Dani raised a lone brow. "And is he a teacher?"

I shrugged. "He's no one. Just someone to occupy my time while I try to finish the year. Do you have anyone new?"

All traces of happiness slid off Dani's face. "No. The only person I'm spending time with is my soccer ball and my team."

"You know," Lo broke our bubble. "We were thinking of coming to one of your games once football is over. Can you send me your schedule, so we can try to make one?"

"Of course, I can. You guys make me feel like shit when I haven't been to one of your games."

"Don't worry about it. You were at every game all through middle and high school. I don't care if you can't make them now. I know you would be there if you could."

Dani gave her brother a sad smile. "You let me off too easily."

"That's what big brothers are for."

"It's too bad UCLA never plays Willow Bay. It's like the universe is against us."

"Yeah, it really is." Oz frowned.

"Alright," Fin boomed. "Enough of this sappy shit. Ford's food is getting cold, and it's too good to waste."

I sat and ate quietly, taking everyone in, wondering what it would be like having Thanksgiving at my aunt's. It would be the first one I could remember at her house. Growing up, mom always worked on Thanksgiving to get overtime. We would have a small meal, usually something she picked up. It was never fancy or anything like that. Being here in this house was the first time I appreciated Thanksgiving.

West leaned on his elbow my way. The smile he wore was genuine, and I already knew whatever he was about to say, I wouldn't like it. "You know, you can invite anyone you want here. This is your home, too. We don't want you to feel like you have to hide any part of your life from us."

"Thanks, that means a lot to me." I gave him my best fake smile.

The guys really were like a real family. They meddled and made me feel guilty, just the same as my biological one.

"But you're not going to have him here, are you." It wasn't a question but a statement.

"It's nothing serious. If anything changes, I'll let you know."

To stop further questioning, I scooped up a large forkful of dressing.

Even though I said it wasn't serious between Xander and me, he had become my addiction. He was in my every thought. My body craved to feel his underneath me, to hear the way he moaned my name, and the way his eyes dilated each time I was near. I wasn't sure how I was going to cope with being away for four days.

I already knew my first stop when I got back to Willow Bay would be Xander's house. I would need to get lost in his body and if he tried to keep me away, so help me God, I would burn his world down.

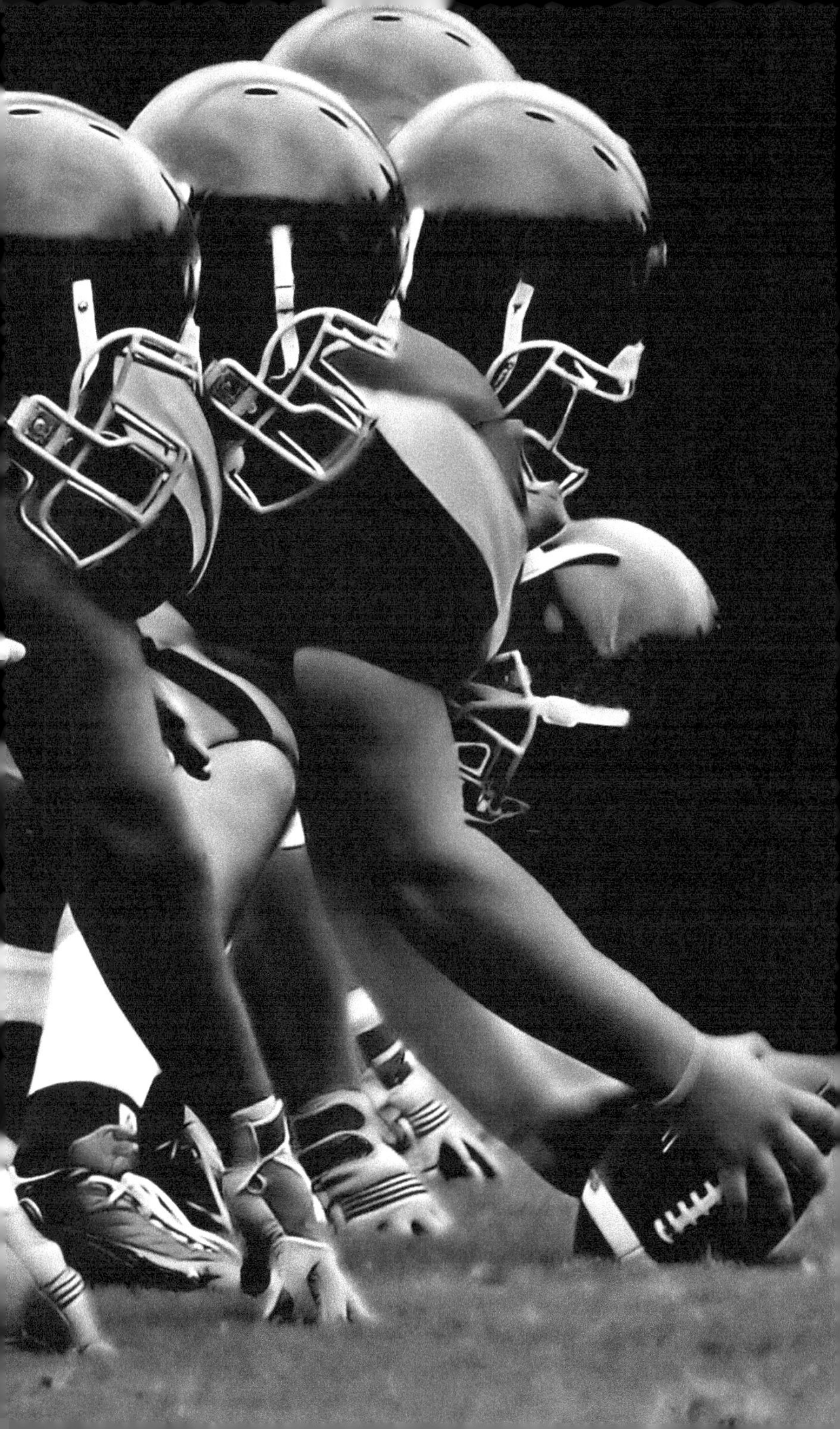

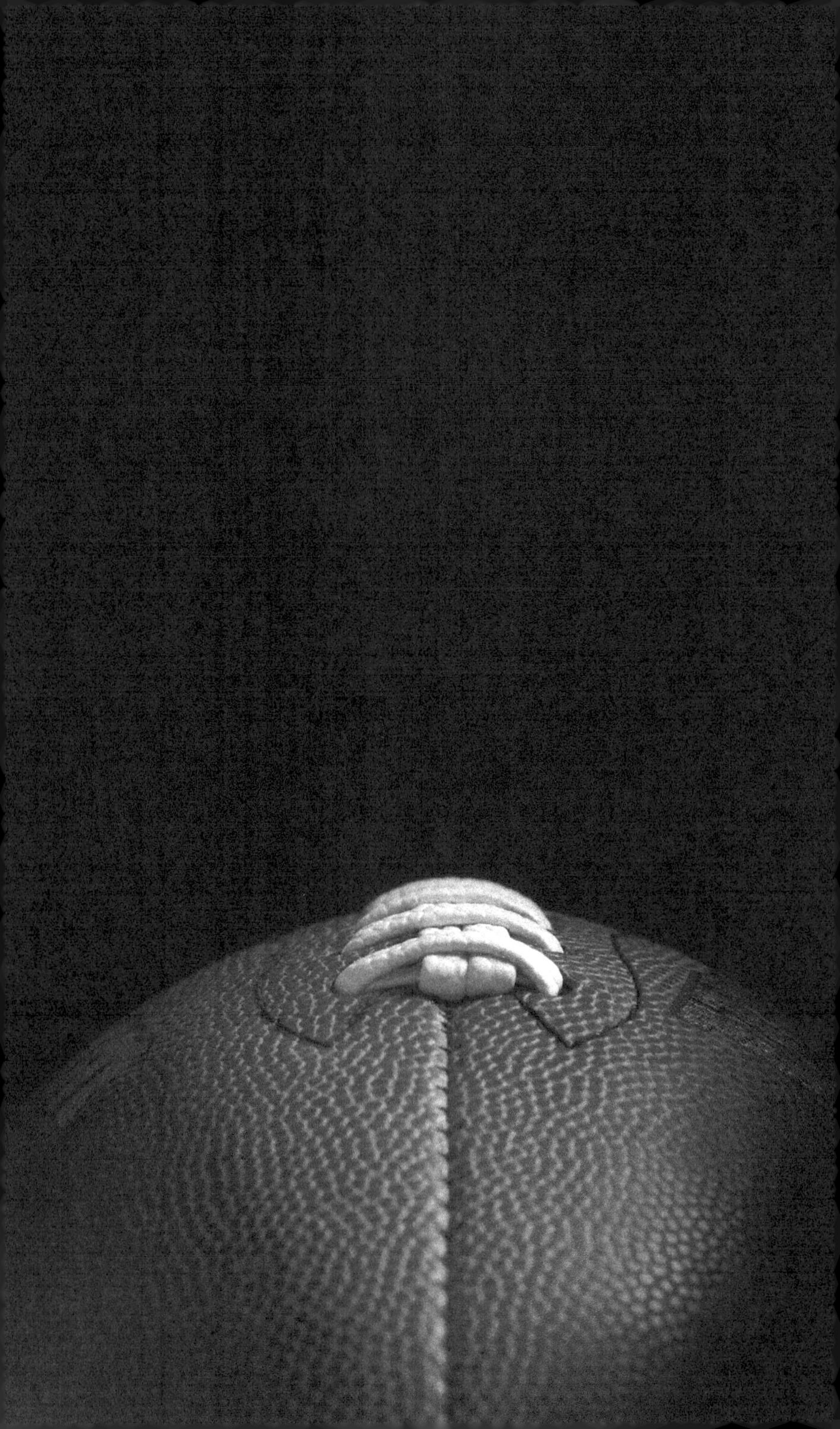

SEVENTEEN
FORD

IF I HAD the money to fly, I would have. It was ten long-ass hours to my aunt's, where I had way too much time to think on my hands. I tried to avoid thinking altogether these days. It was the only way I could stay sane.

Now, as I neared my aunt's, I had cried silent tears for at least an hour of my journey. It was going to hurt to see my aunt. She and my mom almost looked exactly alike, and their voices were nearly identical.

What the hell was I thinking?

Now I understood why Christian and Lucy were upset with me. I was close to having a full-on meltdown with only the thought of coming face to face with my mom's doppelgänger. They had to live with her. I never thought about how hard it must be for them.

Even so, they deserved better than what I could provide. I didn't think they would have been any happier if I forced them on our dad. Not that he would have taken them. He was too busy with his new family to care that his old one was crumbling.

I needed… something. What it was, I didn't know. I thought about calling Oz or West to talk to them, but they were busy with their own families. Plus, what would I say to them? Can you talk to me, so I don't think about my dead mother? Oh, yeah, I failed to mention she's dead, and that's why I can barely function, and I'm a miserable asshole. Although I wouldn't be surprised if Fin had told West. Still, I wasn't going to call them to talk me down. I wanted them to enjoy their time with West's family.

My fingers hovered over Xander's number. I'd never called him or texted him after he'd given me his number. I was sure he expected me to give him mine, but I hadn't, knowing he'd use it to tell me to stay far away from him.

Closing my eyes for a brief second, I hit his name and listened as the sound of a phone ringing filled the silence in my car.

"Hello?" Xander answered with a question in his

tone. I was sure he was wondering who the hell was calling him.

"Hey," I answered back and then had to clear my throat. "Do you have a few minutes to talk?"

"Ford? Is that you?"

"The one and only." I was already regretting my decision, and I'd barely said ten words to him.

"Are you okay?"

Wasn't that the ten-million-dollar question?

"Not really. I've had too much time on my hands driving today. I can't stop thinking. When will it end?" For some reason, it was easier to speak the words I would never have said if I were in front of him. There was no pity to see on his face or any other emotion. All I could see was the wide-open space in front of me.

"I wish I could answer that for you, but I don't think there's a timeline for grief. You're always going to think about your mom, but hopefully, as time passes, the anger will go away, and in its place, you'll think of all the good memories you have of her."

"I know rationally she would be dead by now from the cancer." Why was I opening up to him?

"But it still doesn't take away the hurt from knowing she took her own life."

Fuck, there was no way in hell I would have been

able to do this face to face. And after all that I'd put Xander through, he was being so understanding and kind.

"It kills me to know that she did it to make our lives easier. If I had known, I probably would have dropped out of school to take care of her and my brother and sister," I confessed.

"It was important for her to give you the best opportunity she could."

He was right. My mom was so proud I was the first in her family to go to college. It would have killed her if I had to drop out. Still, it doesn't make it any easier.

"When is it going to stop hurting so much?" I croaked out.

"I wish I could tell you. I'm going to tell you something you don't want to hear, but you need to talk like you are now. You've been bottling it all up for months and letting it fester inside of you." He paused, letting his words sink in. "I'm not going to lie to you. There are still days where it hurts to think about my parents, and they've been dead for almost five years. It was sudden, and I didn't have a chance to say goodbye."

Hot tears leaked down my cheeks as I thought of

the vibrant woman my mother was but hadn't been all summer.

"Why didn't I notice? Why didn't I question her about what was going on? She still went to work each and every day like she was the healthiest person in the world. If I would have known—"

"What would you have done, Ford? I know I didn't know your mom, but I believe she wanted to keep her dignity intact. If she hadn't been able to provide for you and your siblings, it would have only been that much worse on her."

"If she was thinking about us, then she would have realized how much it would hurt for her to keep us in the dark. We weren't prepared. Nothing was planned." She didn't even leave a will. "She ended her life with a snap of her fingers and left me to pick up the pieces."

The pieces were still scattered after all this time, and I wasn't any closer to picking them up now as I was when she took her life.

"She was very sick. I know that's an excuse, but it's true. When people are sick, they're not always thinking logically. Maybe she couldn't take the pain anymore."

That thought was what hurt the most. My mom had hidden her pain from me and didn't want to burden me. At first, she did try treatment, but it was too expensive, and she stopped. She'd been slowly paying the bill and had barely made a dent in it.

Blinding hot rage filled me at the thought that if the treatment hadn't been so expensive, she might still be alive today.

"Talk to me, Ford," Xander said softly over the line.

"I'm angry. At her. At the system and at her doctors. It shouldn't bankrupt someone for them to fight for their life. I had to sell the house to pay off her first round of treatment. When it didn't work, she quit because she couldn't afford it. That's not right," I yelled, my loud voice bouncing around my car. I opened my window and let it out. I wanted the world to hear me. "Why did my father have to leave her with nothing?" I wasn't sure how he got away with not paying any child support over the years. There were points in my life when my mom had three jobs to keep food on the table and clothes on our backs.

"I wish I had an answer for you."

"How can I look at my brother and sister knowing I failed them?" My voice cracked on the last word.

"But you didn't, Ford. You're grieving the same as

them. Talk to them like you're talking to me, and they'll understand. If not now, then eventually. They're hurting just as you are. It wouldn't hurt if you all saw someone."

"I can't. The only reason I'm opening up to you now is because I can't see you or the look on your face. If I saw the pity, I would punch you or something worse."

"There's no pity on my face. All you'd see is understanding and sadness. I want you to know if you ever need to talk to me, be it in person or on the phone. I'm here for you."

Deep down, I knew he was, and that was why I called him. When I first told him about my mom, Xander didn't look at me any differently, and that was what I needed.

"Can I ask where you are right now?" There was worry in his tone that I didn't like.

"I'm driving. Don't worry about me. I'm not going to off myself. No matter how far I fall, I will never take the coward's way out."

"Do you really think it was cowardly on your mom's part? I think she did what she thought was best for her family. In all actuality, it took a lot of courage."

I exploded. My vision went from red to black in a

nanosecond. I wasn't sure how I stayed on the road or didn't break off the steering wheel as my blood roared in my ears.

"How the fuck can you say that? She lied to us for over a year, telling me she was completely healthy. Then she gave up. On treatment, on her children, and on life." By the time I finished those words, my throat was raw from screaming the words at Xander.

There was a long huff of breath down the line before he spoke. "Are you still driving?"

"Yes," I bit out. My hands flexed on the steering wheel, causing my knuckles to turn white. The rage that was swirling inside of me had me close to losing control. I wanted to pound someone's face in to let out the cacophony of emotions. Maybe multiple faces.

"Maybe you should pull over. You're not going to do yourself any good if you wreck."

"I'm fine," I gritted out.

Xander let out an irritated sigh. He was probably shaking his head on the other end of the line, wondering why he was even talking to me. I was sure he regretted ever hooking up with me that first night. "Look, I'm not saying I agree, but I can *maybe* see what she was thinking. I'm not saying it was right she didn't tell you. It wasn't. Maybe if she had someone to talk it out with, she would have seen a different way. What I do know is no one can change the past. Don't let her choices ruin your life or who you are."

That was easy for him to say. How could I let it go when my world was crumbling around me on a daily basis?

"Thanks for picking up." Especially when he didn't know who it was. He probably wished he hadn't bothered. "I'm going to go now. I'm close to my destination."

"Where are you going?" He paused and then took back his words. "Never mind. You don't have to answer that. I'm always here if you need to talk."

I could only grunt. I wasn't sure if I'd call again. The only thing I was sure of was I'd be banging on his door when I got back into town. I would need to get lost in his body to forget about the long weekend.

"Have a good Thanksgiving," Xander called out before I hung up. I shouldn't have called. Now he knew too much. If he looked at me differently the next time I saw him, I wouldn't be able to face him again. It would be over, and I'd need to find a new distraction.

With my arm slung over my eyes, I shifted uncomfortably on the couch. My aunt didn't have any extra rooms, so it was either the floor or her hard as fuck couch. I'd been lying there for the past two hours. At this point, maybe it would be better to try my luck on the floor.

The sound of footsteps above me let me know I wasn't the only one not asleep. If my vague knowledge of the house was correct, I thought Christian's room was right above me. He hadn't said a word to me. Neither had Lucy. Maybe now was a good time to try and talk to him without Lucy or Aunt Cecilia hovering.

Throwing back the blanket, I stood and headed quietly up the stairs. I tapped my knuckle against the door once before I stepped inside. I hadn't been inside or even had a chance to see his surroundings before now. Earlier, when I got the tour, his door was closed.

I took in the clothes strewn all over his floor. There wasn't a blank spot to see if the room was carpeted or hardwood.

Christian lifted his head from looking down at his phone and hissed, "What are you doing in here? Did I say you could come in?"

Standing in his doorway, I crossed my arms over

my chest. "This has gone on long enough, Chris. You act like I'm the one who killed her instead of the person who found her and had to deal with everything."

"And you think we aren't dealing with anything?" He stood from his bed and stalked across the room toward me. He was nearly as tall as I was but skinny. If he thought he could take me, he was sorely mistaken. "We had to move away from all of our friends and into a complete stranger's house all because you thought it was best to sell the house."

My eyes narrowed at my brother. "Do you think I sold the house so I could have a little extra spending cash?"

"No," he flapped his arms at his sides. "I think you used it for *you* to go to college."

He couldn't be more wrong. Was this why he refused to talk to me?

I stepped forward, hitting him with my chest, and pushed into the room. A bitter laugh tumbled from my lips. "You couldn't be more wrong. I sold the house to pay for mom's medical bills. Bills that you can't even fathom the amount. Once those were paid off, I put the rest of the money in an account for you and Lucy to go to college. I admit it isn't enough to do much, but at least it's something." I pushed into him further. "My college is paid through a scholarship, and the only way I can live there is because my friend took me in. He has a house where he's letting me stay in exchange for cooking all of their meals and keeping the house clean. I'm a fucking maid. Tell me how bad you have it here with Lucy by your side and aunt Cecilia. Oh, right, you can't," I hissed out the last.

If Chris thought he had it bad, he was in for a rude awakening when he had to step out into the real world.

"How was I supposed to know that?" He took a step back and put his hands on his hips. "You didn't tell us anything."

"Maybe because you refused to talk to me. How many times have I tried to call you and Lucy? More times than I can count, and each fucking time neither of you answers. If it wasn't for our aunt, I wouldn't even know you're alive."

He hung his head as he spoke. "You don't need to worry about us."

"Of course, I'm going to worry. Look where it got me to not ask questions. I didn't even know mom was sick. She hid it from me the same as you and Luce. It kills me to know she felt there was no other choice than to end her life in order to make ours better." Running my hands through my hair, I pulled at the strands as I looked at my brother, who I realized was just as broken as me. "My life is not better. I hate every second of every day. The guilt of not knowing. Of not being able to help, and then with you two shutting me out. I…" My throat closed up, making it impossible for me to speak.

"We know it's not your fault." Warm arms wrapped around me from behind, and Lucy laid her head on my shoulder. "If anyone should have known something was wrong, it should've been us. You were at school. How were you to know?"

I wasn't sure, but surely there had to be signs.

"I'm sorry we stopped talking to you. We didn't know." Lucy let go of me from behind and moved to stand in front of me. Her big brown eyes filled with tears.

"I'm sorry I didn't talk over selling the house with you. I didn't think about how you'd feel. When I saw all the medical bills, I freaked out, unsure how I was ever going to pay them."

Lucy curled up to my side and gave me another hug. It felt nice after all this time. I wrapped my arms around her. She looked up at me with glassy eyes. "You shouldn't have had to deal with that."

"Maybe not, but if not me, who else? I couldn't

put that on the two of you." I closed my eyes as I spoke. "I should have thought about how moving would affect you both and clued you in on why I was doing the things I was doing. You two have always been so close with your twin thing. I'll admit I'm kind of jealous."

Christian moved in to hug me from the other side. "Fuck, bro, you know we love you. We shouldn't have shut you out. Do you have anyone to talk to?"

Oh, if they knew the way I've changed. How angry I'd been.

"Not really. I've been doing everything in my power to *not* think about… well, anything. I haven't exactly been the best company."

Lucy pulled her head back. "You need to find someone to talk to—a friend or maybe even a girlfriend. I bet the right girl can get you to talk. Maybe you'll settle down once you graduate."

Should I?

I didn't want to hide anything any longer.

"I might not end up with a girl, and I might never settle down. Right now, my focus is trying to become the best chef I can be."

Chris' face broke out into a giant smile. "You need to open your own restaurant." He leaned forward, whispering. "Please tell me you're going to help with dinner tomorrow. While Aunt Cecilia is nice, she's not a great cook. It's been torture eating her food since we've been here."

I chuckled. "I'm not going to step on her toes. If she asks, then I'll help, but otherwise, I'm going to be hands-off."

"Aw, fuck." Chris hung his head. "It's going to be a crappy Thanksgiving dinner, then. She's too proud to ask for help."

"Maybe you can ask if she wants help," Lucy suggested.

"I'll ask, but that's all I'm going to do. I never thought you two would miss my cooking."

Lucy stood up on her tiptoes and kissed my cheek. "We more than missed your cooking. We missed the hell out of you, big brother."

Maybe this visit was exactly what I needed to turn the corner.

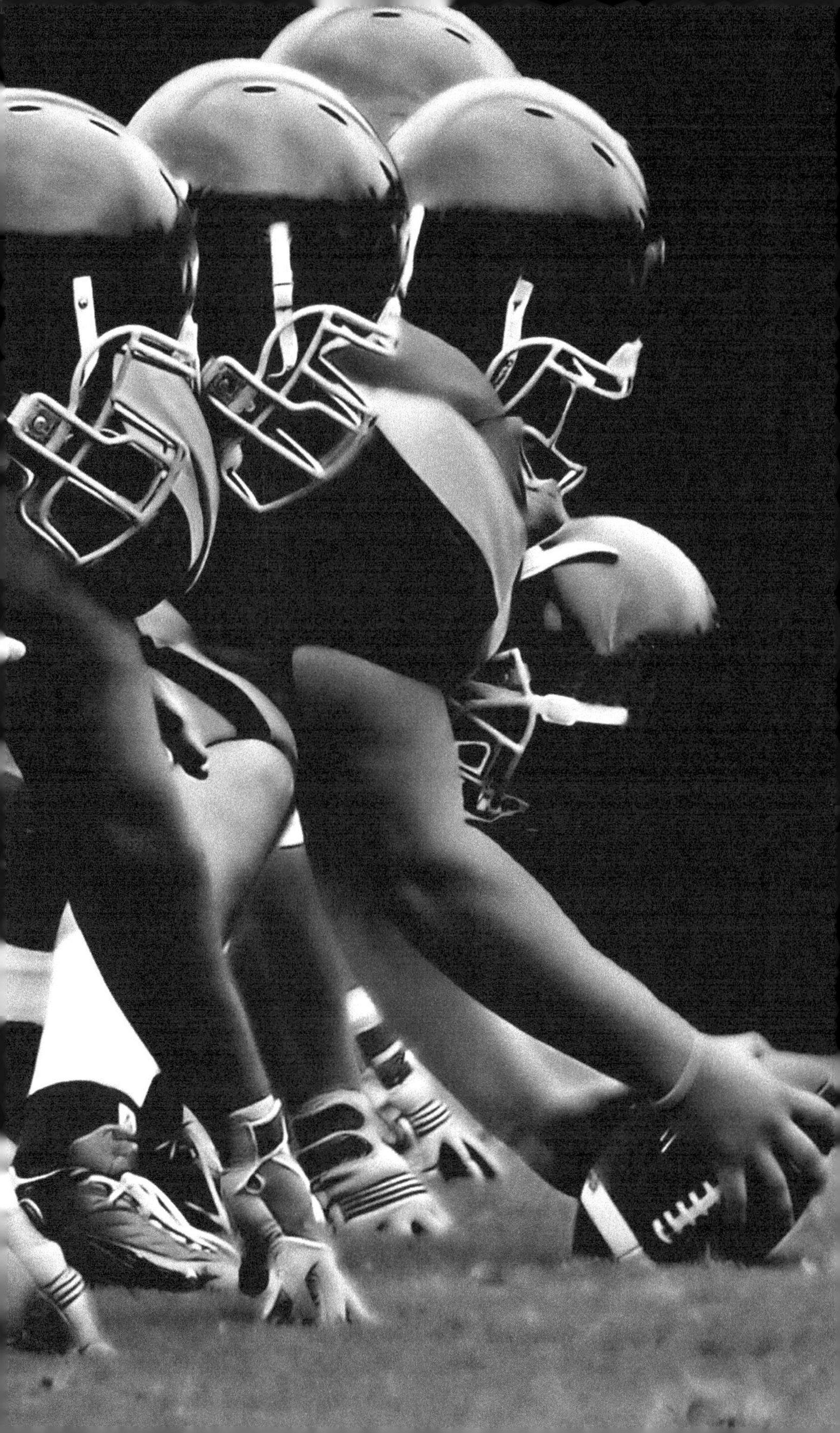

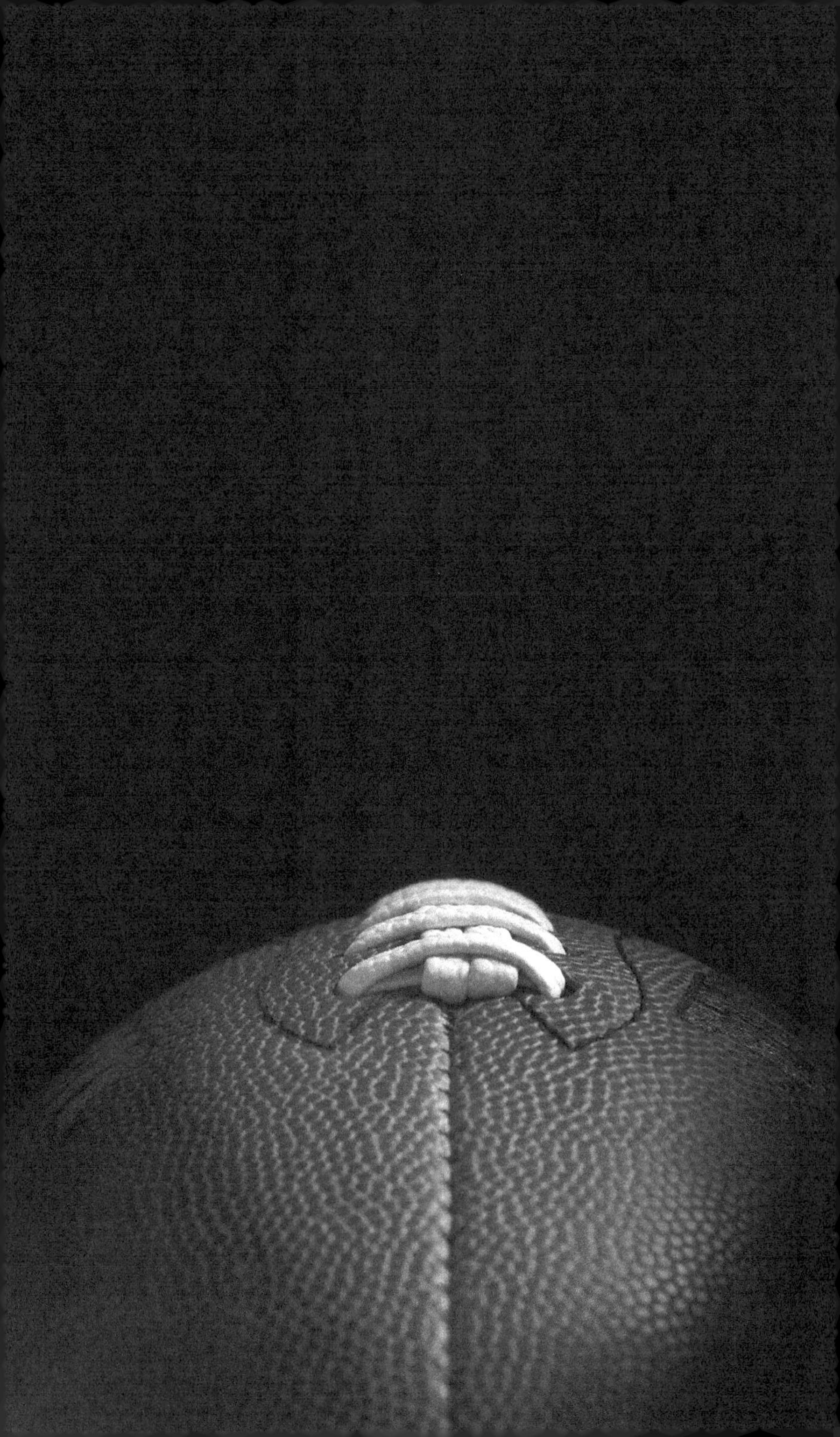

EIGHTEEN
XANDER

ALMOST LIKE CLOCKWORK, I heard Ford's fist pound on my front door. Why he didn't use the doorbell, I'll never know. His knock was impatient as I took my time walking to the front door. It had been three days since Ford called me and revealed more of himself. After being so vulnerable over the phone, I thought I might never see him again.

When I opened the door, Ford was draped across the frame with his nostrils flaring as he took me in. He started at my bare feet and up my gray sweatpants-clad legs, lingering where my cock was starting to stir, and up to my bare chest. By the time his gaze reached my lips, he was pushing me into the living room and down on my couch.

A chuckle left me as I bounced on the cushion. I

looked up at him, my smile wide as I spoke. "Did you miss me?"

"Shut up," Ford growled as he straddled my legs.

"I can't." I ran my hand down his side and gripped his hip. "There's something different about you. You seem… lighter. While I'm not opposed to what you're doing, maybe afterward we can watch a movie or something." I wanted to see if there was an off chance I could be more than just a hole for Ford to forget his problems in. Because no matter how hard I tried, I couldn't fight the magnetic pull I felt toward him. Maybe he felt the same way about me, and that's why he kept coming back.

"A movie, but no rom-com or any shit like that, and certainly no talking about our feelings. That's where I draw the line. Now pull out my cock and show me you missed me," he growled out.

"Who said I missed you? You didn't see me showing up at your house banging down the door." Even as I said the words, I pushed my hand down the front of his pants and wrapped my fingers around his thick shaft.

"Yes, like that," he moaned. "It's been too long."

It certainly had been. My addiction to Ford was scary and had me second-guessing all my choices these days.

"Lift your hips," Ford demanded.

I had no problem complying with his demands. Lifting up, I pushed my sweats down as far as I could with Ford on top of me. My cock sprang free, and Ford's eyes turned black with lust. His warm hand gripped my dick, and I let out a low moan.

Ford stood and stepped out of his jeans and underwear. "Take off your clothes, and lay down on the couch."

Why did Ford giving me orders turn me on so damn much?

I had my sweatpants off and was stretched out on the couch before my next heartbeat.

Ford's appraising eyes took me in as he climbed on top of me. "You're one fine male specimen. Has anyone ever told you that?"

I shook my head, at a loss for words. This was different from the other times. More. Ford didn't compliment me. Ever.

Leaning down, he sucked on my bottom lip as he started to rut his cock against mine. My hands eagerly ran over the smooth skin over his taut muscles. If anyone was perfection, it was Ford. While I was fit, I wasn't sporting a six-pack. My muscles weren't as defined as his, but the way Ford looked at me made me feel like I was fucking Superman.

Cupping the side of my neck, Ford's large hand held me in place as he devoured my mouth. The kiss was full of passion and fire, his want and need.

Slipping one of my hands down between our bodies, I grabbed both our cocks as best as I could and started to stroke. Ford groaned into my mouth, and I couldn't wait a moment longer to have him inside of me.

Breaking the kiss, I panted as I looked up at him and saw the same want in his eyes. "Please tell me you have a condom and some lube in those jeans of yours."

"I wouldn't come without one." He groaned as I ran my thumb along the underside of his shaft.

I wanted to say I had some up in my bedroom, but I couldn't wait that long. I needed him now. I didn't want to break this spell he was under.

"Fuck me, Ford." The way he made me feel and the expert way he worked his cock was essential to my being.

Leaning back on his hunches, he picked up his jeans and removed his tools from the back pocket, never taking his eyes off me. I wanted what he was going to demand of me. I wanted to lie here like this where I could watch every nuance of his face as he fucked me.

"Push your knees up to your chest."

Ford smirked at how easily I complied. It was in these moments I was willing to do anything for him.

"Did you fuck yourself with your fingers while I was gone?" I shook my head. "Do you have a toy that does it for you then?" Again, I shook my head. I hadn't so much as jacked myself off the few days he was gone.

I arched up as he penetrated me with two fingers and started to stroke. "Did you touch yourself while thinking of me?"

"Every fucking day in the shower, but my hand feels nowhere near as good as your ass," he answered.

"Then what are you waiting for?" I asked, even as I rode his fingers.

"And here I thought I was being a nice guy trying to make sure you were ready for me." Taking his length in his other hand, Ford removed his fingers.

I wanted to protest at the loss of them, but Ford didn't leave me waiting for long. He was pushing the tip in before I could make a sound.

Ford's gaze was locked on where we were connected as he pushed in inch by glorious inch. What I wouldn't give for that sight. "Your ass is so greedy for my dick."

I was insatiable for every little thing Ford gave me. He made me feel like I was in high school with an undeniable crush on the captain of the football team, even though he was straight. I never knew what to expect from Ford, but I gobbled up every morsel he gave me.

Leaning over me, Ford braced one of his hands on the arm of the couch as he moved in and out of me in long, slow movements that had me panting.

My hands gripped and clawed at his shoulders, trying to find purchase with each measured stroke. The slow build-up had me close to losing my mind, and the second Ford's hand wrapped around my aching length, it took everything in me not to explode that very second.

I pushed back and up, delirious from all the pleasure coursing through my body. I was awash with heat and ecstasy.

"More," I moaned as he bottomed out, his balls slapping against my ass.

The grip on my pulsing dick tightened as he started to move faster. Ford's hair fell into his face. Without thought, I quickly pushed it out of the way, hoping it would stay in place. His eyes dilated further, and he started to pound inside of me.

"I'm so…" I didn't get to finish my sentence. Ford

brushed against my prostate at the same time he twisted his hand. I came fast and hard all over myself and Ford's hand. He didn't stop moving, stroking every last bit of pleasure inside of me as he chased his own.

The sheer intensity on his face was glorious to watch. He was a beautiful god and my tormentor.

At this point, I wasn't sure I'd have it any other way.

Collapsing on top of me, Ford's heavy breaths landed on my shoulder. On instinct, my arms wrapped around him and started to run up and down his back. He melted into me further with my touch.

Was this a turning point, or would Ford be back to his usual self once the post-orgasmic bliss wore off?

I could feel him start to soften inside of me. It reminded me that Ford was human, after all, not the god he seemed to be during sex.

Ford's thumb grazed the side of my neck before he pushed up onto his knees and removed the condom. He quickly tied it into a knot and placed it on the floor before he plopped down at the end of the couch and pulled his underwear back on. "That was good."

"Yeah, it was." It was so much better than good, but I didn't want to give him too much praise and make him cockier than he already was. "Do you want to go clean up?"

Looking more relaxed than I'd ever seen him, Ford rolled his head to the side to look at me. His face was devoid of anger, which was something I wasn't used to. "I'm good. Do you have any drinks with electrolytes in them? I'm wiped."

Did this mean he wanted to go again? Hell, maybe I needed a drink too. "Sure, help yourself to the fridge. Get me one while you're at it. I'm going to clean up."

While I hustled to remove my drying jizz off me, I had the notion of him leaving to get out of any further connection between us. I was a little shocked to find Ford sitting on the couch with a drink in hand when I came back into the room.

Sitting down beside him, I took the drink he held out for me. "What do you want to watch?"

"No, clue. I don't have much time to watch TV or movies. Whatever you want is fine. Just stick by what I said earlier."

Did he seriously think I liked rom-coms? I wasn't going to subject either one of us to that misery. "Don't worry, I won't, and I also won't make you watch The Notebook," I smirked as Ford rolled his eyes at me. "Do you like horror movies? I'm kind of in the mood to watch something scary."

"Oh, did you want to jump into my lap or curl into my side when something scary happens?" He chuckled and took a sip of his sports drink.

"I don't find them scary, but I like watching them. If they scared me, I don't think I'd watch them. Do you get scared?" Maybe Ford wasn't so tough after all.

He looked at me blandly and then shook his head.

"Alright, this is a lot of pressure since you don't watch much. I saw there was a new movie on HBO that looked good."

"Oh, rich boy here with his HBO. I can say with one hundred percent certainty I haven't seen it." He shrugged. "I can't remember the last time I actually saw a movie."

"Maybe we can go see a movie at the theater over in Loganville. There's a movie coming out around Christmas I want to see. What do you say?"

His brows arched. "Is this like a date?"

"It doesn't have to be. It can be two guys going to see a movie together."

Cocking his head to the side, he smirked. "Are you going to be my sugar daddy now?"

Throwing my head back, I laughed long and hard. "All because I have HBO and want to see a movie at the theater?" The notion had me laughing harder. "If that's all it takes, then sure. I'll be your sugar daddy."

Ford relaxed into the couch. "As long as you don't ask me to start calling you daddy. That's where I draw the line."

I wasn't sure if Ford knew the definition of a sugar daddy. He was a young, poor college kid. Even still, he dominated me in a way no one had ever done before. I had a feeling Ford wouldn't let me pay for anything no matter how strapped for cash he was.

"Done. What do you say we watch this in my bed where we can stretch out and be more comfortable?"

He hopped up and held out his hand for me to take. I didn't hesitate to take his hand and let him drag me up the stairs to my bedroom.

We both crawled into my bed shirtless, with only our underwear on. With our backs against my headboard, I clicked on my TV and searched for the movie I saw advertised earlier. "Can I ask you a question?"

I felt him stiffen beside me and take a deep breath. "You're free to ask."

"But it doesn't mean you'll answer. I got it. Where did you go for Thanksgiving?"

"I went to see my brother and sister. I figured while I had a few days, I'd try to talk to them."

I turned to see him better, making Ford close his eyes as he sunk deeper into my bed. "They weren't taking my calls. I hadn't talked to them since the day our aunt took them to live with her in Oregon."

"And did they finally talk to you?" I wanted to reach out and touch him, but I wasn't sure he'd welcome the touch. While one wall was down, there were a few dozen more to break through.

"Yeah, they did. We had more than one good talk, and we all understand each other better."

It made sense now why he wasn't fighting me at every turn tonight.

"It had to be hard with them not talking to you. I'm glad your trip worked out. How old are your brother and sister?"

"They're seventeen."

My brows rose. "Both of them?"

"They're twins. They have some strange bond. They barely have to speak out loud. They always know what the other's thinking. It's annoying as fuck, but I'm glad they've had each other."

"But who have you had?"

"No one, but I haven't wanted anyone. You and

my roommates have tried to get me to talk, but I couldn't. I still can't. I'm still too angry and…"

"Broken. And you know what, Ford, you have that right. I can't imagine going through what you did. The pain will always be there, but it will get better in time."

"If you want me to stay, then let's stop talking about this. I thought we were going to enjoy a movie, and you were going to pretend you don't get scared while you use me as your human shield."

That sounded like something a girl would do. Still, I didn't comment on it. I didn't want to start anything with Ford. Instead, I hit play as I smirked at him.

"I think it might be you who is in my lap or using my shoulder to hide your ass."

Ford laughed and settled into my bed with his left hand holding my leg possessively.

Maybe things were starting to look up between the two of us.

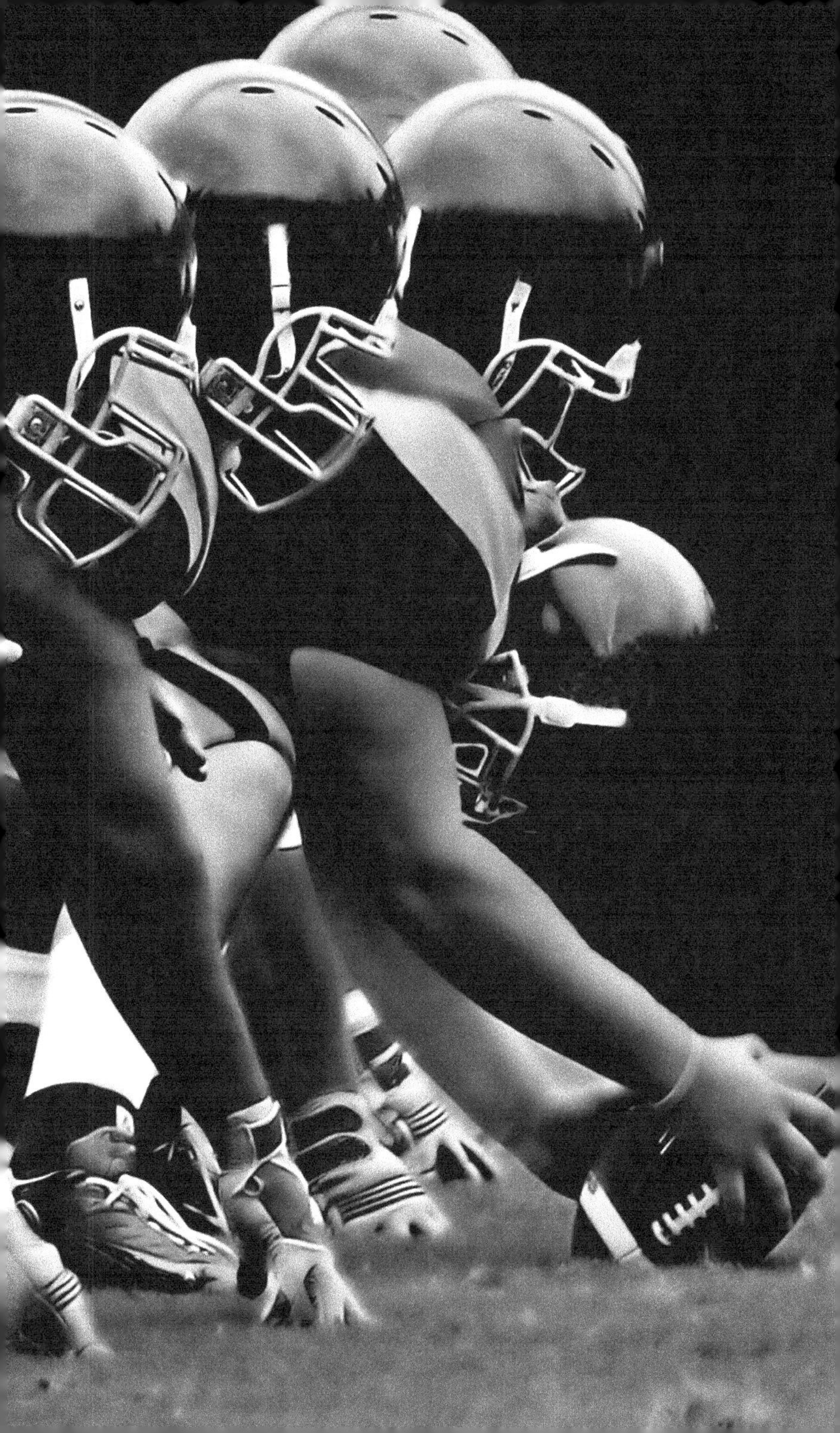

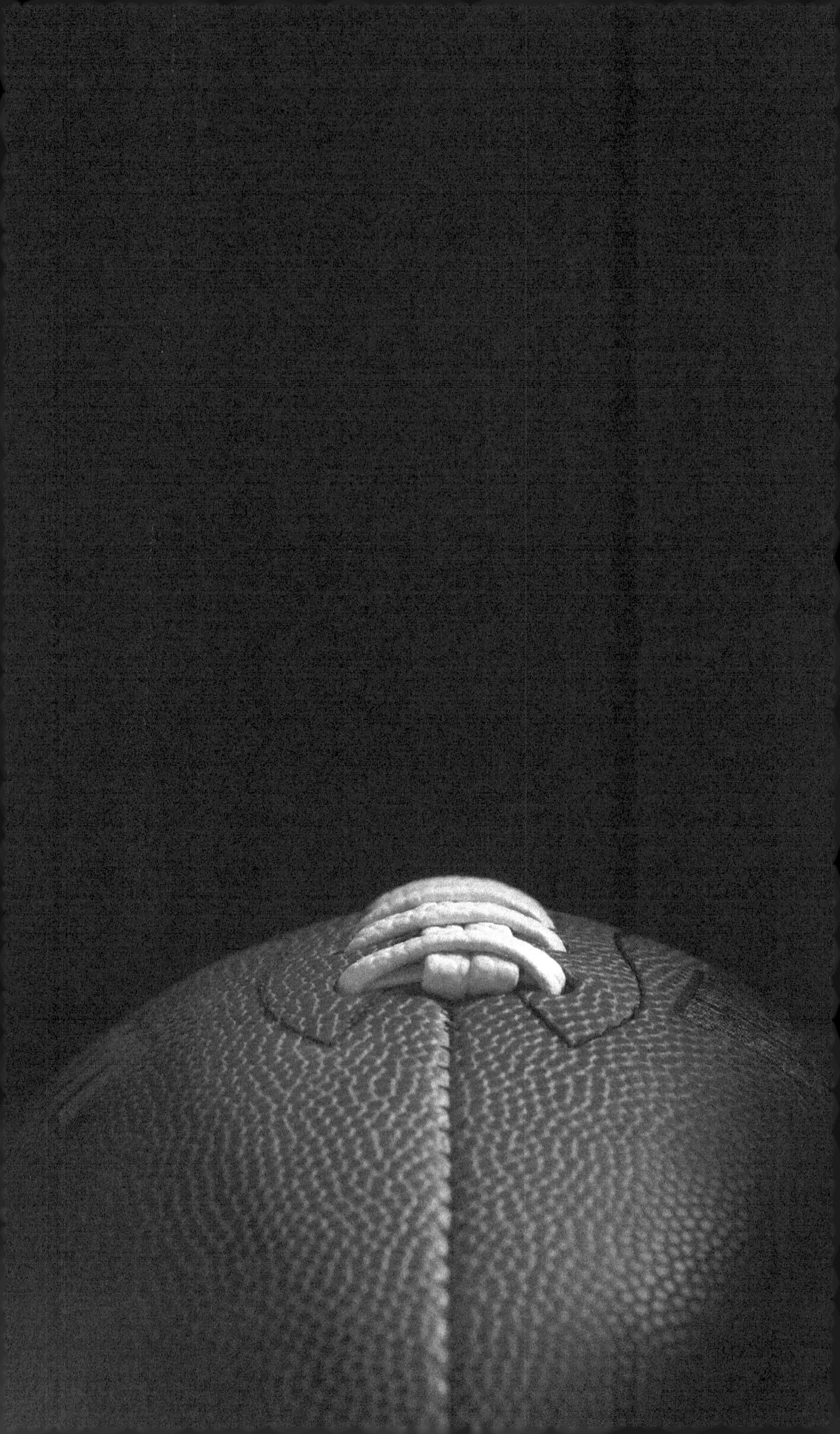

NINETEEN
FORD

WHY DID it bother me so much that I was running late to meet Xander? The movie hadn't started yet, and he'd understand that time ran away from me while I talked to my brother and sister. While I wished I could have stayed longer at Aunt Celicia's, her couch wasn't something I was willing to sleep on for more than a couple of days.

Plus, it was nice to have the house to myself while everyone else was still away visiting their families during winter break.

Parking, I pulled my phone out of the cup holder and looked to see if Xander texted me, and I hadn't noticed. Still nothing. Maybe he really was mad at me. Did he think I was standing him up?

Stepping out of my car, I saw his white SUV

closer to the theater. Maybe he was inside waiting for me or in line and didn't notice my text.

Tonight felt… strange. It wasn't a date per se, but something like it. We weren't two friends hanging out. It was strange having feelings when you didn't want them. This all started with me needing to forget, and now it had turned into Xander being the one I confessed my darkest thoughts to.

I shot off another text, letting Xander know I was here, and a few seconds later, I heard his phone go off. Turning in a circle, I looked around but didn't see him anywhere.

Instead of texting him again, I decided to call. The chimes of his phone going off rang out in the night. Maybe he forgot his phone or dropped it. When his voicemail answered, I called it again as I walked in the direction of where I heard his phone.

The parking lot was dark, making it difficult to see much. Why the hell weren't the lights on at this time of night?

I called again, and this time I saw a light underneath a car a few feet away from Xander's SUV. I jogged over, ready to scoot myself underneath the car when I saw a boot on the ground. I ran faster when I spotted a body between two cars.

"Xander?" I yelled.

A hand twitched, and a low groan escaped the body on the ground. Kneeling down beside him, I could barely make him out, but I could see his face was bloody, and one of his eyes was swollen. The white shirt he wore was dirty, the hem torn.

"Fuck, Xan, I'm sorry I'm late. What the hell happened?"

His eyes fluttered open, and his head rolled to the side to look at me.

"Three guys tried to rob me, and when I didn't give them my wallet, they beat the hell out of me." He tried to roll to his side but cringed and grabbed his side in the process.

"Why the fuck didn't you just give them your wallet? They could have killed you," I growled, putting one hand around his shoulders to help him to his feet.

"Yeah, well, I wasn't really thinking about that at the time." He grunted as he stood. Wrapping my arm around his waist, I guided him out from between the two cars. "I just didn't want to spend the rest of break dealing with the DMV, the social security office, and credit card companies."

"That's the stupidest thing I've ever heard." With my arm around his waist, I guided him toward my car. "Now, let's get you in my car and to the hospital."

"I'm fine." He grimaced as I helped him into the passenger seat. "I just need to go home and rest. I'll be right as rain after a couple of days."

I slammed the car door, pissed he'd been so stupid, and was continuing to do so. I took a deep, calming breath before I got in the car and started it. "When I got to you, I think you were unconscious. You probably have a concussion, which means you need to go to the hospital."

"I'm not spending the rest of my night sitting in an ER. If you're so worried about me, you can keep watch over me tonight, and if you see something alarming, I promise I'll go, but not before then."

"Fine," I growled out. "You can come back to my place. Everyone is still gone for break, so we'll have the house to ourselves. Plus, I'm not sure you can make it up your stairs."

"Me either," he coughed and clutched his side.

Xander's ribs were either broken or, at the very least, bruised badly. "Did they kick you in the side or just hit you?"

He let out a harsh, hitched breath. "Both. My side hurts like a son of a bitch."

"More reason to take you to the hospital," I

muttered, but I wasn't going to fight him. I knew I wouldn't want to go if I was in his position. "Was it only a robbery, or was it more?"

"You mean a hate crime because I'm a gay black man?" He let out a sad sigh. "I can't say for certain. There's no hiding the color of my skin. The same as yours, but I don't think they knew I was gay."

"You know, when I decided to attend school here, I thought I would be away from prejudice, for the most part. But from my time here, I've learned it's everywhere." Even though he was hurt, Xander reached over and placed his hand on my knee. "Did you know that one of my roommates was drugged and beaten up our freshman year because he's gay?"

"I did hear of an incident with one of the football players."

"It wasn't an incident," I growled out. "It was a hate crime, plain and simple. They tried to get him to have sex with a woman in the hopes that once he was inside of her, he'd magically become straight. When that didn't work, they beat him up. It was…" I wasn't sure how I could describe that night and what I saw.

"You don't have to tell me more. I didn't realize it was your friend. I'm sorry it happened to him. No one should be targeted because of their skin color or sexuality."

"I agree wholeheartedly. What I saw when I walked into that room is forever embedded in my brain. I think it's a good thing West can't remember what happened to him. He only remembers waking up and being in pain." What I didn't tell him was how brave I thought West was for being able to leave the house afterward like nothing had happened. After trying to catch their frat house on fire, I was surprised they hadn't retaliated. Especially after my recording of those douchebags confessing, Alpha Mu was never coming back.

"Have you been targeted?" He asked it so quietly I wasn't sure if I imagined it or not.

"Not here, but where I grew up in New Mexico, I did. Not for my skin color, but after a few of the guys in my high school saw me under the bleachers with another guy. After that, I hid my attraction to men until I got here. Until you."

"I'm flattered you chose me even if it was in the most unconventional way."

This hadn't started out on the best of turns. Well, the first night did; what happened after wasn't. I couldn't say I was sorry, though.

Xander cleared his throat and gave me a nervous smile. "Are you attracted to—"

"I'm attracted to a person as a whole. I don't care about the sex." I finished for him.

"So, a woman could walk in the door, and you'd… have you been with other people since the night we met?"

I smirked over at him. "Are you asking if I've been with any men or women or both?"

Xander huffed. "Anyone."

The thought was preposterous. I couldn't help but laugh. Had he been worried about this the entire time?

"When would I have had the time?" I laughed at the absurdity. "I'm in class all day, then football practice. After that, I cook dinner for my roommates, my homework, and then head to your house to fuck you. And then the cycle repeats." I rolled my eye and gave into settling his fear. "But for your information, I haven't been with anyone else."

"There are days when you weren't at my place, and I was fighting you."

So, he thought I'd seek out someone else. It probably would have been easier if I'd found anyone other than Xander, but I knew he was the only one who could make me forget my fucked-up life.

"Just rest. We'll be back at my place soon enough."

Xander chuckled and then moaned. "Is that your way of politely telling me to shut up?"

"Yes," I grunted out. His words were making me uncomfortable. I wasn't sure how to process the emotions Xander brought out in me. I didn't want to like him. It was too dangerous for both of us, but it seemed as if I didn't have a choice.

"You know you can just drop me off at my place. You don't have to do this."

"I know I don't have to," I gritted out, keeping my eyes on the road.

"The thought of traversing my stairs doesn't seem appealing. I'll go to your place, but only for tonight."

I had a feeling Xander didn't like to feel weak. In fact, I was surprised he didn't push back more. He must have been hiding how much pain he was actually in.

"I'll even let you pick the movie," I said to lighten the mood.

"Thanks, but you always let me pick what we watch." His voice was filled with amusement. "Maybe you'd like to pick what we watch tonight."

"Can you log into your HBO account here?"

"I don't see why not. If I do, are you going to start watching TV without me?"

"Like I said before, when would I have the time?"

Seriously, where was all this free time he thought I had? "The only other TV I see is when my roommates and I play Call of Duty."

"Ah, there's where your time goes. It makes sense. Sometimes I forget how young you are."

"Alright, old man, there are plenty of people your age who play video games. I don't play often, but when we all have free time, I do play with my roommates."

"Alright, you don't need to get so defensive about it. I was merely joking about you watching without me. You're certainly hot and cold tonight. One minute you want to take care of me, and the next, you're getting all pissy. Why is that, Ford?"

"Do you expect me to be in a good mood after you got your ass kicked by a bunch of assholes?" I was already regretting my decision to bring him to my house. Maybe I should drop him off and enjoy my alone time.

"No, I'm sorry." He breathed down his nose and looked out the passenger window. "You have every right to be in a bad mood."

"And so do you."

The only problem with Xander being hurt was I couldn't fuck my anger out with him. I'd be in the shower jacking off while he was in the next room, all purple and blue.

"Have you watched that Game of Thrones show we passed by when looking for that movie the other day?"

Xander chuckled from beside me. "Have you never heard of it?"

"Not really, but I didn't have cable growing up, and neither did my friends." I felt stupid saying it, but I'd already brought up the show. "I've heard people mention it in passing like everyone's watched it."

"You might be the only one," he laughed and then held his side. "Fucking hell, don't make me laugh. I'll watch it with you, and we'll see if you like it."

From what I heard, it didn't seem like anyone hated it. Plus, we needed something to watch. Maybe since he'd seen it, Xander would fall asleep and get some rest. And if he were sleeping, I'd be less inclined to fuck him.

"I never thought I'd be back here," Xander said as I pulled up in front of the house.

"Me either." I parked and was at the passenger side, opening the door before Xander could even try to open it.

"You're really taking this whole thing seriously. I

promise I'm fine," he grumbled as I gripped him underneath his arm and helped him to stand.

"Yeah, it really seems like it. I think your face just turned white from pain. Let's get you inside. Your ribs will feel slightly better once I wrap them."

"Fucking hell, that's going to be torture," he hissed as if he could already feel the pain.

"It won't be bad. I'll get you a couple of ice packs and some ibuprofen. You'll be feeling better in no time."

Xander's lips thinned, but he didn't make a sound as we walked inside. Now it was his turn to take in my home. "I didn't get a chance to look around during my escape. Your place is nice."

"Well, I can't take credit for anything but my bedroom." I left him to take in his surroundings as I grabbed the ice packs out of the freezer and went to the hallway closet to find an Ace bandage.

Xander was standing in the middle of the living room, staring at the dog bed on the floor. "I thought you said you clean the house."

"I do, but no one is overly messy. Not even Charlie." I pointed to Charlie's bed. "He's not here right now. Let's go get you cleaned up."

He followed me down the hall and into the

bathroom. Pulling out a washcloth, I warmed the water until it was nice and hot.

"Okay, now this might sting a bit," I said as I dabbed the cloth to the wound on his forehead.

Xan clenched his jaw. "Just a little. Maybe it would be better if I cleaned myself up."

"Whatever you'd like. I'll get us a couple of waters and meet you in my room. Do you remember where it is?"

His eyes flicked up to meet mine in the mirror. "I'm sure I can find it."

Turning on my laptop, I sat on the bed and brought up my browser.

Xander came to stand in my doorway looking cleaned up but more swollen and bruised. "Maybe we should watch it in the living room. I think you'd enjoy the show more if you were watching it on a bigger screen."

It would be better to have distance between us. That way, I'd keep my hands to myself.

Grabbing up the supplies I'd gathered, I walked back into the living room and set them down on the table by the recliner. "Take this." I placed the ibuprofen in his hand and then one of the bottles of water. After he took them, I handed him one of the ice packs. "Here, put this on your eye. If you don't get ice on it soon, it's going to be swollen shut."

His one good eye focused on me. "You're a really good caregiver. You know that?"

I ignored his words. "I'm going to wrap your ribs now."

"Do what you must." He gritted his teeth.

I shifted to pull up his shirt and stopped at the black and blue colors that took up his entire right side. "Are you sure you don't want to go to the hospital? I think you might need prescription pain medicine."

"I wouldn't take it. That shit makes me unfunctional."

"I'm not sure how much you need to function right now. It's not like I'm saying you should take them for two months, but maybe a few days."

"I'll be fine with your over-the-counter meds. Now, can you hurry up, so we can watch TV?"

I knew he really wanted to relax, and the only way to do that was to fix him up. "Sure, try to stay still, and if this gets too tight, let me know." I circled the bandage around his torso, covering the bruising. Once I was done, I pulled his shirt back down. "All done."

Even with the worst of it hidden underneath

everything, I couldn't take my eyes off where the bruising was. Xan had to be in so much pain.

"Do you not want to get treatment because you're ashamed this happened to you?" The thought was out of my mouth faster than I could stop it.

"I'm not ashamed, but I don't need this on record either." I started to open my mouth, but he pressed a finger to my lips. "No more questions. Not tonight."

I could respect that. I handed him the remote. "Download the HBO app while I get us a couple of blankets."

I didn't give him much of a chance to answer. When I came back into the room, Xander was in the recliner with the ice pack on his eye and the other on his side. He looked like he was close to falling asleep. I covered him with one of the blankets and moved to sit in the other recliner.

"Thanks. Are you ready for one of the best shows ever?"

I laughed. He had played it off so well. "Blow my mind."

"Happily."

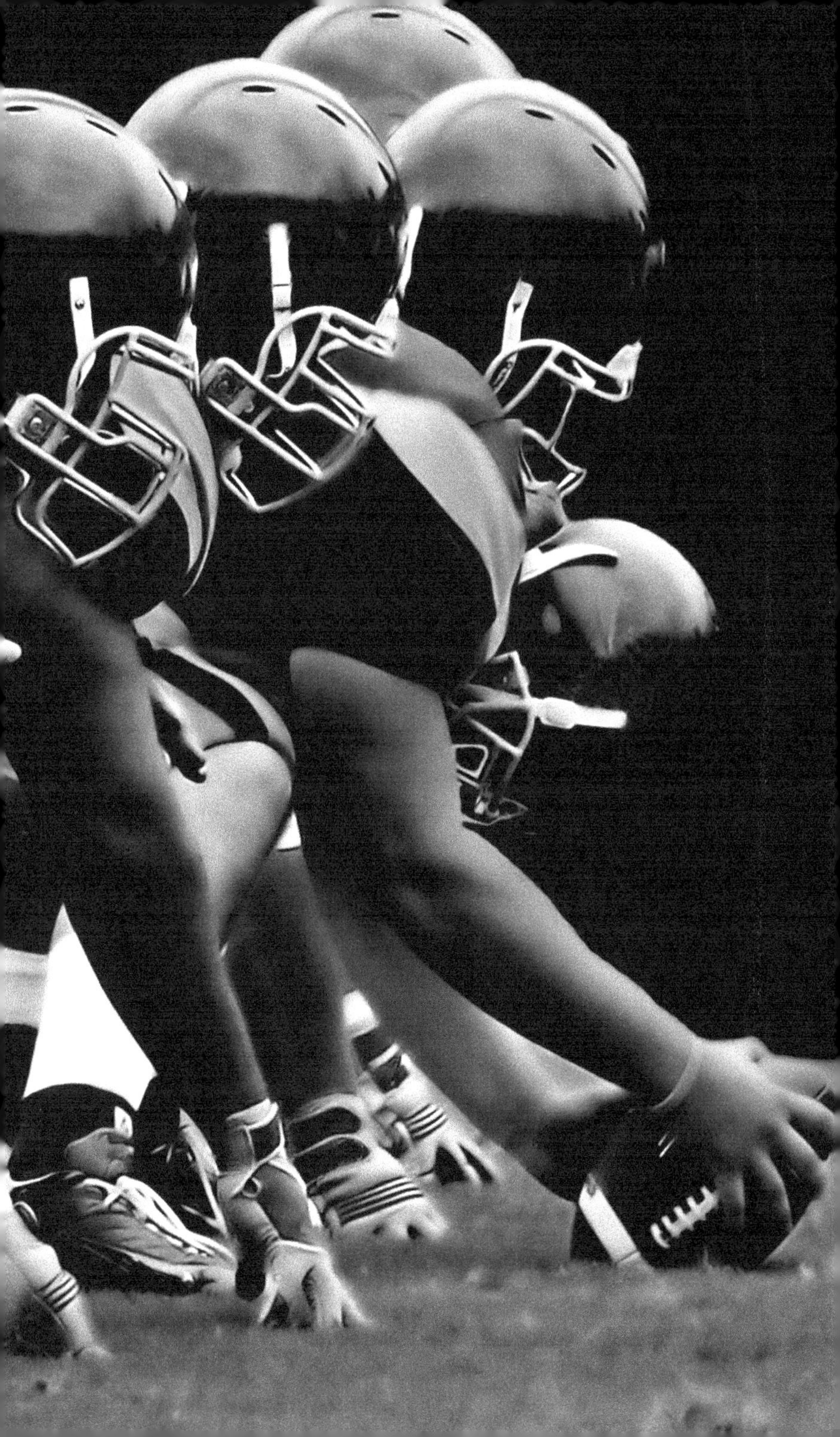

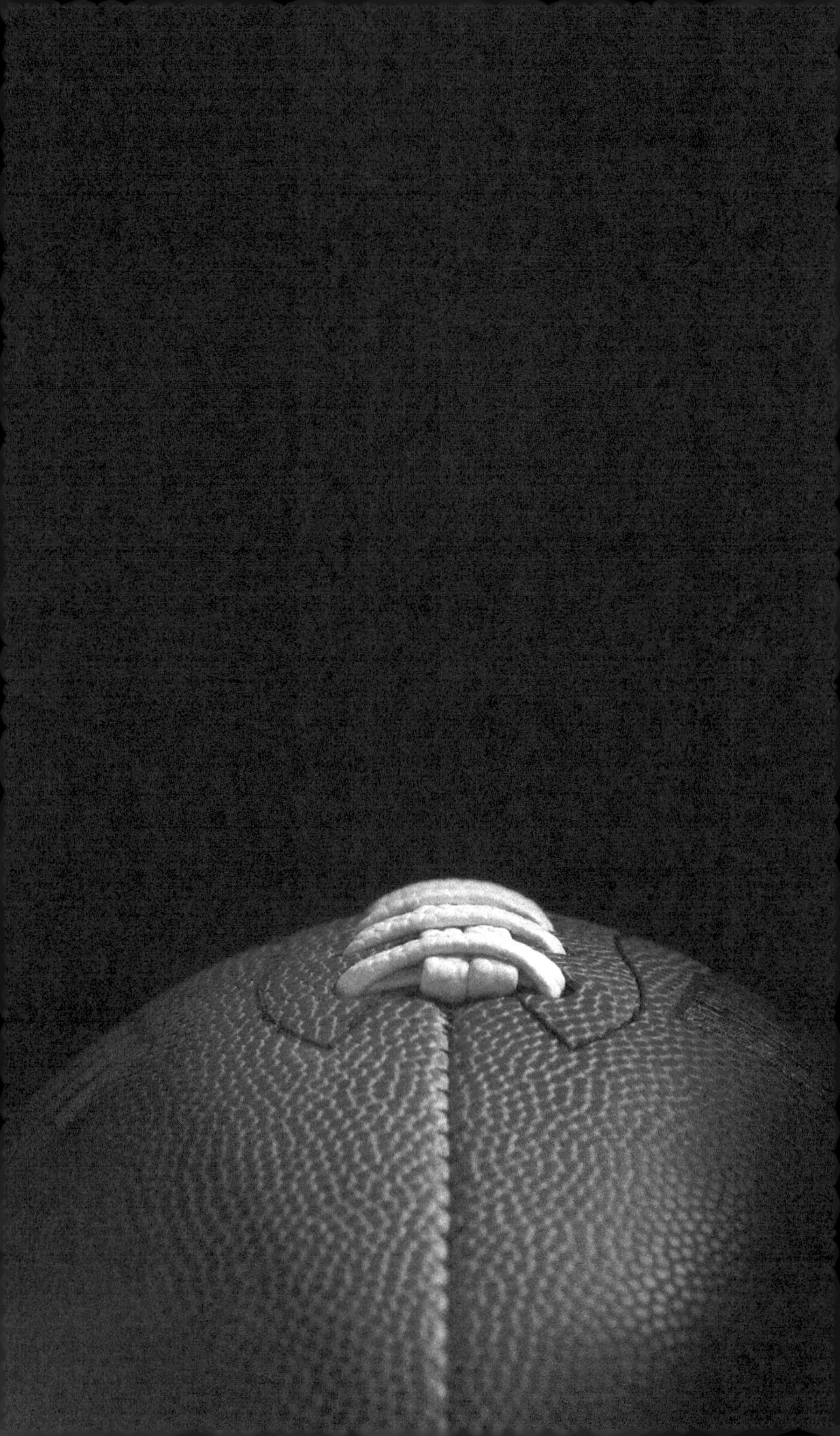

TWENTY
XANDER

FORD ROLLED to his side and covered his eyes with his arm to block out the sunlight. We'd slept in the living room all night. Not the most comfortable, but I wasn't sure I'd be comfortable anywhere. I was surprised Ford stayed when he could have gone and slept in his own bed. I, on the other hand, wasn't sure if I could get out of this chair without help.

"I didn't know you have a dog," I said in greeting.

"He's not mine. He's Lo's, and I guess Oz's but mainly Lo's. She went through something last year, and he got her a dog. He's a damn fine dog at that." His voice was deep and gravelly with sleep. The entire time, his arm stayed over his eyes.

"You should have slept in your room."

"I could have done that, but if you needed me, I wasn't sure if I'd be able to hear you."

That was thoughtful of him. I wanted to tell him that, but while Ford had opened up to me for the last month, I didn't think he was ready for those kinds of niceties.

Slowly, he got out of the chair without looking at me. "Let me take a quick shower to wake up, and then I'll make us some breakfast."

"Hey." I sat up in the recliner and put the leg rest down. "Could you by any chance help me get out of this chair and let me take a piss before you get in the shower?"

Ford helped me up without a word and then sauntered down the hall to the bathroom. I heard the water turn on, which only made me have to go to the bathroom that much worse.

I took one step and knew it was going to be a long day. Everything on me hurt. Each step sent pain through my ribs and made my head throb. By the time I reached the bathroom, Ford was undressed and stepping into the shower. Even with how much pain I was in, I couldn't deny the perfection of his body. His olive skin was smooth over steely muscles. With each move he made, his muscles rippled and flexed, making my morning wood ache with need.

"Why are you looking at me like that? You've seen me naked plenty of times." He looked over at the toilet and then back at me. "Are you one of those people who can't pee with someone else in the room?"

No, I wasn't. I was just having a hard time concentrating while seeing him in his element. The one night we'd been here, the night we met, it had been dark, and we'd been drunk. Now I was fully sober, taking in his magnificent form.

"You'd better stop looking at me like that, or I'm not going to care that you're hurt and shove you up against the wall and fuck you until you can't stand up any longer."

I wouldn't mind that, not one bit.

He breathed down his nose and closed the shower door. "It took you nearly five minutes to walk back here. I don't think that would be a good idea unless you want pain with your pleasure."

I wasn't opposed, but I had a feeling the pain I would be feeling wouldn't be the type that would keep my dick hard.

"Take your piss, and then there are three ibuprofens on the counter there. There's water in the fridge. Do you like coconut?"

That came out of nowhere.

"I like it fine. I don't love it. Why?"

"Because Fin hates coconut, and I've wanted to make a new recipe. How does coconut crepes with maple ricotta and strawberries sound?"

"It sounds like if this is the type of breakfast you make every day, I might become a regular here."

"It's not," he chuckled. "We eat healthy here, especially during the football season. Once a week, we indulge. Otherwise, Lo is my guinea pig here."

I wouldn't mind being his test subject.

I did my business and then let Ford take his shower in peace. I wandered into his tidy bedroom and looked around the sparse room, then headed out before I got caught. It felt wrong to be here even with his roommates gone. I was standing by the table when Ford walked in wearing a pair of sweatpants and a tight t-shirt.

"You've got a nice setup here." I sat down at the table as gingerly as I could, but it still hurt like hell. Even though I didn't want to admit to him, Ford was right; the ibuprofen wasn't enough.

Ford eyed my side for a second before he went back to pulling ingredients out. "Do you want another ice pack for your side before I start cooking?"

"Yeah, maybe then it will be somewhat numb when I eat."

"You know," he continued, setting out a couple of bowls. "I can still take you to the hospital and get you checked out."

"I'll be fine." If there was any time for this to happen, winter break was the best time. I wouldn't want to show up to class like this.

"If you say so. It's not a money issue, is it?" He asked with a raised brow as he handed me an ice pack. Why was that so damn sexy? Ford was right. I was in no condition for sex today or in the near future.

"It's not money." I looked down at the ground as I spoke. "I don't want to explain what happened. It's embarrassing I got jumped."

I could feel Ford's impenetrable gaze on me. One I didn't want to look into. "Why are you embarrassed?"

Because I felt like a pussy. I wasn't as stacked as Ford, but I wasn't someone you'd look at and think they could take easily either.

"I should have given up my wallet. Now instead of dealing with canceling cards and getting a new driver's license, I'm going to be laid up even longer. I was stupid."

"I'm not going to argue with that, but I'm not going to lie. I probably would have done the same thing." That made me look up at him. "I understand why you didn't want to back down. If I saw you in an alley, my first thought wouldn't be that I could take you."

Now he was just trying to make me feel better.

"I'm being serious. First of all, I don't go about attacking people, but you wouldn't be an easy person to take down."

"What if you had your friends with you?" I huffed out.

"If we were those kinds of people, then yes, it wouldn't be a problem. Did you get a good look at any of them?" He moved across the kitchen to kneel down in front of me. "If you won't go to the hospital, then you should file a report with the police."

"If only I had, but they wore masks. They knew exactly what they were doing. Who knows how many other people they robbed last night?" If I thought I could help anyone with any of my knowledge, I would, but I knew nothing except maybe an estimated height for each of them.

"Fuck, I hadn't even thought of them ambushing anyone else," he hissed out. He stood up and stormed back to where he'd been in the kitchen. "Why are there so many fucked up people around here? The thought that any of the shit I've witnessed could happen to my sister or brother kills me."

I stood slowly and moved behind Ford. Wrapping my arms around his waist, I rested my cheek on his back. Ford stiffened for a moment but soon relaxed into my hold. When was the last time anyone hugged him? "I'm sorry. I wish I could spare you from these thoughts. All you can do is warn and teach them and hope they never find themselves in the same position for the atrocities you've witnessed."

"It scares me they'll be targeted due to their brown skin. They don't deserve that. Hell, it could have already have happened, and I wouldn't know." He hung his head.

I held him tighter. "No, one does."

He patted my hand once and then started cracking eggs. "Maybe we can watch more Game of Thrones while we eat breakfast."

I stifled a laugh. It hurt too much. It seemed Ford did indeed like the show. "I have no problem with that. In fact, I think I might go take a shower to see if it will help loosen up some of my muscles if that's okay with you."

Ford looked at me over his shoulder. "That's cool. Call out if you need any help."

Who was this nice guy? Was it strange that I kind

of missed when he was being an asshole? Yes, I knew it was, but I wasn't used to this side of him.

Luckily, I didn't need any help. I wasn't sure my ego could take the blow. Even the simple rinse off and putting my clothes back on took me far longer than I thought it would. By the time I got back into the dining room, Ford was sitting at the table and filling our plates.

"It smells amazing," I said as I gingerly sat down.

Ford flashed a quick smile before he trained his eyes on me. It was unnerving having him watch me eat like this. It was strange he didn't seem to know how to accept the compliment to his cooking, and yet he always waited until I took my first bite.

The coconut and maple burst on my tongue, making me moan. "I was right. Count me in to be here for breakfast every day."

He chuckled and took a bite of his own crepes. His brows scrunched as he looked down at his food. "I think I could have whipped the ricotta more and made them lighter."

"Do you critique all the meals you make?" I asked before eating another bite. I had no idea what he was talking about. I didn't see any way to improve on the breakfast he made for us.

"I didn't use to, but now what I'm hoping to

become a chef, it's all I do." He frowned. "Cooking never used to be stressful. It was just something I liked to do."

During the summer, Ford never worried, or at least he didn't seem like he did. It could have been from the trauma of losing his mom. Now that he was slowly getting better, other stresses were coming to the forefront. "Has someone commented about your food not being… enough?"

"No, but this is my life, and it's not like I can sit and read a book or my notes to drill it into my head. The only thing I can do is practice and hyper analyze my food."

He was going to give himself an ulcer if he kept worrying the way he was. "I wish all my students were as dedicated to their studies as you."

He looked up at me from under his long black eyelashes. "Are you saying I'm one of your best students?"

Ugh. Why did he have to mention me being his teacher?

"And now you look like you're chewing sawdust. You know," he smirked. "You're no longer my teacher. Your Econ class was the only one I had to take that's not part of the culinary degree. I can promise you I won't be in any more of your classes."

Even with that being true, I still couldn't rationalize the fact that I'd slept with a student and continued to do so after I found out he was in my class.

"It doesn't mean we should continue doing this. It's wrong." So, so wrong.

Placing his fork down gently on his plate, Ford drilled holes into the side of my head. "Are you telling me you no longer want to see me?"

"It's not a matter of want. You know I want you." The words I couldn't say were, where was this going? I was thirty-five, and Ford was only twenty-one. We were in two very different places in our lives.

"Then what is it? Do I need to threaten you again?" The muscle in his jaw feathered.

He would go there.

"I don't want things to go back to where they used to be. It wasn't healthy for either one of us."

He hummed. "It was fun, though, wasn't it? And it got you to do what you really wanted."

"I won't deny the sex was fun."

"Then what's the problem now that I'm no longer your student?"

I knew no matter what I said, Ford wouldn't like it. He'd fight me to the very end. Instead of talking, I chewed my food in silence.

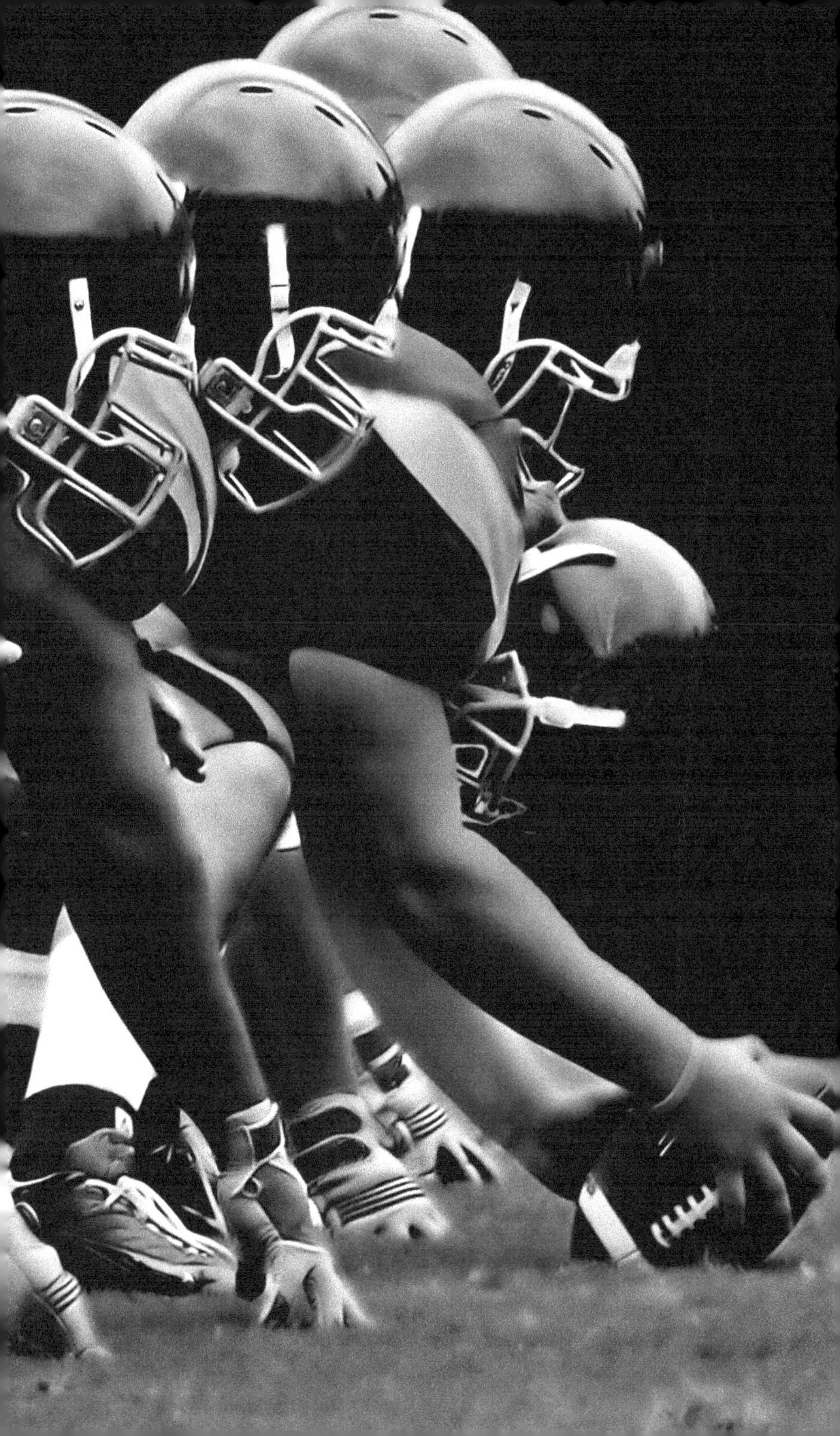

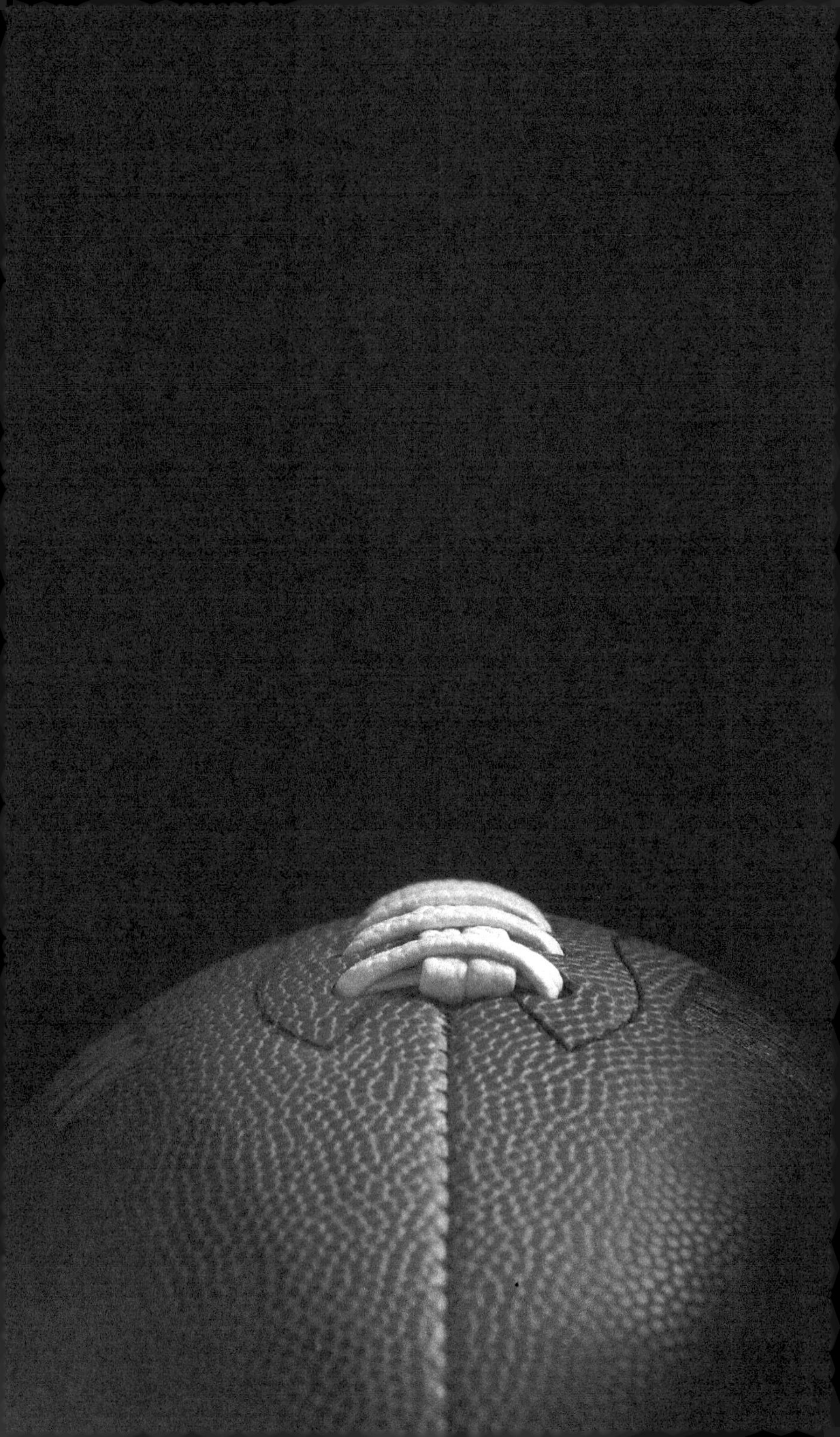

TWENTY-ONE
FORD

HE'S SHUT down on me.

I'm surprised he followed me home after we went and picked up his SUV yesterday morning. He'd barely spoken five words to me all day today. Maybe he just needed someone to take care of him, and once he was better, he was going to leave.

It was strange seeing him in my house, in the living room, watching TV like he'd always been here. He'd fallen asleep while we watched Game of Thrones again. His eye was barely swollen, but that wasn't the issue. It was his ribs that were still a dark purple that looked almost black.

If he weren't injured, I'd pin him down and fuck whatever was wrong with him out, but I couldn't do that.

"Why are you staring at me?" He grumbled from the other side of the living room.

"Why not?" He was hot as hell, even with bruises. But I wasn't going to tell him that.

"I should go home and stop invading your space. The stairs shouldn't be a problem now." What was a problem was the fact that he couldn't look at me while he spoke. His eyes were still closed like he was sleeping. Had he been pretending this whole time while he silently stewed over there?

"I like you here. Besides I was about to cook us some dinner. Do you want to go home to your frozen meals?"

I wasn't sure how Xander was as fit as he was with how shitty he ate. The man lived off prepackaged meals.

His mouth turned down. "You know I can't turn down anything you make."

I did.

Why was he pulling away when I finally opened up to him?

Maybe he only liked it when I was an asshole and threatened him.

He shifted uncomfortably in the recliner. "While I appreciate you taking me in and taking care of me, after dinner, I'm going to go home."

I leveled him with my glare. What the fuck was going on? I didn't like being on this side of things. "And what if I want you to stay?"

"I think we both know it would be best for me to go home. I can't get comfortable here. We always knew this was temporary."

I wasn't sure if he was talking about being at my place or us. Either way, I didn't like it.

"If you don't want to be here, you don't have to wait. You can leave now," I gritted out as I got up from my seat. I didn't look back as I went to the kitchen.

I pulled out my cutting board and one of my knives and started cutting up some peppers and onion. With each chop I made with my knife, the anger only intensified instead of lessening. He was ruining everything.

"I didn't mean to piss you off," Xander said from behind me, startling me.

My knife didn't hit the onion I was currently cutting, but my finger. "Motherfucker," I yelled as I rounded him and went to the sink to rinse off my finger and inspect the damage.

"Fuck, Ford, I'm sorry. I didn't—"

"I know," I cut him off, not wanting to hear his apology. "Maybe you should go now." The cut was deep, and I was trying to decide if I needed stitches or not. Not that I could afford a trip to the ER for fucking stitches because I cut myself by doing the most basic of things in the kitchen.

I felt him behind me this time before he spoke. "Oh, fuck. You need stitches."

"I might be able to superglue it closed." I tried to press the sides together, but it hurt like a son of a bitch. I might as well have cut off my hand.

"Let me take you to get it patched up. It's the least I can do."

I turned on him. It felt like fire was coming out of my ears as I glared at his shocked face. "I don't need your help. You've made it abundantly clear since yesterday that you're done with me. Well, now's the perfect time to tuck tail and leave," I snarled out.

"Ford, it isn't like that," he said quietly, calmly.

"Isn't it? You've barely said a word to me, then you wake up, and the first thing you say to me is you're going to go home. Now's your chance. Go home, and fuck off."

Xander placed his hands on my shoulders and leaned in. His face was a mask of anger and turmoil. "You don't get to tell me to fuck off. Not now, after all we've been through."

I laughed bitterly. "Isn't that exactly what you're

doing to me. You can't wait to get out of here. Well, guess what? I'm not stopping you. Don't worry. I can get myself to the doctor."

"What doctor?" His jaw ticked.

"I don't know." Maybe I'd call Coach and see if he could get ahold of the team medic.

Wrapping a bundle of paper towels around my bleeding finger, Xander looked at the microwave. "If we hurry, you can make it before the urgent care closes in Loganville."

"Thanks, but I can drive myself."

"For fuck's sake, Ford, why are you being so stubborn? Let me help you, and then if you want me to leave, I will."

I wasn't sure why he changed his tune. He was dying to get out of here only ten minutes ago. It wasn't like I was going to bleed out and die on the way. It was only twenty minutes away if there wasn't traffic.

"Fine." I ripped my hand out of his hold and held it up to my chest. "Let's get this over with."

Grabbing my wallet, I slipped my feet into a pair of trainers and waited by the door. I should have left while Xander was putting his shoes on. The only problem was he was parked behind me, and I wasn't going to fuck up my only transportation because he was pissing me off.

I stood impatiently by the door, grinding my teeth into dust. When Xander came out, he took me in and then promptly walked out the front door.

"I don't know why you're angry at me for wanting to go home. It would not be ideal for your roommates to find me here."

"So that's what you're worried about?" I laughed, but there wasn't a trace of humor in it. "They won't say anything."

"You can't be sure of that." He leveled me with a tight jaw from across his car.

I could. I had gone to burn down a house with Fin. There was no coming back from that. I wouldn't give up their secrets, and they wouldn't give up mine. But I couldn't explain any of that to Xander.

Xander got into the car, and I followed suit.

I stared out the passenger window, unsure how I got here. The second I let my guard down around him, Xander was a different person.

"Has it stopped bleeding yet?" He asked as he got onto the freeway.

I held the towel tighter around my index finger. "With the way it's pulsing, I'd say no." I blew out a frustrated breath. "I really don't need another expense."

"Urgent care won't be bad, and if you need—"

"Don't offer because I won't accept. I'm not a charity case. You were ready to drop me like yesterday's trash up until I tried to slice my finger off."

"You know," he worked his jaw. "Up until this moment, you haven't acted like a petulant child."

I would have jumped out and walked home if the car wasn't moving. I didn't care if my finger fell off or I bled out. It would be better than dealing with him.

I held my tongue from saying this was the first time he was acting his age.

"Ford, tell me something." My eyes met his for a brief moment before I went back to looking out the window. "Where do you see this going?"

I let out an annoyed huff. "I don't know. I have no idea where my life is going after I graduate."

"We didn't talk about it, but how are things with your brother and sister? Are they doing better?"

"They're probably doing better than I am. They have each other and our aunt. Plus, I set aside money for them for when they go to college."

"And you didn't put any away for yourself?"

"They need it more than me." I would feel like a shit brother to take that money when I've already taken so much from them. "I have a scholarship, and once the football season is over, I'm going to work in the library for the rest of the school year. Rinse and repeat."

I could feel his eyes on me even as I stared out at the passing scenery. "Okay, and where are you going to live this summer?"

"I'll be at the same house. Fin doesn't plan to sell it until we graduate, if then. After we're all gone, he might rent it to other college kids. I don't really know since it has nothing to do with me."

Why did he care?

"I shouldn't have asked. It's none of my business."

It sure as hell wasn't.

We were silent for a few minutes. While I tried to ignore the fact that I could have done some serious damage to my hand and my lively hood, I decided I needed to quiz him.

"Where do you see this going?"

"I don't know. I guess that's why I was asking you. You still have another year and a half left until you finish school, and after that, you're going to move away while I plan to live here."

That didn't really leave much more to say. It seemed Xander had it all figured out. Just as I was opening up to a future between us, he was closing the doors.

"After tonight, I won't bother you. I won't force you to let me in or let me inside your body." The words tasted bitter on my tongue, but they needed to be said. This needed to end before I made a bigger mess out of my life than I already had. I was too pissed off at him to pay attention to my surroundings and look where I was now: headed to stitch up my finger when I couldn't afford it.

Xander pulled into a parking space and then tapped his fingers on the steering wheel. "I would try to talk to you about this, but I can see you're not ready to listen to what I have to say."

"What's there to say?" I shrugged like the whole situation didn't matter. "We're over. It was good while it lasted." I shifted and placed my hand on the door handle. "Thanks for the ride, but I'll call an Uber to pick me up and take me back to campus."

There was no way in hell I was going to spend another minute with him. I'd take my words back for the chance to be inside of him one more time, and I didn't want to do that. I wasn't going to start the back and forth.

Xander and I had no future, and I was going to

force myself to forget about him once I stepped out onto the sidewalk.

"It doesn't need to be like this, Ford. We're both adults who can put aside our... differences until I take you home."

He couldn't even say it. Whatever *it* was. But I knew what we were. We were nothing. Especially now.

I got out of the car and leaned down until our gazes locked. "I think we need a clean break, and this is as clean as it's going to get.

"Wait, Ford," he called after me.

I narrowed my eyes at him. "You've wanted me out of your life for months, and now I am. You should be happy. If not, then you can fuck off."

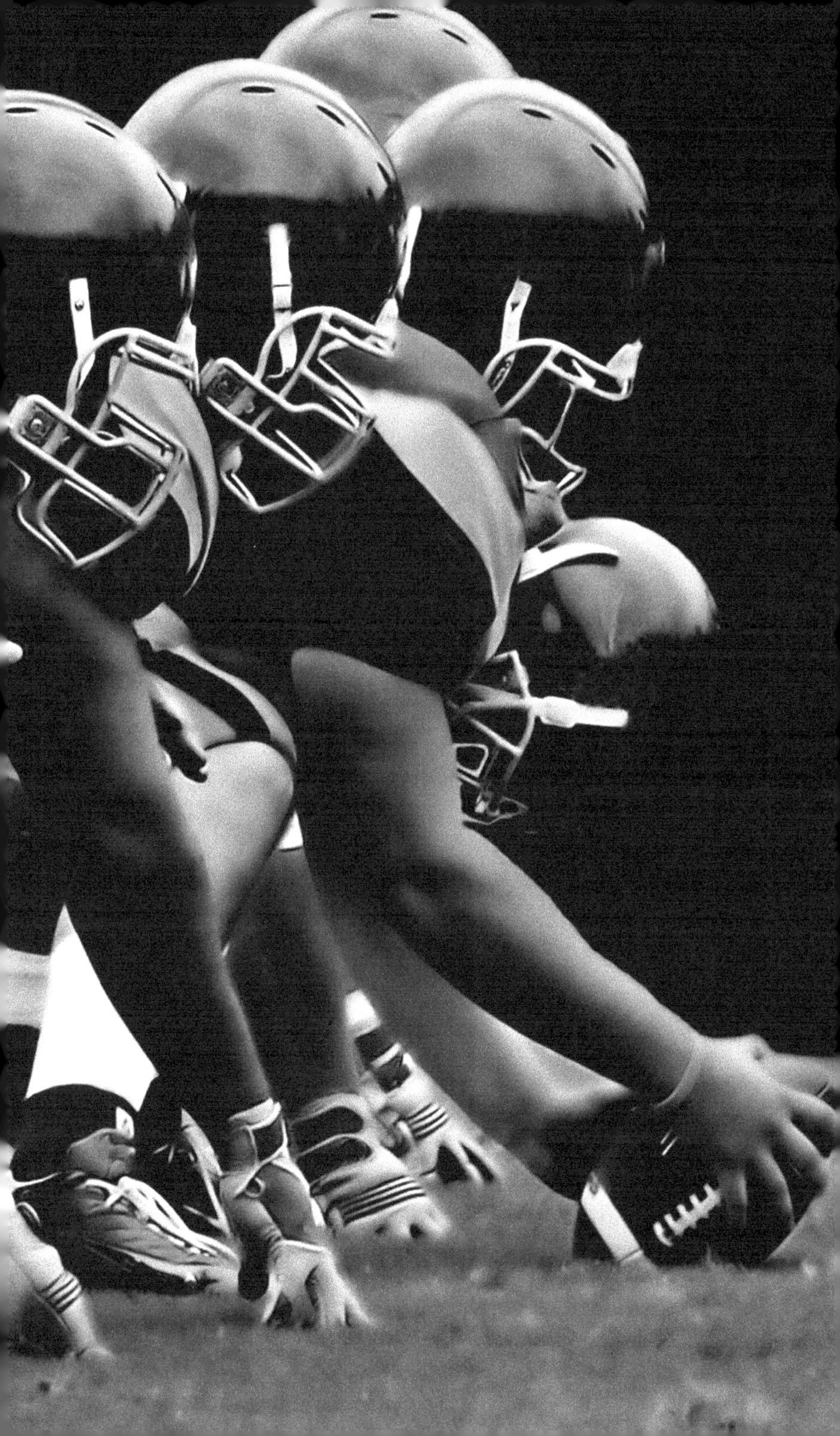

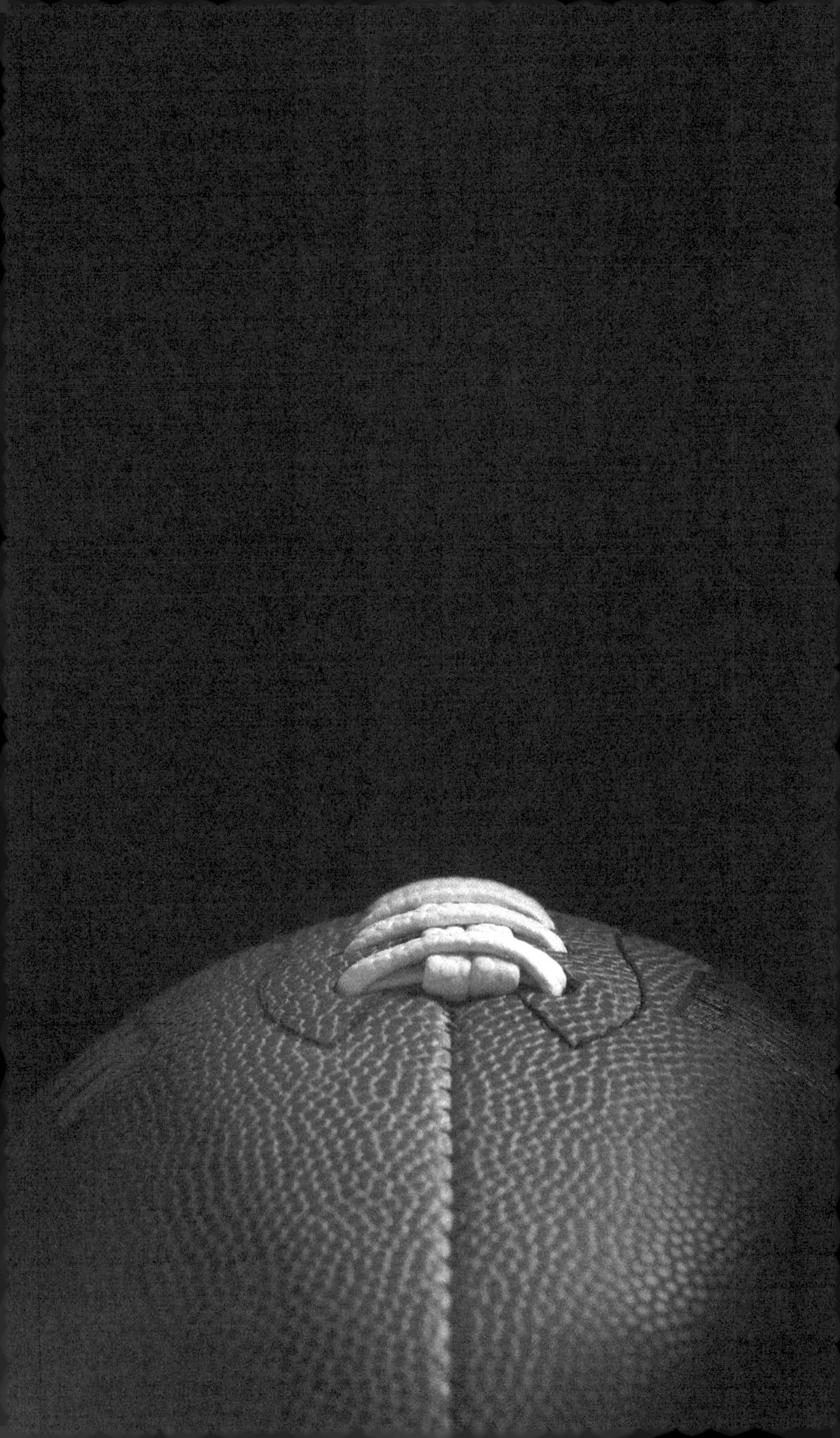

TWENTY-TWO
XANDER

I DIDN'T THINK I'd see Ford on campus since he was no longer in my class, but that wasn't the case. He was everywhere I turned once we got back from winter break.

Today was the hardest by far. I took a shortcut on the way to my office and saw Ford with his arm around a pretty blonde girl who was smiling at him like he hung the moon just for her. I never thought about how I might see Ford with others, and more importantly, women. Even though we weren't together, it hurt to know I couldn't provide him with what he needed and that he'd gotten over me so quickly.

His dark eyes landed on me, and any and all trace of happiness wilted right off his face. The girl said something to him, and it was as if I'd never been there. Ford went back to smiling and talking to her.

It stung to know I was so easy to get over. Especially when I laid in my bed alone night after night, reliving the moments when Ford dominated me and gave me the best damn orgasms of my life. I needed to move on with my life and not let him control me any longer.

On days like today, I wished I didn't live in a small town. I wanted to go out and have no one know me without having to go out of town. Ford had ruined the bar in Loganville for me. There was no way I could go there and not think of him.

Stepping outside my building, I started to cut across the lawn toward my car when the pretty blonde from earlier popped up by my side.

"Mr. Lawrence, can I talk to you a moment?" Her voice was soft and gentle and just as lovely as she was.

"I don't know, can you?" I replied while I picked up my speed. Maybe she'd get the hint I didn't want to talk and leave me alone.

"I'm sorry to ambush you," she looked left and then right before she spoke in a quiet voice. "I know about you and Ford."

I stopped walking and narrowed my eyes at her.

Who the hell did she think she was saying those words out loud?

"I promise I won't say anything to anyone. I'm one of his roommates. I saw you that one morning, and I'm sure it was your house he disappeared to every night. It's just..." she took a deep breath and looked down at the ground for a moment. "I'm worried about him. He told us what happened with his mom." She placed a hand on her chest, and her eyes started to mist. "I'm not sure what happened between the two of you because Ford won't tell me, but do you think you could talk to him?"

"Why would I talk to him when he's no longer my student?" Even though she knew about what once was, there was no way in hell I was admitting it to her. Not here. Not now.

She nibbled on her bottom lip for a moment before she stood tall. "I saw the way you looked at him today as you walked by and the way Ford deflated once you were out of sight."

"I looked at him the same way I do all of my students." I wasn't sure why I denied it, except it felt like my world would implode if I didn't.

"He's been so... not like himself since we all got back from break. Has he ever talked about hurting himself?" A tear escaped down her cheek as she looked up at me.

What had happened for Ford to have her this worried?

"He wouldn't hurt himself if that's what you're thinking."

"I hope you're right. Have you talked to him recently?"

"Not since he got back from seeing his family for Christmas." Maybe something did happen, and that's why he was irrational that night. "He seemed perfectly fine when I saw him with you earlier." Why had I said that now that I knew this pretty girl wasn't someone he was interested in?

Her big blue eyes locked onto mine as she shook her head. "I think that was all a show for you. The second you were out of sight, he was back to being his sad self."

"I don't know what to tell you. We haven't had any communication, and I don't see that changing. I'm sure he's fine. Just give him time." I wasn't sure if I was saying those words for her benefit or for mine.

"Okay, if you think it's nothing." She looked off to the side and then back at me. The worry was back in her eyes even as she tried to reassure me. "I'm sure it's nothing. I'll try to talk to him again and see if he'll open up to me." She nodded like it was a good idea before giving me a tight smile. "I'm sorry I bothered you. You have a good night."

I wasn't sure how I was going to do that when now all I could think about was something horrible might have happened, and would he do something to hurt himself if he was low enough? Ford had said he thought what his mother did was cowardly, but there was only so much a person could take, and Ford had endured more than most at a young age.

Two hours later, after an unappetizing frozen meal, I couldn't stop thinking about what Ford's roommate said. It wouldn't hurt to reach out to make sure he was doing okay. It would put my mind at ease, and then I could go on with my life. I knew he wouldn't answer a text message from me since he hadn't responded to any since I dropped him off at urgent care to see how he was doing, so I decided I'd drop by his place. Once I saw with my own two eyes that he was fine, I'd leave and leave him to live his best life.

Pulling up in front of Ford's house, the driveway was full of cars. I should have come earlier when his roommates weren't home, and now I was outing myself to a bunch of college students. Not the smartest move, but none of them had been where Ford was concerned.

Taking a deep breath, I got out of my car and headed up the driveway. I could hear animated voices as I came up onto the front porch, making me second guess my decision to come. It would be easier if they weren't all right there to see me. Still, I needed to see Ford. If his behavior warranted his roommates to worry after what happened with his mom, it couldn't be good.

Steeling my nerve, I knocked on the front door and waited with bated breath for what was about to happen next. The door opened with two athletic men standing on the other side. I'm not sure what I expected of who Ford lived with, but I didn't expect them to be drop-dead gorgeous. One with light brown skin and striking green eyes spoke. The guy behind him gripped his shoulder in a possessive way.

"Um… Mr. Lawrence, right?"

"Yeah, but you can call me Xander since we're not on school property."

The one with green eyes nodded while the other narrowed his dark eyes on me. He didn't look like someone you'd want to meet in a dark alley. "Is Ford here by any chance?"

"Oh, yeah. He's in his room." He looked over his shoulder for a moment and then back at me. "Are you here to talk to him? He's been… off. Even more than when he came back after the summer."

"I am, although I'm not sure how much good I'm going to do. We haven't spoken in a few weeks." It had been the longest three weeks of my life.

"If he talks to anyone, it will be you," the intense one said.

"I'm not so sure about that, but I'll try." They continued to stand there, their big bodies blocking the entryway. "Are you going to let me in, or are you going to get Ford to come out here?"

"Oh, I'm sorry," the green-eyed one said, pushing the other one back a few steps. "Excuse our manners. Head on back to his room."

I stepped inside and smelled something amazing. Even troubled, Ford still cooked for them. A hand came down on my shoulder, halting me. I turned to see the intense one staring me down. Was this where he threatened me?

"Thanks for coming by."

"Of course. No one should go through what Ford has gone through. If I can help in any way, I will."

I didn't like a room full of people watching me make my way to a room I shouldn't know where it was, but I had to push that aside. They knew about Ford and me, and they didn't act like it was any big deal. No one was looking at me with disgust. Instead, they only looked worried.

Deciding not to knock, I walked right inside Ford's bedroom to find it dark. The only light came in through the crack in the curtains. I spotted Ford lying on his bed, staring up at the ceiling. He didn't move. I wasn't sure if he even knew I was there or if he was ignoring my presence.

Sitting down on the edge of the bed, I turned to angle my body toward his. Ford continued to look up at the ceiling. The only indication that he knew I was in the room was his hands balling up into fists at his sides.

"Ford—" I started but was immediately interrupted.

"Why are you here? Shouldn't you be at home grading papers or on a date or something?"

Okay, so that was how this was going to go.

"I'm here because your roommates and I are worried about you." I placed my hand on his arm and felt his body stiffen underneath my touch. He didn't remove it, so I kept my hand where it was. "Did something happen since the night at urgent care?"

"Life," he chuckled bitterly.

"Do you want to expand on that?"

"Not really, and why do you care? I mean nothing to you."

"If you didn't mean anything to me, I wouldn't be here. You've always meant something to me. Otherwise, I wouldn't have continued to let you dominate my world."

"I'm sure it's been better now that I'm no longer in it," he gritted out between clenched teeth.

I knew I'd have to open up if I expected the same from Ford. "I've been miserable. I've missed you, and not just the sex and cooking," he scoffed at that. "Well, not just that, but having you in my space and your scent on my pillows."

He threw his arm over his eyes as he spoke. "If you're saying all that shit just so I'll open up to you, it's not going to work."

"I'm saying it because it's true. So, you'll know how I've been feeling without having you in my life. You know you're the one who ended it with me, not the other way around."

Ford slammed his fists into the mattress. His eyes hit mine, and he glared at me. "Why the fuck wouldn't I end it when you were talking about how it wouldn't go anywhere? I was doing us both a favor."

I saw his point, and he wasn't wrong. Those were my words, but once he ended it, I knew I didn't want it to happen deep down in my heart. I wanted to find a way to keep Ford in my life. It wasn't ideal with him being a student, but damn if I didn't want to try.

"You're right, and I'm sorry. I was overwhelmed by my feelings for you and the fact that you're a junior at the college where I teach. I'm not sure what the rules are for dating students that aren't in your class, but it has to be highly frowned upon. I've been so scared of losing my job that I never thought of how I'd feel when I lost you."

Ford rolled to his side, facing me. "I opened up to you when I couldn't with anyone else. Why couldn't you do the same?"

Because I was a coward.

"You're braver than I am." My hands itched to touch him, but I kept them at my sides. "Is our being apart the reason you've been upset?"

"I wish," he scoffed. "It's my family. Always them."

"What happened?"

"Why should I tell you? Are you going to report back to my roommates and then slip back out of my life?"

My brows knotted. "Did you hear a single word I just said?"

"I did, but what's changed? Are you going to let me into your bed every night and then pretend I'm just another student during the day?"

"I don't know, Ford." I picked up his hand, unable to hold back any longer, and ran my thumb over the back. "We don't have to figure it all out tonight. Right now, I want to help you. The rest can come later."

"You can't help me. I thought everything was good when I saw Christian and Lucy for Christmas. They were back to being their usual selves, and then I got a call." My heart sank as I waited for him to finish. Lacing our fingers together, I held them on my thigh. "Lucy's pregnant by some kid and wants to keep the baby. I can't tell her what to do with her own body, but I feel like she's ruining her life. I don't think she realizes how hard her life is going to be."

There was no magic fix for his teenage sister being pregnant.

"Has she been to a doctor yet?"

"My aunt is taking her tomorrow, and they'll find out how far along she is. When she told her boyfriend, he dumped her. What kind of asshole would do that to a girl?"

Plenty, I imagined.

"I understand not wanting this for your sister, but what I don't understand is why you're taking it so hard. It's not—"

"I should have been there for her. My aunt doesn't know my brother and sister the way I do. She's being friendly and letting them get away with murder, hoping that they'll like living there with her. They don't need a friend right now."

My lips tipped up. "I never would have thought tough love would be your parenting style."

"Well, look where the other way got my baby sister. I hate this for her." He ducked his head so I could no longer see his face.

"I hate it for the both of you, too. But I know there are many young mothers who go on to be successful and wonderful parents, and I have no doubt your sister will be one of them." I shifted, wanting to be closer to Ford. He moved back, giving me space to lie next to him. Stretching my body out next to his, I cupped the side of his neck and waited for him to look at me. I wanted him out of his head and here with me.

"Thanks for coming to check on me." His big brown eyes looked up at me through his long lashes.

"You shouldn't have done that when I've only been an asshole to you."

"Maybe I like your brand of asshole." Letting my hand slide around to cup his jaw, I leaned in and brushed my lips to his. "I like you, Ford, no matter what my actions or words might have inferred."

His arm moved to drape around my waist as he spoke with a gravelly voice. "Likewise, Mr. Lawrence."

It was all kinds of wrong for him to say my name like he wanted to fuck me. and yet I loved it.

"Fuck, I want to fuck you right now." He rutted against me.

"What's stopping you?" I asked as I pressed my hips against his.

"The fact that we have an audience in the other room. You coming here is one thing, but them hearing what I want to do to you is something altogether different. I won't do that to you."

At least one of us was thinking about my reputation at the moment. Ford made it so easy to get lost in the moment. If what we had was going to continue, I needed to keep my head on straight.

"What would you say if I invited you back to my place?"

Pressing his steel cock into my leg, Ford smirked up at me. "I would say I like the sound of that."

He started to get up, but I pushed him back down. His dark eyes looked at me questioningly. "You told your roommates about... this summer?" I didn't want to ruin the moment, but I was shocked he'd opened up to them.

"I did, and tomorrow I'll tell them about Lucy, but tonight I want to get lost in your body. We really need to get out of here before I throw caution to the wind and fuck you where you are." His hand ran up my side and rested on where my ribs had been bruised. "Are you all healed up?"

"I'm not one hundred percent yet, but it only hurts occasionally now." I didn't care about any pain inflicted on me as long as I had Ford deep inside of me. "What about you?"

He ran the tip of his finger over my bottom lip. "It's as good as new."

I nipped at the end of his digit and then sucked the sting away. "I can't wait for you to put it to good use."

Pulling his finger out, Ford grazed his teeth along my jaw as he spoke. "Your mouth is going to be put to good use. You just wait and see."

I couldn't get out of there fast enough.

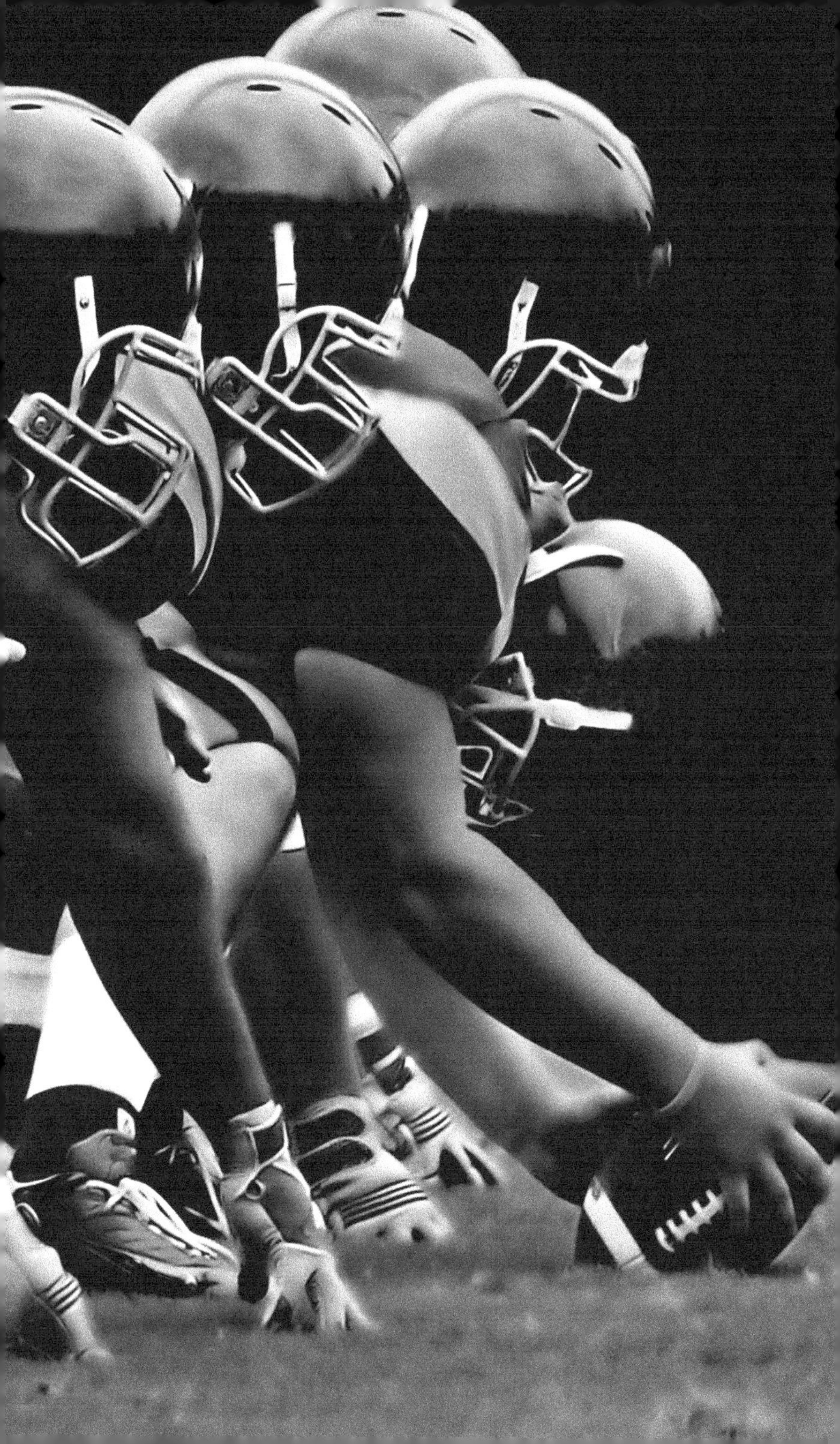

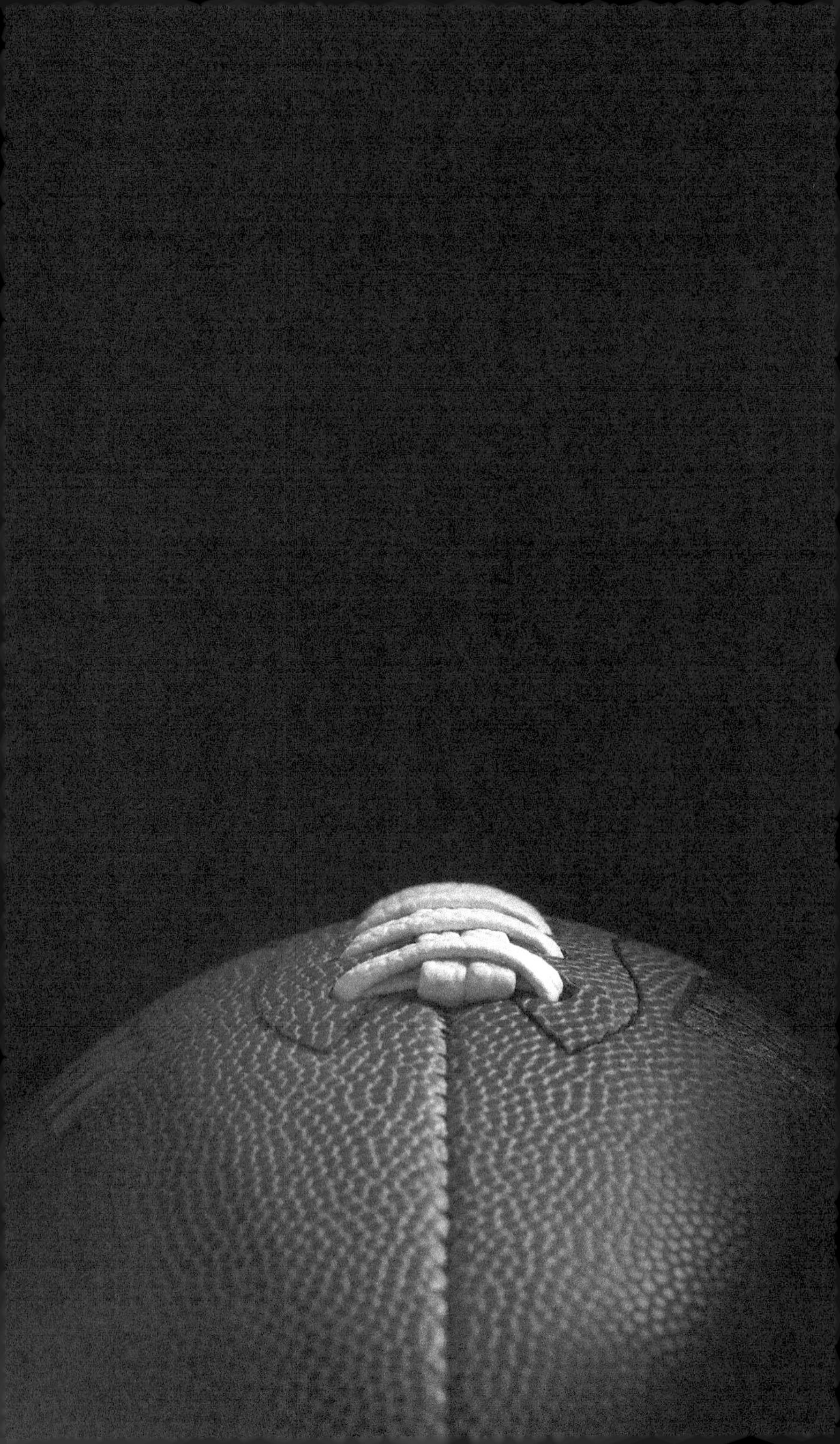

TWENTY-THREE
FORD

ZIPPING UP MY BAG, I stopped in my tracks. The energy of the room was something I couldn't explain. It was almost as if someone had died. "What's going on?"

Oz's blue eyes were red-rimmed as he looked up at me. The corners of his lips turned down. He shook his head before he buried his face into Lo's shoulder.

What the fuck? My body filled with tension as I waited for someone to explain. They'd only been back a day from spring vacation, but last night everything was fine.

Lo ran her fingers through Oz's hair while Charlie sat at his feet and leaned into his leg.

Someone needed to start talking, and soon.

Lo's voice was quiet as she met my gaze from

across the room. "Dani was admitted into rehab today."

I slumped down into the empty recliner, unable to believe what I'd just heard. "For what?"

"Anorexia," Oz spoke with a voice so gruff it didn't sound like him. "She's lost so much weight since Christmas and blamed it all on her training with her soccer coaches." His sad eyes flicked up to mine. "It's not healthy. We had to get her out of there. Once she's out of rehab, she'll be moving here."

"You do whatever you have to do for your family. I totally understand."

Oz sat up and wrapped his arm around Lo's shoulders. She leaned into him. Both their eyes were glassy as they looked in my direction. Oz cleared his throat. "I know you do. You've been through the wringer with yours. We're going to try and clean up the basement to make room, but none of us are…"

"Construction workers," I finished for him. "She can have my room, and I can sleep on the couch when I'm home."

Fin's head popped up from where he was sitting with West. "You haven't been spending many nights here. Are you staying with Teach?"

I rolled my eyes at him. He knew damn well I was with Xander. "Yes, I'm at Xander's house. The walls in this place are paper-thin, and he's still doesn't like that you know about us." They all opened their mouths, and I knew what they were going to say, so I stopped them before they could speak. "No matter how many times I tell him that you won't say a word."

"Maybe if you bring him around more often, he'll see we aren't so bad," West said.

"Maybe." We were still in that stage where we couldn't keep our hands off each other. There was no way in hell Xander would let me touch him the way I wanted with an audience. I knew Xander was waiting for me at his house, but I felt bad leaving when they were all so sad.

"Go enjoy your man. You deserve it," Oz said. "My problems aren't going away." He stood and helped me to stand before he grabbed me up in a hug. "Thank you for giving up your room for my sister. It means a lot to me, and it will to her as well." He pulled back and tried to smile at me but failed. "I don't feel so bad since you're rarely here at night anymore."

"It's the least I can do after everything you've all done for me." I wanted to talk to Lo about how she was doing. Over spring break, they'd caught the guy who raped her, and he was in jail for raping five other women. They thought there were more victims. She was doing so well I didn't want to bring it up on the off chance it would trigger her.

I brought Oz back into another hug and spoke into his ear. "I've been wanting to talk to Lo, but I wasn't sure if it was okay or how to go about it."

"I'll let her know. She's relieved he's been caught but feels guilty that he wouldn't have raped anyone else if she had come forward. And now this with Dani." His eyes went glassy before he looked down.

"It's not either of your faults. If there's anyone to blame, it's her coaches." I hadn't seen Dani recently, but she was already too skinny when I saw her at Friendsgiving. How she continued to play soccer was beyond me. I wasn't going to ask how this would affect her chances of going to the Olympics. They didn't look good, but what did I know?

"My head knows you're right, but my heart is telling me I should have been there for her more. I should have seen the signs as she closed herself off and tried to get out of seeing any of us. I know how demanding a sport can be, but I never thought she was starving herself. Why would they want her like that?"

"I wish I knew, man. I'm sorry. I'm here for you any way you need. You just let me know." I stepped back and spoke so everyone in the room could hear me. "I know I don't always act like it, but you all are my family. If you ever need anything from me, I'm here. All you have to do is ask."

West stood and gave me a brief hug. "You're our family too."

"This feels weird—like I'm never coming back, but I'll be here after class tomorrow to make you dinner just like I always do."

"We know, and if you ever want an entire night with Mr. Lawrence, you don't need to ask. Just tell us we have to fend for ourselves," Fin added.

I didn't like the thought that they'd eat some shitty meal because of me, but I appreciated it, nonetheless.

"Thanks, I'll do that."

"You should probably go before your teacher wonders where you are," Fin laughed.

"Ha, ha. You know he's not my teacher, and he never will be again." But he was probably wondering where the hell I disappeared to. "I'll see you tomorrow." I waved as I walked out the door. Tonight felt different. Our lives were changing yet again with the addition of Dani. Maybe this summer, I could use my free time cleaning out the basement and making myself a room down there.

I pulled up to Xander's ten minutes later to find him sitting on his front porch waiting for me.

"Trouble at home?" He asked it in a playful tone, but he had no idea.

"Something like that." I took in my surroundings. Today was the first day I realized I had never seen anyone outside. It was like Xander lived on a movie set, and the rest of the houses were for show. "Why are your neighbors never outside?"

"Because they're all old and are in bed by the time you get here," he chuckled before his face went stoic. "Let's go inside, and you can tell me what happened."

For the first time, I didn't mind opening up with how I felt. While I still wasn't over my mom killing herself, I wasn't filled with anger every time I thought of her. Thanks to talking to a therapist, Xander, and my friends, I could breathe now.

I followed him inside and set my bag down by the door before heading into the kitchen. With football season over, I could eat a little freer and tonight was my night to splurge.

After telling Xander everything that had happened while I was at home, he sat quietly at the kitchen counter while I finished making our dinner.

"That was nice of you to offer up your room. Are

you really going to try and fix up the basement?" One brow rose as if he thought I wasn't capable. He was right. I probably wasn't. "I didn't even know that house had a basement."

"That's because when you've been there, you've been busy, and no one goes down there. It's a total wreck, but I don't need much. Just a place to lay my head at night and electricity."

I was busy straining the pasta and making sure the sauce was just how I wanted it when I noticed Xander was gone. I pulled the garlic bread from the oven and searched for him. After making two meals tonight, I was ready to eat.

I found Xander upstairs in his room, standing in his closet. I leaned against the door frame and took him in. His face was drawn in concentration as he stared at his clothes. "Dinner's ready."

He nodded and moved a couple of shirts before he turned to look at me. His Adam's apple bobbed as he looked at me while he tapped his index finger on the side of his leg.

Why was he nervous?

Xander cleared his throat. "I know you said you could make the basement yours or sleep on the couch, but what if you slept here when Dani moves in?"

"I sleep here more often than not, so yeah, I'll probably want to stay over more if that's okay with you." I turned to go back downstairs. The smell of the garlic bread was causing my stomach to growl.

The corner of his mouth curled up. "That's not what I meant. I... I'm asking you to move in with me."

That stopped me in my tracks. He couldn't mean what he was saying. "What if someone finds out?"

"I don't plan to hide my relationship with you forever, Ford. If someone finds out between now and you graduating, we'll figure it out." He cocked his head to the side. "You haven't answered my question, though. Do you want to move in?"

"Of course, I do, but I don't want you to ask me because you feel sorry for me. I can handle living in a dark and damp basement for a year."

Xander laughed and stepped out of his closet. Putting his arm around my waist, he pulled me to his side as we walked out of his bedroom. "I would feel horrible if you lived down there while I have all this space here. You're here almost every night, so why not make it permanent?"

I turned before we headed downstairs and placed my hands on his shoulders. "Don't ask this if you're not ready because once I'm here, I'm never leaving."

I laughed, but I was only half-joking. I wasn't sure when it happened, but I was so far gone for Xander. I'd barely admitted to myself, afraid that at any moment, he'd freak out about me being a student and end this. Now he was going all in. Was it possible he felt the same way about me?

"Why would I want you to leave? Fuck, Ford, what do I need to do to show you I love you?" His eyes blazed as he waited for me to speak.

I nearly swayed on my feet as I asked the question. "You love me?"

Xander stepped closer until the tips of his toes brushed my shoes. "Why else would I put up with your moody ass?"

"Because you're addicted to my dick." I looked back to his bedroom, wanting to get lost in him. My hunger forgotten, I wanted Xander more than ever.

"While that's true, I love you more." He tapped my chest right above my heart before he grabbed my hand and started down the stairs. "Let's eat first, and then we can celebrate you loving me and moving in."

"I don't remember saying anything," I shot back, and I trailed behind him. Had I said I love him?

"Maybe not verbally, but your body did." He stopped on the bottom step and looked up at me. "I've known for a while."

"And you didn't say anything?" I stepped down and headed to the kitchen. How did he know me so well?

"I wanted to give you time to work it out for yourself," he called after me.

"Thanks, I guess. I'm trying to work out this entire day. A lot has happened since everyone got back from spring break. First, they caught the guy who raped Lo, then Oz's sister. It puts my pregnant sister into perspective."

"And then I ask you to move in and say I love you." He closed his eyes and breathed deeply. "I should have said it earlier. I knew when I couldn't move on in December, and now it is April. I've wasted so much time not telling you."

"Don't be so hard on yourself. You act like one of us is dying, and this is the last time you get to say those words. It's not. You can tell me every day, as many times as you want." Placing the noodles and then the sauce over them in my bowl. I moved to sit at the bar while I watched Xander get his food. "I've never had anyone love me except for my family."

He stopped what he was doing and smiled. "Sometimes, I forget how young you are."

I hated it when he reminded me of our age difference. "So, you've been in love before?"

He sat down beside me. His arm rested against mine. It was so easy to be around him. He made me forget everything. Even without being inside him. "A long time ago, but it was nothing like this."

"This feels pretty great."

"Yeah, yeah, it does," he agreed.

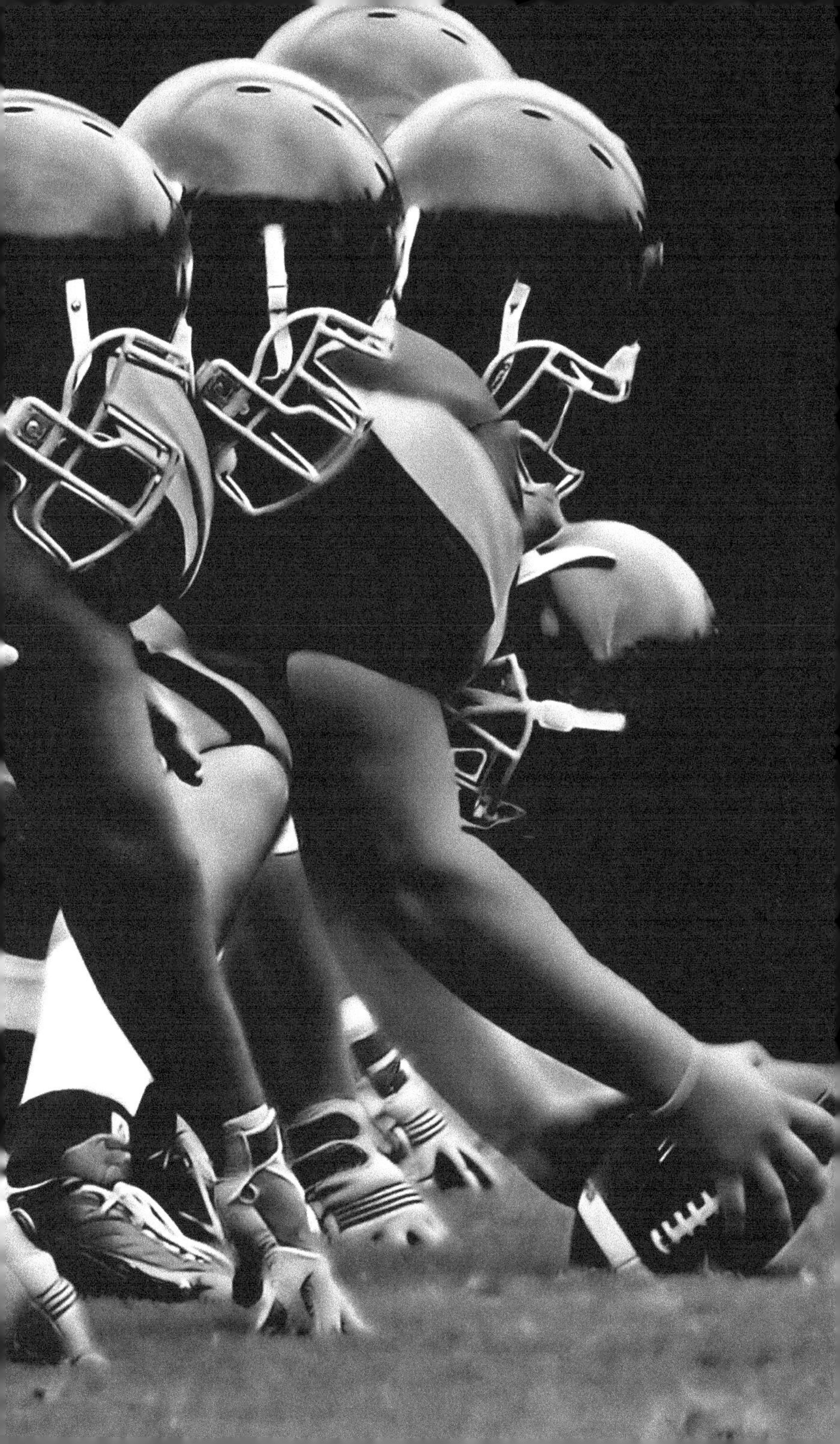

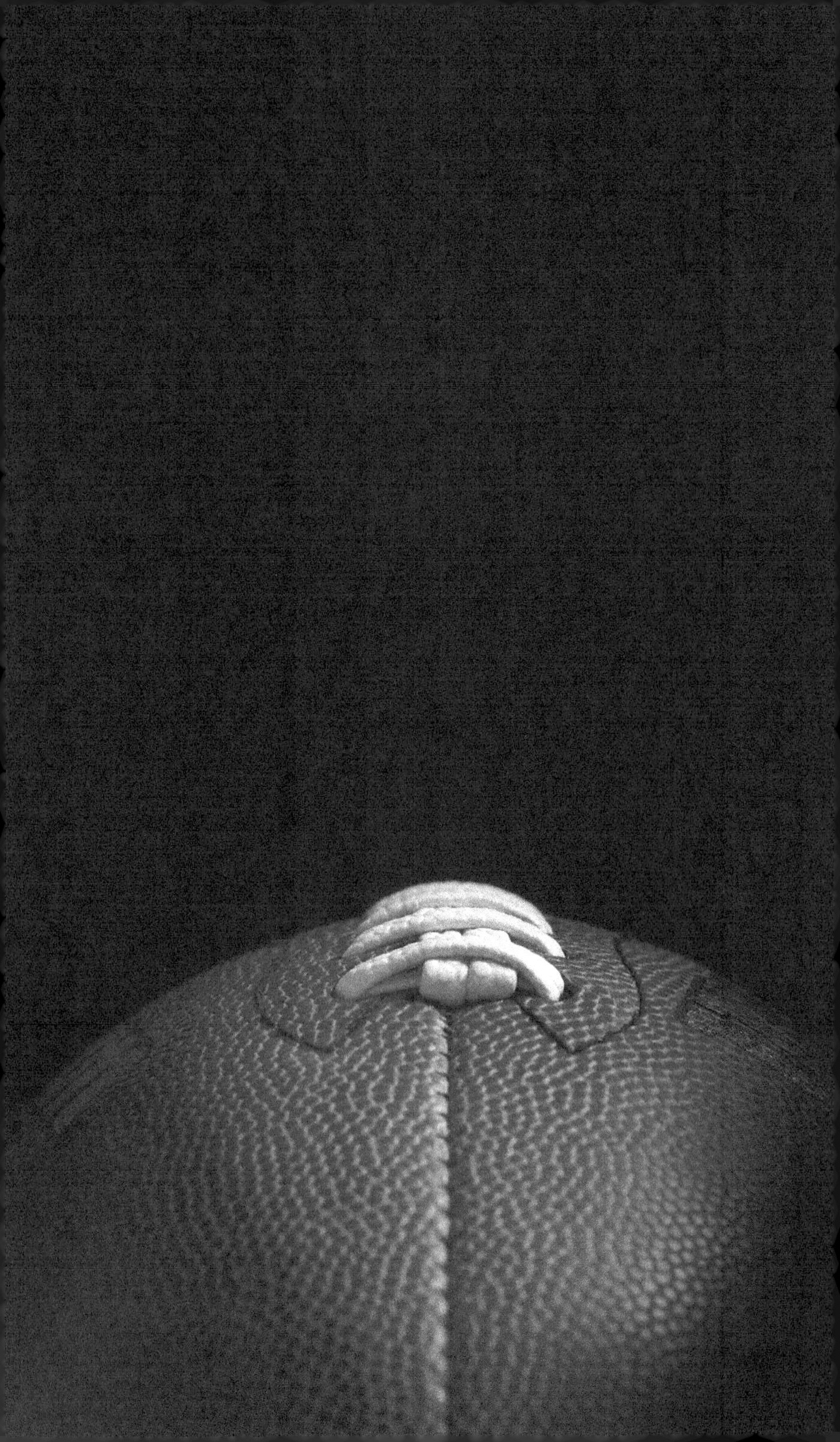

TWENTY-FOUR
FORD

WITH THE LAST of my things in my arms, I made my way out of my room and into the hall. Dani was standing there in an oversized sweatshirt I was sure she was wearing to hide her overly thin body. I placed the box on my hip and leaned against the wall.

"What's up?" I didn't know her well. I'd only met her a few times, but she was one of my best friends' sisters, so she felt like family to me even if I didn't know her.

"You don't have to do this because of me. I hate that I'm running you out. I could sleep on the couch until—"

"I'm not doing it because of you, and if I was

staying, there's no way in hell I'd let you sleep on the couch. I'd give up my bed to you in a heartbeat."

Her small, soft hand landed on my forearm. "That's really sweet of you. Hopefully, we'll get to know each other now that we're in the same zip code."

"I'd like that. Plus, I'll still be over at least once a week cooking dinner." I wanted to say how I'd be trying to get her to gain weight, but that wasn't my place.

"You know, I think they're the lucky ones with the deal you made. Having your own private chef isn't cheap."

I chuckled. "Maybe that's what I'll do instead of opening up my own restaurant."

Her blue eyes, which had been dim up until now, lit up a small fraction. "You should." She looked down, and when she looked back up at me, Dani's eyes were filled with sadness. "What little food I've had of yours has always been the best I've ever had. I'm sorry about Friendsgiving. I promise I'll eat more this year."

"It's okay. I understand, and so does everyone else here. Try not to get too mad at them while they hover over you the first few days. They only have your best intentions at heart."

"I know," she choked out. "I'm just thankful I got to come here instead of having to be home with my parents. They keep asking me what they did wrong over and over again. It doesn't matter that I tell them my eating disorder has nothing to do with them and more to do with me."

And her coaches at her old school, but I didn't bring them up. The most important thing was Dani got the help she needed and was with people who cared about her. They wouldn't let her backslide.

"I'm glad you're here." I adjusted the box that was starting to get heavy on my hip.

"Oh, I should let you go. You probably want to get settled in at your boyfriend's house."

She was right. I did.

Dani leaned forward and whispered. "He's really hot. I can't believe you bagged a professor."

I chuckled escaped as I started to move down the hall. "Thanks, and let's keep it to ourselves about how I'm seeing and living with a teacher."

Dani made the motion of zipping her lips. "Your secret is safe with me. And if you ever want a threesome with a girl, I'm always down."

"Not on your life," Oz growled from outside. "You touch my sister, and you're a dead man."

"Hey," I laughed, sidestepping around Oz, who

was glaring at me. "Don't be mad at me. Those words didn't come out of my mouth. That's all on your sister."

Oz narrowed his eyes at Dani in a playful way. "You're going to keep me on my toes, aren't you?"

"You wouldn't have it any other way," Dani laughed. I was happy she was here where she could be herself and around people who loved her. Life wasn't going to be easy for her anytime soon.

Oz pulled his sister into a hug and whispered something in her ear. It reminded me I needed to call Lucy and see how she was doing. And Christian. I knew they had each other, but I wanted them to know they always had me as well.

After putting the last box in my car, I closed the trunk and turned around to find all of my roommates standing in a line in the yard.

"You all look like you're going to miss me," I laughed.

"We are," West said, stepping forward and hugging me. "But we're also happy for you. It's nice to see a smile on your face every day now."

I patted him on the back. "I want to thank you all for giving me the time to come to you when I was ready, and thank you for caring. You're my family. Now and always."

"Same man," Oz said, coming in for a hug. I gave him a back pat and started to move back, but Oz held firm. "Thank you for giving your room up for my sister. I know the act means a lot to her."

"It's my pleasure, and if you ever need anything, just let me know," I said as I pulled away.

Lo jogged up and hugged me around my waist. "I'm going to miss you," she whispered, her fingers tangling in Charlie's hair.

"I'll miss you too—all of you. This isn't goodbye. I'll be here so often you won't even know I'm gone."

"I hope so." Lo wiped under her eyes, and not two seconds later, Oz had her in his arms. "Go before Xander wonders if we've decided not to let you go. Which I'm considering, by the way."

"I'll see you guys this weekend when you come over for dinner. Just keep the teacher jokes to a minimum." I needed to get the hell out of here before I started to get emotional.

They all laughed as I got inside my car and turned it on. The air conditioning blasted me in the face as I pulled out of the driveway and gave them one last wave before I moved on. After being unable to pay rent and Fin continuing to let me live in the house rent-free, I wasn't sure where I'd go once I graduated. I knew I'd still have no money once the time came, and yet here I was, already moving out at the end of my junior year into a home I planned to never leave with a man I loved. It was unreal.

What was my sister's life going to be like trying to finish high school with a baby? Would she go to college?

Picking up my phone, I hit Lucy's name and listened as the call rang through the speakers of my car.

"Hey, what are you doing calling me? I thought you were moving today," Lucy answered.

"I am. I'm on my way to Xander's house as we speak. I didn't have a whole lot to pack. Xander took the first load, and I've got the rest in my car."

"Are you two still coming up here in a couple of weeks to visit?" She asked quietly. Unsure. As if anything would keep me away.

"We are, but enough about me. I was calling to see how you're doing. Have you heard anything from the father yet?"

"He's still ghosting me. I'm sure he'll feel differently when I'm asking him for child support," she laughed bitterly. "I think I felt the baby kick yesterday."

"Oh, yeah. What did that feel like?" I wasn't sure

how I'd like the feeling of a human being inside of me kicking my insides.

"Weird and cool," Lucy laughed.

I wanted to ask her if she was scared, but I knew she was. Who in their right mind wouldn't be? Instead, I said what I called to tell her in the first place. "You know you can call me for anything, and I'll always be here for you, right?"

"I do. Thank you, Ford. I thought for sure you'd be pissed at me."

"Oh, I'm pissed. Livid, but I have to respect your decision, and the only thing my anger is going to get me is time apart from one of the most important people in my life. I wish you were closer, so I could be there for you every step of the way."

"Me too, but I know why you can't. I know I've said it before, but I'm sorry I shut you out of my life when you needed us the most. I can't imagine how hard it must have been to make all of those decisions while grieving."

Excruciating.

But I wasn't going to tell her that. It was my cross to bear, and I was coming out of it from the other side now.

"I know you are, and I should have tried to

explain to you what was going on. If I had been able to talk, maybe things would have been different."

I pulled onto Xander's street, which was our street now, and smiled at the fact. It was amazing what a difference a year could make. I never thought this would be possible after the heartache I'd been through after my mom killed herself.

"I'm going to let you go, but if you need anything, let me know."

"I will."

"And can you do me a favor?"

"Anything," she replied back quickly.

"Can you make sure that Chris knows I'm here for him too?" I hated putting her on the spot, but I needed them both to know. I'd tell them again and again until I was blue in the face.

"He knows. We both do. Just like we're here for you. Anything you need. If you need to talk about mom or vent about your boyfriend." She giggled, and I knew she was shaking her head on the other end of the phone. "It still sounds weird to say you have a boyfriend, but I better get used to it. Once I do, then he'll probably be your husband. I can't wait to meet him in person."

I almost choked on my tongue. While I loved Xander, I'd never thought of him as my future husband. I wasn't even sure that was something he wanted. Hell, maybe tonight we needed to sit down and see what we saw in our future.

"Are you still there?" Lucy asked. There was laughter in her voice as if she knew what she'd done.

"I'm here. I'm not sure we're at the point in our relationship where we'll talk about marriage."

"You should probably graduate first," she offered. It was the same way I felt about her starting a family before she was out of high school, but she knew that. This I could control, unlike her circumstances.

"You're right. I should. I'll call you in a couple of days to see how you're doing. If you need anything, call or text," I said as I pulled into the driveway.

"I will. Bye, Ford. I love you."

"I love you too, Luce." I disconnected the phone call and exited the vehicle.

I grabbed one of the boxes from the backseat and headed inside. I scanned the downstairs, and when I didn't see Xander, I headed upstairs. Xander was in the closet, hanging up all of my clothes. It was surreal to see them beside his own clothes. We definitely didn't have the same style. I was always in shorts, t-shirts, or sweats, but Xander had a whole other side to him for work. He always wore a button-up shirt with slacks, ones that always showcased the magnificent body he had underneath.

"Hey, you're back," he greeted me.

"Sorry that took so long. They got a little sappy as I left." I set down the box and moved across the closet to him. Xander's soft lips pressed to mine as his hands roamed down my back and straight to my ass.

When I pulled away from the kiss with my arms wrapped around his shoulders, I asked. "Do you want to get married?"

"Married?" Xander sputtered. "Where did that come from?"

"I was talking to Lucy on the way over, and she said something." I took a step back in order to read his face. "It made me realize I have no idea what you want. Do you ever want to get married or have kids?"

"Married one day? Yes, but kids I'm not sure about. What about you?"

"I've never thought about kids, even when I was with girls. I'm not opposed to children one day." I shrugged. "Maybe we'll see how we feel in a few years. If we want one then, we can come back to this conversation."

"I agree." Xander's dark brows dipped. "Was that a proposal?"

"Most definitely not. If I were going to do that, it would have been much smoother. Plus, I should probably get through college first before we make any more life-changing choices."

"I couldn't agree more." He backed me out of the room and over to the bed. "But I do know of one thing we can do in the meantime."

"Oh, and what's that?" I asked as I stepped out of my tennis shoes and pushed the elastic of shorts down past my hips. My cock sprang out and angled itself toward Xander. I enjoyed watching Xander's brown eyes turn black with lust as he took me in.

"Christening every room in *our* house," he said as he pulled the hem of his shirt over his head.

"I like the way you think. How many rooms do you think we can do in twenty-four hours?"

Xander shook his head while laughing and crawled up the bed until every inch of me was covered by him. "I don't know, but I'm sure willing to find out. And what we don't cover now we have the rest of our lives to do."

I liked the sound of that. I had my forever. Xander was my happiness rolled up into a big, dark satin skin covering lean muscles, kind eyes and heart with a perfect dick.

Pushing up on my elbows, I crashed my mouth to his. Unable to express what I was feeling in that moment, I put it all into that kiss: love, devotion, hunger, and hope. When we broke for air, panting and smiling, I cupped the side of his neck. "I love you, Xan."

Leaning into my touch, his eyes softened. "I love you, too."

Smoothing my other hand down his spine, I gripped his hip and rolled Xander onto his side. Straddling his waist, I took his cock in my hand, gripping it hard, and started stroking. My thumb ran over the head and along the underside. Xander's eyes shut as he bucked his hips.

His eyes opened and locked on mine. "How do you always know the right way to touch me?" He moaned.

"I'm talented that way," I smirked. "Let me show you what else I'm good at." Leaning down, I started to place kisses down his chest and licked along both sides of his obliques.

"Fucking hell, you know how to torture me too." His large hand gripped my hair as he tried to push me down to where he really wanted me.

My eyes flicked up to his, and I smiled. "All good things come to those who wait."

"I've waited my entire life for you. I think that's long enough. Now suck my dick."

Gladly.

Sweeping down, I licked along his shaft and then wrapped my mouth around the tip of his cock, sucking and licking until he was desperately arching his hips up for more. Only then did I open my mouth and take all of him in, swallowing his length until he hit the back of my throat.

Xander let out a grateful groan, threading his fingers through the strands of my hair. He didn't push, letting me take my time. One hand went to his balls, and the other slid down to his tight ring of muscle. Xander pressed against my finger, needy for me to be inside his ass.

I liked how needy he always was for me. I wondered if it would ever start to fade. I craved him more and more with each passing day, and I hoped he felt the same way with me.

"God, I need you inside of me," he groaned as I scissored two fingers deep inside of him and then curled them, knowing I'd hit him in just the right spot.

Letting his dick go with a pop, I kissed my way

back up his long torso until I swiped my tongue through his waiting mouth. Grinding our dicks together, I reached over to the nightstand and grabbed the bottle of lube. I kept my mouth on his, devouring his taste as I slicked myself up. I rubbed my fingers along his hole before I pressed inside slowly.

I laced our fingers together and anchored them above his head. The entire time, I never took my mouth from his. I couldn't get enough of Xander, knowing he was mine. If he could get me through the darkest part of my life, I knew there was nothing we couldn't beat together.

Once I was fully sheathed inside his tight ass, I slowly started to rock in and out of him. I pressed his legs open further to get as deep as possible. "Fuck, you feel amazing." How was it possible that being inside of Xander while loving him made it so much better? The way he looked at me with wonder and pleasure mixed on his face had me wanting to quicken my pace, yet at the same time continue to draw out every ounce of pleasure from him slowly. I wanted to remember today for the rest of my life. Today was the start of a new beginning. Our beginning.

Xander's hands trailed with fervor down my back

until he cupped my ass with each hand. I couldn't hold back any further as the blunt tips of his nails dug into my skin. There was plenty of time to make love to him now that we had forever. Now was the time to fuck him hard like we only had today. This moment.

I pulled back and then slammed into him, letting Xander know I was giving him exactly what he wanted. One of his hands moved from my ass to grip his cock. Pulling back onto my knees, I kept my gaze on the way he touched himself and watched my cock disappear into him over and over again. I wasn't even finished, but I already knew I'd be ready to go again after I unleashed inside of him. That's what Xander did to me. I forgot anything and everything when I was with him.

Xander's body started to shake beneath me, and I knew he was close. I joined my hand with his, and after one stroke, hot cum shot out over both our hands and his stomach. Seeing his cum painted over his abs was so fucking hot. I unleashed, shooting my load while he squeezed my cock like a vise grip.

Leaning down, I slipped my tongue between his parted lips and tasted every inch of his mouth. I couldn't get enough. Only once my dick started to soften and slip out did I pull away. Rolling off

Xander and onto my back, I pulled him against me, loving the way his hard muscles felt against mine.

"If you keep that up for the rest of the night, you just might just kill me," he chuckled against the crook of my neck.

Tilting my head, I rested it on top of his head. "We can't have that now, can we? I guess I'll just have to go easy on you from now on."

Xander pulled away and leaned up on his elbow so he could look down at me. "Don't you dare. I wouldn't have it any other way."

"I won't," I promised. "I was powered by all the feelings rushing through me, but damn, I gotta say it was hands down the best sex I've ever had. I wouldn't mind always trying to do better."

Xander's eyes softened before he laid back down. His hand moved to rest over my rapidly beating heart. "It's the same for me, too. Sometimes it's scary how much I feel for you. Especially in the beginning."

I could only imagine. I wasn't sure why he let me in night after night sometimes. Now I knew. There was no denying us. It was always going to happen, no matter the circumstances. Only ours didn't start off with a nice little meet-cute. No, ours was built on pain and pleasure.

"I wouldn't change our story." I must have been quiet for too long because Xander's hand moved up to cup my jaw. His thumb caressed over my stubble, soothing me and lulling me into a trance that was close to putting me to sleep.

Placing my hand over his, I pulled it up and kissed his palm. "Me either. The pain was worth it now that I have you."

Xander slipped on top of me and started to move against me, our stomachs sticking together from cum and sweat, but I didn't care. For the rest of the night and into the early morning, we fucked and made love wherever our bodies fell, on whatever surface one of us pushed the other onto. We couldn't get enough of one another, and we did the same the next day and the next. It was a high unlike any other. One I never wanted to be without and never would.

Our summer was bliss. We went camping several times and saw my brother and sister. I wasn't sure what my senior year would bring for Xander and me. We had to be careful so no one would find out we were together. My sister would be giving birth soon after she started her senior year in high school. After everything we went through, I knew we could get through anything.

. . .

The Willow Bay series isn't over yet. Up next is Danica and Declan's book in Off Sides. Would you like to see the siblings of our favorite characters get their own books in Willow Bay's second generation? If so, I'd love to hear from you.

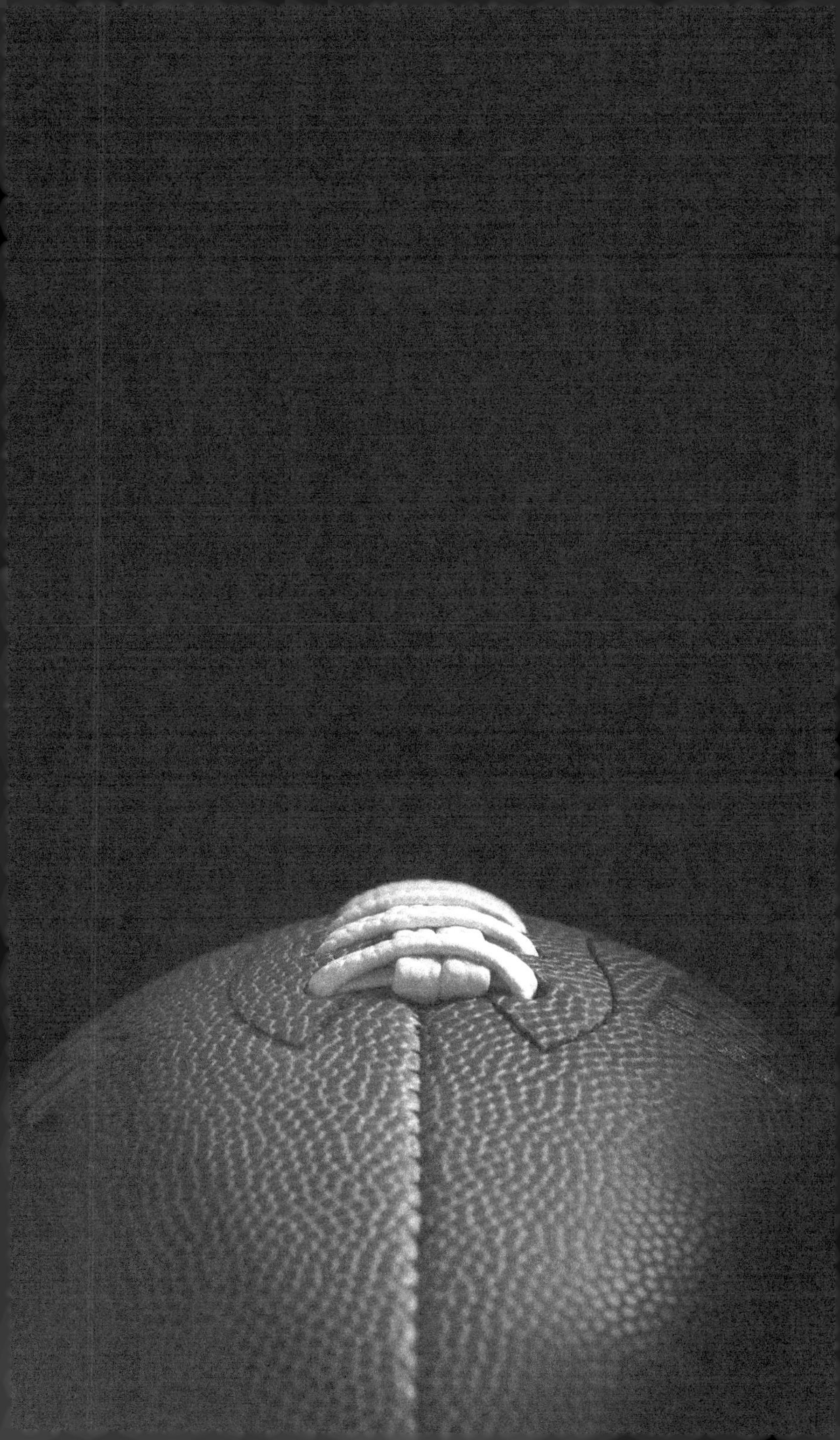

Did you enjoy OVER TIME? If so, please consider leaving a review on Goodreads, Amazon, or BookBub. Reviews mean the world to authors especially to authors who are starting out. You can help get your favorite books into the hands of new readers.

I'd appreciate your help in spreading the word and it will only take a moment to leave a quick review. It can be as short or as long as you like. Your review could be the deciding factor or whether or not someone else buys my book.

To stay up to date on all my releases subscribe to my newsletter.
https://harlowlayne.com/newsletter/

ACKNOWLEDGMENTS

My family- your support means so much. Thank you for all of your encouragement and giving me the time to do what makes me happy.

To my **girls**: Kelsey Cheyenne, Carmel Rhodes, QB Tyler, and Erica Marselas. I love each and every one of you. Thank you for all of your support.

Thank you **Kristen Breanne** for making my story into a book.

To all my **author friends**, you know who you are. Thank you for accepting me and making me feel welcome in this amazing community.

To **Wildfire Marketing Solutions and Shauna**, thank you for all your knowledge and for helping me make Away Game a success!

Lovers thank you for always being there.

To each and every **reader**, **reviewer**, and **blogger** - I would be nowhere without you. Thank you for taking a chance on an unknown author.

ABOUT ELLA

Ella Kade is a forbidden and dark romance writer who enjoys writing captivating characters with sinful intent.

Read Ella to get immersed into her words where she ruins lives and slowly puts them back together.

ALSO BY ELLA KADE

<u>Willow Bay Series - Forbidden Romance</u>

Away Game - MM, Bully

First Down - Sister's Best Friend

Over Time - MM, Student/Teacher - May 13, 2022

Off Sides - Second Chance, Forbidden - November 2022

The Elite's: Year Two - July 12, 2022

Sin's Sacrifice - MC, Second Chance - July 15, 2022

CPSIA information can be obtained
at www.ICGtesting.com
Printed in the USA
LVHW021425050522
717841LV00069B/4419